THE REVIEWS ARE IN...
THE CRITICS LOVE AMANDA!

"ENTERTAINING. There are similarities to *Bridget Jones's Diary* and *Sex and the City*...but AMANDA BRIGHT@HOME is deeper and more honest in its portrayal of one woman's life."
—Bookhaven.net

"RUEFULLY FUNNY. Now mothers (and fathers) everywhere can laugh and cry along with Amanda as she experiences the daily trials of adjusting to her new life at home—and discovers that success isn't always measured in the workplace."
—*Human Events*

"ENGROSSING....Readers...will enjoy the escapades of [this] sympathetic mom of two."
—*Booklist*

"A WONDERFULLY HONEST and funny, fully rounded character. Any parent who has been faced with the heartrending choice of career versus family will relate to...Amanda Bright."
—FictionAddiction.net

"YOU'LL LOVE [AMANDA'S] INSIGHTS, UNDERSTAND HER INSECURITIES....Like a dear friend who shares her deepest thoughts and darkest secrets, her story is an incredible reminder that, no, you're not alone."
—*First for Women*

amanda bright@home

DANIELLE CRITTENDEN

WARNER BOOKS

NEW YORK   BOSTON

This book is a work of fiction. Names, characters, places, and incidents are the product of the author's imagination or are used fictitiously. Any resemblance to actual events, locales, or persons, living or dead, is coincidental.

Warner Books

Time Warner Book Group
1271 Avenue of the Americas, New York, NY 10020
Visit our Web site at www.twbookmark.com.

Printed in the United States of America

Originally published in hardcover by Warner Books

First Trade Printing: May 2004

10 9 8 7 6 5 4 3 2 1

The Library of Congress has cataloged the hardcover edition as follows:
Crittenden, Danielle
    amanda bright@home / Danielle Crittenden.
        p.   cm.
    ISBN 0-446-53074-3
        1. Washington (D.C.)—Fiction. 2. Mother and child—Fiction.
    3. Married women—Fiction. 4. Housewives—Fiction. I. Title.

PS3603. R58 A43 2003
813'.6—dc21   2002033106

ISBN: 0-446-69246-8 (pbk.)

Cover design by Flag, Jackie Merrie Meyer and Shasti O'Leary Soudant

For David

amanda bright@home

Chapter One

IT HAPPENED every time Amanda came home: she felt asphyxiated by her small house. She stood for a moment in the front hall, her arms full of grocery bags, pushed from behind by two small children and thwarted from moving forward by a minefield of rubber boots, stuffed animals, and scattered blocks.

"Ugh! Kids! Why do you leave these things right here where Mommy can trip?" Amanda dropped the bags on the floor and turned sideways to allow the children to burst past. "Just *go*—go upstairs, do something, watch a video, I don't care."

Amanda bent down and swept aside the offending objects. She did not glance into the living room, knowing it to be in even worse condition than the hall. She would get to it later, after this—but when? And where would it all go? The children's shelves were already full. The area beneath Sophie's bed looked as if it had been attacked by Suicide Bomber Ken: plastic body parts, shoes, purses, and broken pieces of doll furniture were strewn everywhere. Amanda knew from experience that to sort toys consumed as many trash bags as it did hours, and still you were left with uncategorizable little piles of childhood detritus—goggly-eyed fast-food figures, tiny cars, baseball cards, rubber snakes—objects that you couldn't throw away, but you didn't know where to put exactly, either. Four years spent earning a bachelor's degree had not prepared her for a career as a domestic curator.

"And don't make any more mess!" she called up the stairs, to no reply.

It took two more trips to the car to bring in all the grocery bags. Amanda stacked them wherever she could find room in the kitchen: on the narrow counters, the stove, the breakfast table, the floor.

The kitchen, like the rest of the house, remained in what the real estate agent had described as its "original condition."

Amanda and Bob had bought the house during the Washington real estate slump of the mid-1990s. The "three-bedroom, Old World charmer/lots of detail" turned out to be a typical Woodley Park semidetached brick job from the 1920s crammed up alongside another semidetached brick job from the 1920s. There wasn't much to recommend it except that it was not—repeat not—a tract house in the suburbs. Never mind that if she and Bob were different sorts of people they could have afforded a spanking-new, Palladian-windowed, four-bedroom, two-and-a-half-bath "Manor Home" in a development named Badger Run Estates. They had looked at such a place precisely once during their transition from apartment-dwelling, one-child family to house-dwelling, two-child family, and had driven away so quickly that their car left tire tracks in the freshly planted sod.

"I don't want to spend my life commuting," Bob muttered as they sat waiting for the light to change at a six-lane intersection near a strip mall where you could buy, right away, with no money down, a reclining mattress.

"I don't want to be more than two blocks away from a good cup of coffee," Amanda replied, and that was all they said for the next forty-five minutes until the bridge that would take them back over the Potomac hoved into view.

By comparison, the Woodley Park house *had* seemed charming: the plaster moldings, the slanting walls, the cubbyhole kitchen, the urban backyard of flagstone, bushes, and gap-toothed fences. "Eventually you might want to push out the back here and create a sunny breakfast room overlooking the garden," the agent said airily as Amanda wondered whether they could afford to pull up the scuffed linoleum.

That was before Amanda knew Christine Saunders and her custom-built mock Georgian on its two-acre ravine lot, with its "media room," "chef's kitchen," and "in-law/au pair suite" in which Christine stored her holiday decorations. Christine lived in the suburbs—but not the suburbs that advertised in weekend supplements. Her neighbors were artfully hidden behind the glades of an adjoining golf course. Inside her house everything vanished as well: children, toys, noise, even Christine's husband, who kept an office somewhere in the vast basement. The few times Amanda had met him were as he emerged, blinking like a ferret, to ask if anyone had seen his car keys.

Amanda no longer felt any of the defiant pride she had once taken in the clutter of her own house, the clutter that announced, *I am not a homemaker. I am "at home" to care for my children—not to "make a home." One day I will be returning to the office, where I belong. Until then we can get by with the pressboard bookshelves from college and the pullout loveseat we bought when we moved in together, and my grandmother's lamp, and the milk crates we thought made creative record holders. As for the toys everywhere, they just show what affectionate, nonauthoritarian parents we are.* It was the same pride Amanda had once taken in driving an old Volvo wagon instead of the suburbanite's vehicle of choice, the minivan.

Now, as Amanda stared into the overcrowded racks of her twenty-year-old refrigerator, wondering where the new gallon of milk would fit, she felt a nasty pressure building inside her head. She had spent most of the day by the swimming pool at Christine's club. It was the first Tuesday after Memorial Day, and the children had been given one of those mysterious holidays from school ("Teacher Resource/Development—no classes" according to the soggy flyer retrieved from Ben's knapsack). She had stood all morning, knee deep in the kiddie pool, trying to look dignified as Ben spat arcs of water and Sophie screamed in terror at the tiny ripples lapping at her shins. As usual, Amanda and her children were the only ones creating a spectacle. The other mothers rested upon their chaise longues as still and majestic as the gilded figures on Egyptian sarcophagi.

At lunchtime Christine commanded her nanny to take the children to the clubhouse. Amanda joined Christine by the adult pool, where she eagerly accepted a glass of white wine. (Christine was a firm believer in "maternal restoratives," and Amanda was pleased to find that the wine worked upon her like a mild sedative.)

"They can bring us a sandwich here if you like," Christine said, shielding her eyes from the sun.

"Thanks—I'm not hungry yet."

"Me neither."

Christine resumed her talmudic studying of the latest issue of *W;* Amanda closed her eyes, lulled by the distant hum of a lawn mower perfecting the tenth green in the valley below.

"Aren't you loving this weather?" a voice called out.

Amanda turned and squinted. A tall woman in a black string bikini was passing by their little encampment of bags and towels. The bikini set off, like jeweler's velvet, the glistening facets of the woman's figure. Amanda sucked in her stomach. Her own practical one-piece was faded and stretched after many summers of propelling toddlers through the shallow end of her public pool.

"Fabulous," Christine replied.

The woman drifted away.

"She looks too good for fifty," Christine commented.

"*Her?*" Amanda sat up to take a second look at the disappearing form of the woman.

"No—her." Christine pointed to a photograph of an aging starlet in the magazine, hunched catlike on a bed and dressed in a plunging leopard-print bodysuit. "It's either surgery or airbrushing. What do you think?"

"I can't tell."

"I'd say both."

Amanda took another gulp of wine and settled back into the cushion but it was no use; she still felt self-conscious. She picked up the novel she had brought along, an experimental work by an expatriate Chinese woman—highly praised by the *Times*—but she could not concentrate. She could only think about how the white dimpled skin of her thighs resembled raw chicken.

"You want a swim?" Christine asked, rising. "I'm burning up."

"You go. I'm fine."

Amanda watched Christine weave her way through the prone bodies, marveling at her sense of ease. Christine had been a lawyer in an earlier life, specializing in intellectual property, "before it was fashionable," as she put it. Bob told Amanda that his colleagues at the Department of Justice still cited an article Christine had written for the *Chicago Law Review*. Yet in the year since the two women had met, at a play date demanded by their sons, Amanda had never once heard Christine express doubt about the surrender of her career. The only time Christine ever made reference to it was to remark how poorly her job had prepared her for motherhood: "It's not like knowing the doctrine of contributory infringement helps me get Vaseline out of Victoria's hair."

It was not an ease Amanda could share. All her life Amanda had felt herself on a steady trajectory toward some professional goal. The goal wasn't always visible, but she knew it was there. It was why she had studied calculus and biology. It was why she had made herself ill with worry after a poor exam. It was why she and Bob had spent the past ten years paying off her student loans rather than saving for a bigger house. (Her mother had been so proud: a daughter at Brown!) And it was why, at age thirty-five, Amanda could not lie beside a pool on a weekday afternoon without feeling restless.

What of these other women? Amanda cast her eyes over their gleaming haunches. They reminded her of prized thoroughbreds, retired from the track, content in their new vocation as broodmares. When they were not grazing by the pool, they were wandering serenely over the landscaped grounds, hair glinting in the sunlight, a genetically perfect clone or two trotting along at their heels. Personal trainers kept their bodies buffed and sculpted purely for aesthetic pleasure, not because the women had any need to exert themselves physically. Where would they exert themselves if they could? Out here in the suburb of Potomac there were not even sidewalks. When a woman was not at the club, she was chauffeuring her kids, flexing, at most, her right foot upon a gas pedal.

Christine reappeared, dipped and glistening.

Amanda attempted the first page of her book. *In the tiny village in Szechwan province where I was born, there were no dreams. My childhood was dreamless. This is the first thing you must understand about me.*

A burst of howls announced the return of her children.

Good God, it was nearly six. She had to get dinner started. The broiler chicken she had scooped up on the way home suddenly seemed ambitious. Maybe they should just order takeout— although it would be the second time this week. How would she justify it to Bob? *Sorry, but I spent all day drinking at the club and didn't have time to make dinner.*

Her head pounding, Amanda looked through the cupboards for something that would be easy to prepare. Pasta. Canned tomatoes. They had been eating a lot of that lately. She opened the fridge again. Despite the fresh infusion from the supermarket, there was still little that would constitute dinner for two adults: peanut butter, bread, yogurt, juice boxes, eggs, the congealed remains of last night's cheese pizza. Amanda searched through the fridge drawers but came up with only a head of Boston lettuce, some apples, a bag of carrots, and an unripe avocado. Her elbow knocked over a full container of grated Parmesan, coating everything in the fridge with white powder, like a snow globe.

"Damn!"

"Uh-oh, Mommy use bad word." Sophie wandered into the kitchen stark naked, trailing one of Amanda's scarves.

"*Sophie,*" Amanda said tensely, "why did you take off your clothes?"

"I'm playing Indians with Ben." The little girl shook her long brown curls. "I'm an Indian princeth. Will you tie this on me, Mommy?" She held up the scarf.

"No, Mommy will not tie this on you. It is Mommy's good scarf," said Amanda, snatching the scarf away. "And you are *not* Indians," she added irritably. "You are *Native Americans.*"

Sophie burst into tears. Amanda sighed and wrapped the child in her arms.

"B-b-but I want to be an Ind-d-d . . . a-a-a Natif Merkan *princeth.*"

Amanda dabbed at her daughter's tears with her sleeve and draped the scarf around the thin, shivering body, arranging it, as artfully as she could, to resemble a three-year-old's conception of what Natif Merkan princesses would wear if Natif Merkan princesses shopped at Nordstrom's.

"Just this once, Sophie. Next time use a towel."

"Natif Merkans don't wear *towelth.*"

"Well they don't wear Mommy's good scarves either, sweetie. Off you go."

"I'm hungry," Sophie replied.

The telephone rang. Upstairs, Ben began shrieking for his lost princess. Sophie did not budge.

"Go!" Amanda pleaded.

"I'm hungry!"

Amanda answered the phone. It was Bob.

"Hi, hon. What's going on there? It sounds like you're surrounded by Apaches."

"Actually, I am." Amanda pushed Sophie out the kitchen door and closed it, keeping it firmly shut with her foot. A second set of shrieks joined the first.

"Can you talk for a minute?"

"Uh, yeah—sure."

"Do you think we could go out for dinner tonight? Alone? I've got some great news."

Amanda brightened. "I'll have to find a sitter—"

"Maybe Hannah could come over from down the block. We won't stay out late."

"Okay, I'll call you back. But what's the news?"

"I'll tell you when I see you."

Amanda hung up and fetched the vacuum cleaner from the hall cupboard. She stepped over Sophie, who lay theatrically on the floor weeping, and ignored Ben's howls. The only upside of vacuuming, she realized, was that it drowned out the screams.

Chapter Two

THE SHEIK KABOB was the restaurant they went to on the rare occasions they could afford to go out to dinner. It was only a few blocks away from their house, in a grotty stretch of old storefronts that had been converted into a grotty stretch of eateries, each one offering a fast-food version of some foreign specialty. Depending on your mood, you could sear your tongue on oily lamb vindaloo or order soggy pad thai while staring into murky aquariums of condemned fish. When Bob and Amanda had first moved into the neighborhood, they'd sampled every restaurant before deciding that the Sheik Kabob was the place in which they were least likely to contract food poisoning. A proud array of yellowed reviews taped to the front window declared it one of Washington's TOP 100 CHEAP EATS of 1988.

On a warm spring evening like this one, tables were set outside under a torn awning festooned with Christmas lights. By the time Amanda arrived, those tables were all taken, and the restaurant's tiny front entry was jammed with customers waiting to be seated. Amanda politely elbowed her way through and found Bob standing at the bar among a line of young men assessing their nightly vodkas.

"How long is the wait?" she called out, by way of greeting.

"Fifteen minutes," he called back. "It may be longer," he added, as she drew near. "I just got here."

Amanda squeezed in beside him and felt, as always, the immediate relief of his presence. She loved meeting him this way, in a restaurant after work, as she had done when they were dating. Bob complained about having to wear a suit and tie to the office, but she liked seeing him in these clothes. He looked so grown-up, so civilized, and yet still youthful. His dark hair curled over the back of his collar. His face, open and gentle, rested upon enough muscle to save it from appearing soft. Good-natured, but no pushover—that was Bob. Amanda only half jokingly likened his arrival home in the evening to the landing of the marines. Almost instantly, order and discipline would be restored among the rebellious natives, and she would greet him like a besieged and grateful villager. As for Amanda, she felt it was an achievement simply to have changed into something clean. Tonight, between feeding and bathing the children, she had managed to pull on a pair of batik drawstring trousers, a black T-shirt, and sandals. She clipped up her unruly brown hair in a messy bun, and, just before running out the door, smeared her lips lightly with gloss. She had long since ceased trying to compete with the stockinged-and-moussed working women. Amanda possessed a whole closet full of business suits that grew more hopelessly outdated every year— padded shoulders, short skirts, zippered blazers, all very eighties. Every fall she vowed to give them away to charity, and every fall she changed her mind. One of these days she *would* return to work. These suits might come back into fashion. They could be altered. And so the suits remained, hanging in their plastic dry-cleaning bags like bodies in cryogenic suspension.

"We could go next door for Mexican," Bob shouted through cupped hands, above the laughter of a boisterous party of six that had joined them at the bar.

Amanda recalled the sight of her stomach in a bathing suit. "No, let's wait. I feel like having one of their salad platters."

Bob nodded as if he had heard her. By the time they were finally led to a table, they had worked their way through two glasses each of the house's sour Chianti. The buzz saws and hammers that had set to work on Amanda's brain after leaving Christine's returned to punch through her skull.

"You okay?" Bob asked as they sat down.

"Just tired."

He grasped her hand across the table. "Well, this should cheer you up."

Amanda was eager to hear his news, of course, but five years of constant interruption from small children had taught them both to wait for the right moment to talk. It was not exactly the right moment now. The back of the restaurant was not much quieter than the bar. The small tables were jammed up against each other like domino tiles and shook unnervingly whenever the Connecticut Avenue subway rumbled below. It had been a long time, Amanda realized, since they could afford to eat somewhere quiet.

"I just got word from Frank . . ." Bob began. He was cut off by the arrival of a waiter, who thrust between them two vinyl-bound menus the size of phone directories.

"Vould you like to 'ear our speshools thiz ev'ning?"

Bob glowered at the waiter, an affable if overworked-looking man wearing the red vest, black bow tie, and green trousers of a lawn jockey.

"I think we know what we're going to have," Bob said, taking both menus in hand. "My wife will have the large Mediterranean salad, and I'll have the mixed shish kabob platter, thank you."

Bob turned to Amanda. "Would you like anything more to drink?"

"No, *thank you*," she said curtly. "Water is fine."

"In that case I'll have a beer."

The waiter took back the menus and left. Bob shot Amanda a quizzical look. Her eyes, which had awaited his news with such interest, were averted and annoyed.

"Are you mad at me?"

"No."

"Are you sure? You seem—"

"I'm not." Amanda rubbed her temples. "It's just, well, you didn't have to be so rude to him. He was only doing his job." What she was really trying to suppress was her irritation with Bob for ordering for her.

"Rude? I wasn't rude! *He* was rude, cutting me dead in the middle of a sentence and dropping a ten-pound menu in my face. Why don't they ever teach these guys to wait for a break in the conversation? Why do they always have to barge in?"

"That's really—*really*—oh." Amanda stared at him, offended. "I can't believe you'd criticize someone who obviously works hard for a living, for, like, sub-minimum wage. Maybe if the job paid better . . . maybe if he didn't come from a different culture . . ."

"Amanda, please," Bob said, taking her hand again. "Let's not turn this into a lecture on the evils of Western privilege. You know me better than that, and I have very important news I want to tell you. *Please?*"

Amanda removed her hand from his grasp. "All right."

Bob carried on, stammering a little before regaining his earlier enthusiasm. "It's finally going to happen," he said. "Frank"—Frank was Frank Sussman, Bob's boss at the Justice department—"is ready to launch a serious investigation into Megabyte. Finally! It took some pressure from the Judiciary committee, but Frank now agrees that what Megabyte has been doing warrants DOJ action, maybe even an antitrust suit. But— wait for it—here's the best part. Guess who's going to be leading the investigation?"

"Who?"

"Me."

"Are you *serious?*"

"Very serious."

This time they barely noticed when the waiter arrived with Bob's beer and their plates of food, which he dealt to them like playing cards. Bob looked as happy as Amanda had ever seen him. No, that wasn't quite it: he looked as if he had just received a hundred volts of electricity to his entire being, and there was so much energy coursing through him that he had to struggle to restrain even his smallest physical gestures, like raising his glass to his lips, lest he inadvertently knock out his teeth.

"When does it start?"

"Right away."

"Well—cheers, hon. You certainly deserve it." She held up her water.

"Cheers."

Amanda pushed some hummus onto a triangle of pita and ate in thoughtful silence. She was happy for him, thrilled in fact, really, but she felt a tugging inside her chest that compromised her sense of joy.

She understood the magnitude of his triumph: Bob had spent the past two years tracking the unsavory business tactics of Megabyte, the largest computer software company on earth. His efforts had been received with almost total indifference by his superiors, many of them holdovers from the last Republican administration. Amanda herself had begun to doubt that Bob would ever turn up solid evidence. She certainly believed in the cause, at least, to the degree that she could comprehend it. Bob had once tried to explain the case to Amanda by sketching it on a paper napkin in this very restaurant. He used terms like *bundling browsers* and *licensing source codes* and *application programming interfaces* ("Those are called APIs," Bob said helpfully), and drew ballpoint arrows shooting this way and that. None of it made much sense, except for Bob's analogy that Megabyte was "the Standard Oil of our time," with its owner, a former hippie named Mike Frith, standing in for the top-hat-and-striped-pants-wearing John D. Rockefeller. *That* Amanda got. What troubled her was that Bob's sole witness and lone ally was an eccentric attorney from Silicon Valley named Sherwood J. Pressman.

Sherwood J. Pressman (and he insisted on using the whole ridiculous name, right down to the middle initial) was a five-foot-three package of paranoia who represented a group of small computer companies, all of which blamed their failures to expand on Megabyte's chokehold on the market. Pressman had written up his clients' complaints in a document that read more like a potboiler novel than a legal brief. Somehow a copy had found its way to Bob's desk. Bob was intrigued, if skeptical ("I find it hard to believe that even a guy like Mike Frith would say something as hokey as, 'If you don't do what we say, we'll cut off your air supply,'" Bob had remarked as he read through the manuscript one evening in bed). Still, Bob contacted the companies involved and gradually became convinced that they had a case, although he told Amanda he would have come to the conclusion more quickly if it hadn't been for the annoying Pressman. Pressman was obsessed with Megabyte and frequently called Bob in the middle of the night to describe the company's latest wrongdoing. Amanda had learned to hand over the phone when it flashed Pressman's number, too tired to express her exasperation that he had woken the baby—and her—for the fourth time in a week. That all of this had at last come to something—well, that was a surprise.

Yet so was her reaction—here, now, watching him. Bob was waiting expectantly for her enthusiasm to catch up to his, but it couldn't. She felt—what? *What?* She tried to fashion a smile.

"What turned them?" Amanda asked suddenly. "Why now?"

Bob finished chewing a mouthful of meat and took a sip of his beer. "A few things, I think," he said, swallowing. "First, as you know, we've now got Frank. He's a lot more interested in these issues than Chuck Mendelson ever was." Chuck Mendelson was Bob's last boss. "Second, Frank's pissed that Megabyte just announced it's going to launch its new software, MB-98, with all these bells and whistles that violate pretty much every promise the company has ever made to us. Third, we've got the attorney general from Texas on our side. There are a couple of big high-tech companies in his state, and they're furious with Megabyte. They're willing to go on the record, which has been a problem because everyone is so frightened of standing up to Mike Frith. And if the big guys go on the record, we can get the little guys to go along, too. They're already organizing themselves."

He shook his head at the wonder of it all. "Basically, we've got live bodies now instead of just weird Sherwood J. Pressman. And Frank's really pumped. He's going to hold a press conference tomorrow."

"That is amazing."

Amanda watched Bob spear his last bit of meat. He seemed so alive and crackling with purpose that she felt . . . envious. Yes. Envious. When was the last time she had felt so alive and crackling herself? Amanda tried to banish her envy—she thought it unworthy—but she could not banish the feeling that Bob's advancement reflected some failure on her part to advance in equal measure. He was not just pulling ahead of his colleagues but soaring past her, and Amanda found herself unconsciously gripping the edge of the table, bracing herself against being buffeted by the force of his slipstream.

"The downside," Bob continued, "is that this is all going to fall heavily upon you. You're not going to see much of me over the next few weeks—except on television. I'll be the shadowy guy standing behind Frank Sussman."

"That's okay." Amanda hoped she sounded like she meant it.

He took her hand again and squeezed it. "How was your day, by the way?"

Amanda flushed. What would Bob say about the pool, the club, the wine?

"Oh, you know," she murmured. "The usual."

Chapter Three

AMANDA STOOD IN the entry hall of her children's school, awaiting noon dismissal. She had been coming to this same spot twice a day for two years, to pick up Sophie at twelve and then again to get Ben at three. Amanda had a lot of errands to run this afternoon and would have liked to fetch Ben early to spare herself a second trip, but the school was as strict about dismissal as it was about everything else. Amanda had already been issued one warning about pulling Ben from his nursery class "unnecessarily."

The Center for Early Childhood, as the school was called, was housed in a converted mansion along one of the oldest streets in Cleveland Park, the fashionable neighborhood to the north of Amanda's. Built at the turn of the twentieth century by a sugar tycoon with political aspirations, little remained of the mansion's historical grandeur except for the white-columned veranda and elaborately worked lunette above the main entrance. Whatever elegant paths and gardens might once have constituted the front yard had been pulled up to accommodate a cement driveway and ramps for the handicapped; its brick

facade was stained by the generations of pigeons that had con-
gregated on an ugly fire escape tacked to one side. All the wood
trim had been poorly patched and painted over the years, lend-
ing the whole house a shabby, institutional air. This shabby,
institutional air, however, was what contributed to the school's
chic among the Washington elite. As the center reminded parents in its annual fund-raising letter, it ranked among the top
preschools in the nation. It prided itself on accepting only the
most academically gifted students. That these students were
chosen almost without exception from Washington's most
gilded and prominent families was presumably a coincidence.

Amanda and Bob were neither gilded nor prominent, but
they had something nearly as good: a connection. The director
of the center, a woman named Sheila Phelps, was an old friend
of Amanda's mother from their feminist marching days. Phelps
agreed to enroll Ben and Sophie as financial-assistance students
because, as she put it bluntly to Amanda, "If it hadn't been for
your mother, I'd still be a housewife."

The few other financial-assistance students came from the city's
poorest neighborhoods and were accepted, Amanda suspected, to
lessen the incongruity between the school's racially sensitive curriculum and its otherwise all-white classrooms. Yet as generous as
Phelps's aid to Ben and Sophie was, it caused Amanda great discomfort. None of the other parents was aware of the financial
arrangement—Phelps naturally wanted it kept quiet—but it was
glaringly obvious that Sophie and Ben had not been admitted
because of their parents' money or reputation. That left only one
possibility, one that even Amanda herself would admit was
unlikely: that her children were exceptionally bright.

Phelps had been blunt on this point, too, at least as it related
to Ben (school policy allowed Sophie, as the younger sibling, to

be enrolled automatically, regardless of her abilities). "Under normal circumstances, you understand," Phelps had said, "we could not accept a student like Ben."

Bob and Amanda had been sitting nervously in Phelps's office, staring into a wall of certificates and awards, as Phelps went over the terms of Ben's admission. She indicated a manila file at her elbow, labeled with Ben's name. "Here," she said, shoving the file across the desk. "Why don't you just take a look."

Inside was the seven-page application form Amanda had filled out the previous winter. It had asked her to list, among other things, "references" for her then three-year-old, as well as to describe his "academic strengths." Amanda prided herself on being an easygoing mother and had always refused to rise to the bait whenever other mothers boasted that *their* toddlers were swimming or reading or speaking fluent French. But then, she had never before had to confront the Private School Application. What was she to write? "Can peel own bananas. Makes choo-choo noises. Barks at passing dogs."

"You'll see the results of Ben's interview just below that," Phelps directed.

Ah yes, the "play interview." Amanda already knew it had not gone well. For twenty minutes, Ben had hunched shyly in his chair opposite the school's psychologist and resisted instructions to stack plastic cubes and draw shapes in crayon. His poor performance was minutely recorded in two columns on a pink sheet, with a number scale that graded him on everything from eye contact to "motor patterns." Amanda skimmed to the end, where the psychologist's felt-tipped scrawl concluded that Ben suffered from "acute social anxiety" and possessed "poor scissor skills." Before he could be admitted to the center, Phelps informed them, Ben would have to seek occupational therapy for his scissoring. The social anxiety, Phelps said, was something the school could take care of itself.

Amanda did not end up enrolling Ben in occupational therapy—occupational therapy for scissoring cost eighty dollars per hour. Instead she spent a few minutes with him each day over the summer cutting pictures from magazines. Ben mangled every bit of paper handed to him and, what was worse, seemed to delight in mangling the paper. "Look," he would say proudly, holding up a face he had cut in half. Amanda would lose her patience, and Ben would burst into tears. She left off the exercises a few weeks into Ben's first term and did not hear anything more from the school about his scissoring. By then there were other problems. The teacher called to say that Ben had pushed a child during recess. Next he was rolling balls of plasticine into missiles and launching them at the blackboard. He barged into lines. He would not join in singing during "circle time."

Ben's behavior inflamed the suspicion with which the other parents viewed Amanda. Except for Christine, whose son formed a fierce and immediate friendship with Ben, most parents resisted having their children play with him. Amanda launched a lobbying effort on Ben's behalf. She volunteered at every school event and gamely manned a face-painting booth at the PTA winter carnival. The mothers she met were unfailingly friendly. They would exchange anecdotes about child rearing. But they would not take the further step of arranging a play date or suggesting a get-together for coffee. Amanda had attempted that step many times, only to be deftly rebuffed. ("I'd love to but with the kids' soccer schedule everything is crazy right now. Maybe in a month or so . . .") Amanda would wish, yet again, to pull her children from the school and send them somewhere else. But as Bob would patiently remind her, they could not actually afford a cheaper education for their children.

"He's too young for public school, and we're not eligible for aid at another school, so we're stuck," Bob would say. "Look, I don't like our kids knowing only a bunch of Austens and Courtneys and Olivias, either. But what else are we going to do?"

And Ben had to go somewhere: Amanda did not need a professional to point out that her son was developing "issues." Bob scoffed at the psychologist's assessment of Ben and took his teacher's reports lightly. "I was always getting into trouble at his age, and I turned out okay. We'll speak to him about it, but don't worry. He'll be fine. Really." And yet Amanda didn't know if Ben would be fine, really. Those were the same words Bob and others had used to comfort her through the first two years of Ben's life, back when she was working full time. Amanda did not like to recall those days when she used to sit in her cubicle at the National Endowment for the Arts, crafting press releases for events that would not get covered, while her toddler molded clay into dinosaur families and wondered where his mommy had gone.

She and Bob would drop off Ben every morning at seven-thirty, at a day-care center in a local church basement. She chose this center because of the women who worked there, silvery-haired church matrons whose voices never lost their soothing lilt as they pried Ben's fingernails from her calves. *Come let's see what's in the dress-up box. Look at the beautiful pictures Josh is making with finger paint.* Amanda could hear Ben's cries from the parking lot. Bob, guiding her by the elbow, implored her not to go back. "It will just make it worse—he'll be okay in a few minutes." But when the scenes didn't improve, Amanda, at the church ladies' insistence, ceased to accompany Ben inside. Bob took him in while she waited in the car with the windows rolled up and the radio switched on. Bob would come sprinting back, leap into the driver's seat, and pull away before fastening his seat belt. "He's getting much better," he would say, without looking at her.

All day Amanda would monitor the clock in her office, imagining what Ben was doing—play, snack, lunch, play, nap, snack—and assuring herself that the separation was good for both of them. Ben needed to be with other children in a world bigger than his own; she needed to be in the big world, period.

Then came summer, and the dappled green mornings that just begged you to come outside before the air grew thick and everything was stilled by the heat. On the drive to work Amanda would glimpse mothers pushing their babies to the playground or jogging with strollers along Rock Creek Parkway. They looked so unharried; their day seemed to stretch out before them like a bather on a towel. By contrast, there was not a single minute during the week that Amanda felt she could stop, hold, enjoy. When she came home at night, Amanda craved half an hour— just half an hour!—to change her clothes, go through the mail, reorder her thoughts. But there was dinner to make, and those dishes that had been sitting in the sink since breakfast, and the backed-up toilet, and the note reminding her to call the plumber whom she had forgotten to call again. Mostly, though, there was Ben, desperately tired and hungry, but equally desperate that she not leave his sight. He insisted that Mommy—and not anyone else—give him his bath; that Mommy—and not anyone else—put him in his pajamas and read him a story; that Mommy—and not anyone else—sing him his lullaby. Ben virtually ignored his father when she was around. Bob tried. He pleaded with Ben to let him, just this once, put him to bed. But Ben would have none of it. Amanda could not help but relent. Her son loved her with more physical intensity than any lover she had ever known, yet what he wanted from her was so simple and innocent: to hold her hand, to smell her hair, to fall asleep in her arms.

What was Amanda to do? Everyone else insisted she should keep working. Her mother was adamant. Why, when *she* was thirty-two, Ellie Burnside Bright was founding the first-ever natural-birth clinic in Manhattan—*and* she was divorcing Amanda's father. Imagine how strange it would feel *not* to go to the office, her mother warned. I did that, Amanda, I stayed home with you, and it practically killed me. Thought I'd bloody well go out of my mind sitting around the apartment reading women's magazines, waiting for you to wake up. Remember when I nearly *did* go out of my mind? (Yes, Amanda did. Amanda had been four, or maybe five. Her mother left her with the cleaning lady and went AWOL for a day. Years later, her mother admitted to Amanda that all she did was walk through the park and wander up and down Madison Avenue, stopping somewhere for a coffee. Amanda might not have even noticed her mother's absence if the cleaning lady had not been so distressed. She called Amanda's father at work and said she had to get home and where was Mrs. Bright? Amanda played by the apartment door until she heard the key turn in the lock. Her mother burst in, and Amanda exclaimed, "Mommy, we were so worried!" Her mother pushed past her without a word and slammed the door to her bedroom, where she remained for the rest of the evening. The cleaning lady went home.)

Amanda was too embarrassed to confess to her mother that she no longer took pleasure in going to the office. She was too embarrassed to confess it to herself. It cast doubt on the glorious certainty she had experienced the first day she had stepped through the Romanesque arches of the endowment's building: *At last,* she had exulted, *this is where I'll be. This is who I am.* Now when she passed under those same arches, she could only mutter weakly, *This is who I must try to be*. How, Amanda wondered, did the other mothers do it? How did they work through the pain without folding up like circus tents and taking the whole show home?

Then, one morning, three months into her pregnancy with Sophie (and hey, what a barrel of laughs that was, running to the executive bathroom to vomit and dozing off at her desk after lunch), Amanda realized she could no longer do it. She experienced what her mother, in her feminist heyday, used to call a "click" moment, except in reverse: Amanda was waiting as usual for Bob to come running out of the day-care center like a hero in the "money shot" of an action movie just before the building explodes into a giant fireball. She was eating a package of soda crackers to quell her nausea. The entire scene suddenly struck her as absurd. *What on earth am I doing?* Ben needed her—needed *her!* This new baby would need her, too. Nothing else seemed important at that moment except those two facts.

"Bob," Amanda said, as tires screeched against pavement, "I can't do this anymore."

She saw he knew exactly what she meant.

They didn't discuss it until later, when they sat down at the kitchen table after dinner to work it all out. Bob conceded that Amanda's modest salary only covered the child care and the weekly cleaning lady, bills they no longer would be burdened with if Amanda stayed home. He earned enough to pay the mortgage and their household expenses. But if she quit there would be no extras: no new car as they had hoped, fewer dinners out, no refurbishing of the house. Government, Bob reminded her (as if she needed reminding), was not like the private sector. He could not increase his billings or hope for a bonus. His salary was his salary. They would just have to pray that none of the pipes burst.

As Amanda watched Bob punch away at the calculator, scratching down the numbers that represented their livelihood, it occurred to her for the first time the sacrifice she was asking of him. He had fallen in love with a woman whose ambition matched his own. And now she had just rolled the boulder of their shared expenses completely onto his shoulders and was expecting him to carry it without resentment or complaint. She searched his face for a reaction, and it came when he glanced up at her across the table: Amanda saw confusion in his eyes, as if he were trying to realign his vision of her, like someone attempting to refocus his binoculars on a bird whose quick flight had caused its image briefly to split in two.

Amanda's colleagues reacted to her decision with less-disguised bewilderment. They shook their heads sorrowfully, as if they had just lost another comrade in battle—*All that promise, to be cut down so early in life!* Her boss, a childless woman of fifty, added to the mood of requiem by praising Amanda for her "great courage."

Predictably, Amanda's mother took the news the worst. *This is not rebellion, Amanda,* she lectured over the phone. *This is reversion. You can always have a husband, you can always have children, but you can't always have you. And Amanda, you are throwing the you part away. Throwing it away! Where is that daughter of mine who used to talk about making a difference in the world? Where is the little girl who marched around the bedroom chanting songs about women's power? What do you have to say to her?*

The truth was: nothing. Nothing at all. Amanda remained silent as Ellie Bright begged her to reconsider, just as some years before she had begged Amanda to reconsider getting married so young, at twenty-six, the first in her circle of friends.

"Mom," Amanda interrupted. "Aren't you always saying feminism is about choice?"

Ellie Bright paused. The pause, in its way, was more intimidating to Amanda than her mother's yelling—the short silence that precedes an even greater explosion.

"So isn't what I'm doing a choice?" Amanda ventured, a little more timidly.

Her mother snorted. "Of course feminism is about choice. It was just never about *this* choice.

"But suit yourself."

And with that, her mother hung up the phone.

For the first few months of her unemployment, Amanda tried to persuade herself that she was really, truly exercising a choice that should be available to all women. She took even a brief, rebellious pride in her decision and complained to Bob about all the ways society discriminates against mothers, just as she used to complain to him about all the ways society discriminates against minorities and the poor. But as the novelty of her situation wore off, and as Amanda sang "Itsy Bitsy Spider" for the umpteenth time to Ben while longing to lay her miserably fat pregnant body down upon the bed, she had to admit that it wasn't bravery or rebellion that kept her going through these long and unproductive days. It was guilt. Guilt had driven her to leave her job. Guilt kept her singing mindless songs and playing clapping games with Ben. Guilt was the emotion that eclipsed all others in her heart when she anticipated the arrival of the new baby. Amanda was home because she feared the hurt and anger in fifteen years, when two sets of eyes would look upon her and mutely ask, *Why did you do that to us?*

Amanda drank the last dregs of a take-out cappuccino. Glancing around the school's entry hall, she recognized a couple of mothers in tennis whites chatting by the water fountain. Clusters of nannies formed an archipelago around the front doors. Amanda nodded at a father whose daughter Sophie occasionally played with. He was the only male among them, referred to in whispers by the other women as "the at-home dad." Usually he sat alone, on the floor in a corner of the lobby, gazing straight ahead with the subdued, gentle eyes of a Labrador. He was married to a fierce trial attorney whom Amanda had met once, at parent–teacher night. The woman had arrived directly from the courtroom in sharp heels and an expression that had not finished grilling its last witness. Occasionally, Amanda and the dad waited together. They had discovered, in the snatched moments between picking up and delivering children, that they shared a mutual interest in politics, and Amanda enjoyed his semi-ironic takes on the day's news. Today, however, he was trying to pacify his eighteen-month-old son, who was writhing and thrashing to free himself from his stroller. Amanda crumpled her cup and tossed it in a trash container next to the women in tennis whites. They acknowledged her with the briefest of smiles. Amanda returned to the spot where she had been standing, beside a huge potted palm.

The bell rang, and instantly the narrow stairwell became a downspout gushing noisily with nursery students.

"Mommy!"

Sophie gripped the banister while struggling to carry a huge cardboard—gosh, what was it? A butterfly? Children jostled past the little girl, but she steadied herself and edged sideways down the steps.

"Mommy, look!" Sophie tried to hold up the cardboard to show Amanda. A boy raced by and nearly sent girl and artwork flying. Amanda rescued both at the bottom of the stairs.

"What have you got, darling?"

"It's the divethtive system!" Sophie exclaimed, recovering herself.

"The *digestive* system?"

"Yes!"

"It's beautiful." And it was, sort of, with its colorful squiggles and bits of glued-on pasta to represent what Amanda guessed was food passing through the intestines. She wondered vaguely where she would hang it.

"Are you hungry, honey?"

"Yes!"

A mother of one of Sophie's classmates stopped them on the veranda.

"Hey," she said. "I saw your husband on television this morning."

Amanda stepped to the side of the exiting stream and the mother joined her, clutching her own son's hand. She was attractive in an expensive way, her frosted hair cropped and feathered and her eyes nearly invisible behind tortoise-rim sunglasses. Amanda could not remember the woman's name.

"You did?" she replied, surprised. "Bob was on TV?"

"Uh-huh. I was at the gym so I couldn't follow it that well. It was some press conference—something to do with Megabyte?"

"Oh—yes, the antitrust case. Bob's leading the Justice department's investigation." Amanda wondered why she felt the need to stress that.

"Wow." The woman nodded, impressed.

"Mommy, can we go to Burger Chalet?" Sophie interrupted.

"Yes, sweetie. I mean no, sweetie. We're going to go home and then do some errands. The vacuum cleaner's broken and we need to return your library books."

"And we've got Suzuki, don't we, Christopher?" the woman said to her son. "Violin," she confided to Amanda. "He's very gifted but he *won't* practice."

Sophie tugged impatiently on Amanda's arm. The mother smiled in understanding and gave a gentle wave of her hand.

"We should get our children together sometime. Christopher and I often lunch at the club, don't we, Christopher?"

Sophie kept up a steady chant to go to the Burger Chalet. At the top of the school's driveway, Amanda hesitated, waiting for the other mother to pull out in her silver Mercedes wagon before she went to her own car.

"Mommy, ith over there!"

"I know, darling. Let's let the others go first."

Amanda unlocked the Volvo and managed to wedge the digestive system into the trunk. She strapped Sophie into her child seat. Sophie fished around the upholstery and came up with a half-gnawed cookie.

"Oh, Sophie—don't. How long has that been in there?"

Sophie bit into it. "Ith good."

Amanda sighed and settled herself in the driver's seat. She switched on the car radio.

"I want ducky music!"

"No ducky music. Mommy wants to listen to the news."

"Ducky music!"

"No. *Daddy* is on the news."

"Daddy on the news?"

"Yes. Listen."

A male announcer was giving the five-day forecast.

"That Daddy?"

"No. Wait." Amanda scanned the other channels but it was past the hour and the news was already over.

"Okay," she relented. "Ducky music."

Amanda merged into the street to a chorus of singing water-fowl.

Chapter Four

BOB MIGHT HAVE at least called her to give her a heads-up, Amanda thought irritably. Maybe he had called her.

When she arrived home later in the afternoon, after picking up Ben, there was a message on the phone but it wasn't from Bob. It was from Susie. How long had it been this time? Five weeks? Six? Susie lived only a few blocks away but Amanda heard from her less frequently these days than when they had lived in different cities. Susie never rang up just to chat. She would burst into Amanda's life without warning, like a fire truck roaring down the street, sirens howling. *Amanda how are you I need to see you right away.*

Actually there was not one but three messages from Susie. "Hi, are you around? Thought I might come by this afternoon. Got some news I want to tell you." "Amanda, where are you? If you get this, try me on my cell." "Amanda, you won't be able to reach me for the next little while. Why don't I just stop by your house around four?"

It was closer to five when Susie arrived, right at the moment when Amanda decided her friend wasn't going to show up after all. Amanda was about to race out to the supermarket—there was nothing for dinner again—and, well, here was Susie. Amanda made iced tea and sent the children upstairs to watch a video. The two women sat down in the back garden, and Amanda waited for Susie to reveal the reason for her visit.

"Gorgeous day."

"Yes."

"I've wasted most of it inside, at the spa." Susie extended her long fingers to display a fresh manicure. "Tangerine. What do you think?"

"Very summery."

"I think it suits me."

"It does."

"You should go there—they do a great facial." Susie rambled on for a few minutes about the other treatments she had received—everything, it seemed, short of having a new face applied. Her skin had been sandblasted clean like a Chelsea warehouse and troweled with Austrian mud. "It's fabulous. It sucks out all the impurities . . ."

"How Germanic."

". . . then there's this new vitamin C cream they slather on you that really makes your skin radiant."

Susie paused, expectantly. Amanda agreed she looked radiant. "But you don't need creams for that. You always look stunning."

It was true. Amanda had known Susie long enough to become inured to her looks, but she could never be unaware of them completely. Susie possessed the kind of beauty that affected the very molecules in a room. The child of a white mother from an old New England family and a black professor of economics from Chicago, Susie had been blessed with the unexpected features that elevate great beauty over run-of-the-mill prettiness:

bronze skin and silky hair, eyes that were widely spaced apart, a full mouth set in a delicate chin. Had Susie ended up in a city like New York or Los Angeles, she might have faced more serious competition from starlets and fashion models seeking bigger prizes than best-looking girl in Wichita or Kalamazoo. But Susie's ambition to be a political commentator had brought her to Washington, where beauty is notoriously scarce outside cherry blossom season. Her unconventional package—this face, this figure, *plus* an opinion on the latest education bill!—had taken her very far indeed.

"Thanks, but it's getting harder."

"Come off it."

Amanda shifted restlessly in her deck chair, wishing Susie would get to the point. Long experience had taught Amanda that Susie wouldn't anytime soon. Once Susie had gained her attention, she would keep it, indifferent to the maternal alarm clock inside Amanda that was frantically ticking off the minutes she had left to get to the store, the minutes before the video would end, the minutes before the next round of demands would come clumping down the stairs.

"Have you heard from Liz lately?" Susie asked, changing topics. Amanda wondered what Liz had to do with Susie's news. Liz was a friend from college who had moved to upstate New York and joined Amanda in the ranks of unemployed maternity.

"I spoke to her last week. Why?"

"I just wanted to know how she's doing."

So the news wasn't about Liz.

"She's fine."

"Still obsessing over her house?" Amanda didn't quite like the edge to Susie's tone. Susie seemed interested in Liz these days mostly as an object of sport.

"I wouldn't call it 'obsessing.' She's re-covering her sofa, if that's what you mean. And you know Liz—she's doing it herself, the slipcover, everything."

"I knew it!" Susie exclaimed in triumph. "I knew it would be something like that. She can never talk about anything else. It's either decorating or the kids. That's why I stopped calling her. She's like some prefeminist nightmare. It's hard to believe she has a degree in women's history. Thank God *you're* not like that."

"Her kids are still very young," Amanda said in her friend's defense, but she was pleased by the compliment. *Susie doesn't think I'm like that!* "It's hard when your children are that age to do or think about much else."

"You've managed to keep your brain alive."

"Not always. I seem to remember some anguished discussions with you about potty training."

"Yes, but I could always count on you to snap back. Five minutes later you'd be going on about the election."

Susie had nearly finished her glass of iced tea. Amanda glanced toward the house expecting to see the children by now but there was no sign of them yet. Her eye caught the rip in the screen that Sophie had made three months ago. The rip bothered Bob—not that he nagged her about it, he was too New Man for that. He only ventured to point it out once, courteously, as something Amanda "might see about getting fixed." Every time he passed it, though, she was aware of him noting it with a little sigh, as if to say, *I'm not trying to suggest you're not busy at home with the children all day, and honestly, I respect what you're doing, but couldn't you find time to make one lousy phone call? It's not like I don't have endless trivial things to attend to in my day, too.*

"How's Brad? . . ." Amanda prodded. Brad was Susie's occasional boyfriend and the usual reason for Susie's emergency calls.

"Brad?" Susie seemed puzzled by the mention of him.

"Yes. *Brad.* The man you've been dating for, what is it now, two years?" Amanda had spent hundreds of hours with Susie parsing Brad. She knew he had a mole on his backside and that he had once bought Susie thong underwear. She knew all about his previous girlfriends and his reasons for breaking up with them. She knew how much he made at his law firm, that he was trying to lose ten pounds, that he played squash and not tennis, that he preferred solid blue shirts to striped ones, that he didn't like Susie's taste in ties, and that he preferred Campari-and-soda to gin-and-tonic. Amanda was pretty sick of hearing about Brad—frankly, more sick of Brad than she was of Liz's sofa. The sofa would be good for another ten years at least, which is more than she could say about Brad.

"But I haven't seen him," Susie said, not taking Amanda's hint. "Not since you and I last spoke anyway."

"Isn't he who you wanted to talk about—the reason you came over?"

"Brad? Oh no, not *him.*" Susie laughed. "Brad's the same as always. I've got *much* better news than Brad."

Amanda gave Susie an imploring look. "What is it? You've met someone else? *Tell* me."

"All right. Sorry. It's just that it hasn't happened yet, but it's going to, and I had to tell *someone,* but keep it a secret—okay?"

"I promise."

Susie leaned toward her, as if even the shrubbery had ears. "You know how Megabyte is launching a new cable channel—?"

"Yes, of course—MBTV."

"Well—" Susie hesitated, then burst out, "They're giving me my own show!"

"Oh, Susie, that *is* great news."

Amanda felt a flush of jealousy.

"Well, it's almost my own show," Susie corrected herself. "I'll have a cohost. Do you know Johnnie Johns, from the music channel? He's a veejay, but he wants to do more-serious stuff. Our show will focus mostly on political and current events—the things I'm good at."

"That's wonderful."

"Yeah, it's going to be a lot of fun. The producers are trying to appeal to the younger market, you know, the twenty-somethings who are turned off by boring talking-head shows like *Live from the Hill*. They should rename that show *Dead from the Hill*, if you ask me. We're going to be way more hip. Our set is really cool, too. It looks like a loft."

"Fabulous."

Amanda's attention drifted briefly to a clay pot containing straggly pansies she had not yet replaced with begonias. A broken plastic rake lay next to it, alongside the deflated remains of a kiddie pool she had tried to set up earlier that afternoon. She told herself that she did not envy Susie her show—truly, she didn't, her ambitions did not run in that direction—but it was the second time in less than twenty-four hours that she had endured the blow of someone else's good fortune. For a few seconds she felt winded.

"They want to launch it as soon as possible," Susie continued. "We're looking at next month. They haven't nailed down the slot yet but I'm not worried. They've promised buckets of money to promote it. If there's one thing MBTV doesn't lack, it's money."

"That's for sure. Mike Frith and his billions. Funny."

"What's funny?"

"It just occurred to me—you know Bob is—" Amanda thought better of what she was going to say. "Well, Justice and the whole antitrust thing. Bob's involved in that."

"Separate branch. Doesn't affect cable."

"I guess that's right."

"Anyway, it's great—great for me," Susie said. "Because you know if you're not on TV, you don't exist in this town."

Amanda brushed away a wasp from her slice of lemon. She ignored Susie's little jab, convincing herself, as she always did, that Susie was unaware of it. Beauty reduces everyone else to a supporting role. Amanda, Bob, Brad, the whole dancing circle— in Susie's eyes, they were all just extras in her ongoing drama. Like many supporting actresses, Amanda reconciled herself to her role by telling herself that hers was the more complex character. Susie was clever, but not as clever as Amanda. In college, Susie would entrance men with a light, quick remark, but it was Amanda who followed up with the strong argument. The only time they had a falling-out—a prolonged falling-out—was after Amanda met Bob. Supporting actresses are not supposed to get the man; certainly not before the star herself. Much, much later, Amanda would ask Bob why he had been attracted to her and not to Susie. "That's easy," he had answered. "Susie's the sort of girl you look at but not the sort you get involved with."

"Why not?"

Bob shrugged. "She's work. You can tell just by looking at her."

"Some men might think her worth it," Amanda persisted, concealing the pleasure she took in his answer. "She's very beautiful."

"Yes, she is. But it's fashion-model beauty. It's not the kind of beauty that you actually want to touch."

Amanda's unwelcome romantic subplot caused Susie to pull away, and for the next few years Amanda encountered her friend more often in gossip columns than in person. After Susie graduated, she landed a summer internship at the Negro Progress

Fund, a stodgy but respected civil rights organization. Between photocopying and fetching coffee, Susie sold an article to *Harper's* titled "Growing Up Black and White." The article was illustrated by a grainy but heart-stopping photograph of Susie, in a daringly unbuttoned Oxford shirt, brooding over her struggle to find a racial identity. The article—or rather, the photograph—caused a flutter in the national media. Susie was made communications director of the fund by its president, who declared Susie "the face of the next generation." Suddenly Susie was receiving more requests for media interviews than her boss, an elderly giant of the rights movement who had once marched with Martin Luther King Jr. And once the cameras caught sight of Susie, they would not let her go. A network hired her away from the nonprofit world to give broader commentaries on politics. Somehow she pulled this off: Susie's secret weapon—to the surprise of men who unwisely condescended to her—was the quick comeback, and her beauty and poise distracted even critical viewers from listening too carefully to what she had to say.

Pretty soon Susie was being groomed to be a daytime anchor, and then a host of her own show. But Susie—as Amanda knew well—was not gifted at asking questions of other people; too often, she talked over them, answering her own question, leaving her guest mute and irritated. The television critics made fun of her and the show was canceled after one season. Six months later a glossy magazine published an especially mean-spirited article—"Whatever Happened to Susie Morris?" Susie took her revenge by dating rich and prominent men. Amanda eagerly followed these boldfaced romances—until they sputtered out. There was a dot-com tycoon, then a senator well known for his womanizing, followed by a network executive and a mining heir (who later turned out to be of ambiguous sexuality).

Amanda accepted the loss of Susie's friendship—she could not envision even a bit part for herself in Susie's now star-studded life—but it was Susie who eventually circled back, like a seagull seeking respite on an old, familiar pier. By then Amanda had given birth to Sophie and the old dynamic could reassert itself: in Susie's eyes, Amanda was once again playing the unthreatening number two to her commanding lead.

That was fine—Susie's life was nothing if not diverting—but on this afternoon, Amanda's patience was wearing thin. Susie showed no inclination to leave. She had removed her sunglasses and closed her eyes, tilting back her face to absorb a radiant shaft of sunlight filtering through the trees. Lit this way, against the humble backdrop of Amanda's backyard, Susie resembled a golden messenger dropped to earth by the gods.

"Mommy?" Ben emerged from the house with a saucepan on his head.

"Ben, what are you doing?"

"Playing knights." He looked at Susie without interest and then back at his mother. "Can Sophie use your umbrella?"

"No, Ben, no. Not in the house—"

"Ben!" interrupted Susie with mock indignation. "Is that any way to say hello to me?" Susie was given to eruptions of maternal affection toward Amanda's children that lasted only so long as Ben and Sophie were willing to endure them. The rest of the time she regarded them as sweet but intrusive pets who, after a scratch under the chin or a small treat, should be content to go away and lie down.

Ben ignored her. "Outside can she?"

Sophie appeared behind Ben, stark naked as usual.

"Sophie!" Susie gushed. "Are you going to give Susie a better welcome than your brother did? Give us a hug."

Sophie trotted over and hugged Susie.

"Did you bring a present?" the little girl asked artlessly.

"Maybe." Susie rummaged through her handbag. "I know I brought something . . ." She produced a ballpoint pen.

Sophie looked as pleased with the pen as if she had been presented with a diamond tiara. She turned it over in her hand to admire it.

"Say thank you, Sophie."

"T'ank you."

"What about me?" Ben stared greedily into Susie's handbag.

"I'm sure there's something in here for you, too." After another search, Susie came up with a small packet of breath mints.

"Yuck," said Ben. "I hate those."

"Ben—"

"I'm sorry but that's all I have, sweetie." Susie snapped her handbag shut.

"Maybe we should go inside," Amanda suggested. "That way the kids can play out here."

Susie followed her into the kitchen, where Amanda began tidying up the mess the children had left. Susie sat at the table and watched. Amanda balked: couldn't Susie *see* how late it was? Then she caught herself. Why *would* Susie race home? Awaiting her was a perfectly decorated Georgetown row house sitting perfectly undisturbed. Amanda visualized it all—the sleek beige sofa with its row of silk cushions, unsullied by small fingerprints; the terry robe hung over the treadmill; that day's mail scattered over the polished wood floor. Lining the bookcases were framed photographs of Susie with politicians, Susie with her parents, Susie at parties, grinning wildly, her arms flung around friends. Late at night, in the dull shadow cast by a single lamp, these pictures would attest to a life of such fun and glamour that Susie could shut out, for a moment, the unbroken hum of the refrigerator and the male voice in the bedroom, trailing down the stairs from the TV.

"What are you doing for dinner?" Amanda asked.

"I've got a horrendously busy day tomorrow," Susie answered, evasively. "I was planning on going to bed early."

"Would you like to have dinner here? I'm just going to eat with the kids. Bob will be late."

"Oh, hey, sure. I'm not that hungry. I was just going to pick up something on the way home anyway."

"Then stay. Only, I've got to run to the store."

"Fine. We can take my car, if you like."

They packed the children into the narrow backseat of Susie's convertible. "Yippee!" shouted Ben. Susie popped in her "driving music."

"Do you think the kids will be safe without their car seats?" Amanda yelled over the blast of electric guitars.

"They're fine. They're belted—besides, we're only going four blocks."

Amanda allowed herself to relax and enjoy the fragrant summer air blowing in her face. She could get used to going to the supermarket like this. But when she glanced over at Susie, who in her sunglasses looked like a starlet touring the Côte d'Azur, Amanda realized that she had been reduced once again to the supporting role in yet another Susie Morris production.

When Bob got home, the children were asleep and Amanda was in bed, reading. She came downstairs and found him foraging through the fridge like a hungry bear.

"I saved you dinner." Amanda indicated a covered plate on the counter.

Bob kissed her cheek and pounced on the plate. He tore back the foil. His face fell.

"I wish I'd bought stock in Fresh Farms," he grumbled, staring at the familiar cold helping of sesame noodles, mixed beans, and boneless chicken breast from the whole foods supermarket where Amanda did most of the grocery shopping. "If as many people lived off their prepared food as we do, we'd be rich by now."

Amanda bristled. "I didn't have time . . ."

"No, no, it's fine, it's fine." Bob rummaged through the cutlery drawer for a knife and fork and opened the fridge again.

"Are we out of beer?"

"Oh gosh, yes, Bob," Amanda apologized. "I must have forgot."

"No problem, no problem. I'll have a Scotch. I think I deserve one tonight."

He reached above the fridge to the high cupboard where they stored their few bottles of hard liquor. Most of them had been given to Bob and Amanda as gifts and still had little bows attached.

"Thank you, Uncle Joe." Bob poured himself a large finger of Scotch and drank it down quickly. He filled the glass again with water and sat down to his meal at the small table in the corner of the kitchen.

"How was your day?" he asked, his mouth full.

Amanda poured herself a glass of water and joined him at the table.

"Busy. Not as busy as yours, I bet."

"Yeah, what a day."

"You were on television." Amanda hoped that bluntly asserting the fact would save her from having to admit that she had missed seeing him.

"I was?" Bob paused in his eating.

"Yes. At the press conference."

"Huh. I thought I'd be out of the shot. How did I look?"

"Good." Amanda sipped her water.

Bob scraped up the last bits of food with his fork and looked up hopefully. "Is there any more of this?"

"In the fridge."

Bob fetched the plastic containers and scraped the leftovers onto his plate.

"I thought it went pretty well," he said, sitting down again. "Frank did much better than I'd hoped. He's been pretty squeamish about the whole thing."

"I thought you said he was enthusiastic."

"He is, he is. But today he really had to take the plunge. I mean, going after Megabyte is no small thing. You want to make sure you have firm evidence."

Bob was speaking to her with a slightly cocky air, like a star athlete explaining to an announcer how his team was going to win.

"And he has the evidence, right?"

"Pretty much."

"What do you mean, pretty much?"

"We still have to get the depositions," Bob allowed, "you know—from all the companies Megabyte's been kicking around. But we'll get them. You saw the press conference. It's not just that Mike Frith wants to tell everyone they have to use Megabyte software. Frith would love to control all online commerce as well. That's really the issue. Imagine if Mike Frith stood to gain a commission from every sale that was made on the Internet. *Every* sale—new cars, airline tickets, clothes, you name it. He could do it, too, if we don't put a stop to it. And I'm telling you, we will."

Amanda listened, uneasily. She had never seen Bob so fully caught up in his work or willing to align himself so completely with his employer, using *we* instead of *the Justice department* or simply *Justice*. Bob had always tended to approach his work with a detached attitude, one that took pride in never seeming to be in the pocket of anybody, one that had greeted unexpected problems and surprise betrayals by his colleagues with an ironic smirk, as if he had expected them all along.

Bob shoveled the last of his noodles, burbling about the assurances he had received from Sherwood J. Pressman. Now that Justice was "serious," getting the depositions would be "a piece of cake." Faith in Pressman—that was something new, too.

"You done?"

Bob stared at his empty plate like a small boy, wishing it would magically refill itself. "I guess so."

She took it from him and stacked it in the dishwasher.

"Anything go on here today? Kids okay?"

"Kids are fine. Susie was by."

"Huh."

"She had good news—"

"What, Brad finally popped the question?" For a moment Bob seemed interested.

"No. About her work. She's starting a new show."

"Oh." Bob found a blueberry muffin in the bread drawer and proceeded to devour it. "Hope it's better than the last one."

"You're always so hard on her."

"I'm not hard—just honest. Her last show was a dog."

Amanda agreed but would not say so. "This one sounds better. It's about current affairs and she has a cohost—a veejay from the music channel."

"A veejay? On current affairs? Why is that a better idea?"

"It's different—"

"I'll say."

"You're being negative again."

"Look, Amanda, I can't see how it will succeed. The audience for political talk shows—aside from Beltway wonks like me—is mostly retirees like my father, and believe me, they have no interest in what some moron veejay has to say about their Medicare."

"Well, that's the point," Amanda returned, tired of Bob's ever more far-ranging assertions of expertise. "The show isn't aimed at your father. It's airing on Friday evenings, for one thing. It's aimed at younger people who don't usually watch these shows—the sort of people who—"

"—are at home on a Friday night and eager to hear Susie's views on the Federal Reserve?" Bob grinned.

"I'm sure it's not going to be like that." Amanda wiped up some crumbs with her hands. "Anyway, I just hope it works for Susie. She needs this."

Chapter Five

CHRISTINE LED THE group of mothers into an enormous vaulted room replete with enough slipcovered sofas and chairs to fill a hotel lobby. Everything about the room felt as if it had been purchased in its entirety from a decorator's showroom and reassembled here, right down to the artificial bonsai on a side table and the gilt-framed row of botanical prints above the mantel. Even the photograph of Christine's children, propped on a grand piano, looked borrowed from a photographer's studio. Amanda could only imagine the struggle and bribery that had produced such a wholly unnatural portrait of Austen, smiling cherubically in a sailor suit with his hair neatly combed to one side, a beribboned Victoria in his lap, her hands clasped in the folds of an elaborate velvet dress.

Amanda settled herself in an armchair and was nearly swallowed up in its cushions.

"My mother always warned me to avoid 'drinking' play groups," Christine said as she poured out wine. "She knew one. Half the women in it got divorced, and the other half got cancer. Cheers."

The women tittered and raised their glasses. The toast was broken by a shrill scream from somewhere in the nether regions of the house.

Amanda knew right away that the scream did not belong to Ben or Sophie; but she also knew that if a child screamed beyond the parental perimeter, Ben was the odds-on favorite to have caused it. Sure enough, a little girl came running into the room wailing, "Ben did it! Ben did it!"

"Meredith!" The girl's mother rose anxiously. "Ben did what, sweetie?"

"Hit me with a truck!"

"Oh, Meredith, come here and let me see." The mother cast an accusing look at Amanda.

Christine sighed and topped up Amanda's already full glass. "Now you're in trouble," she whispered. "Your boy has injured the hundred-thousand-dollar child."

Christine's private nickname for Meredith Ripley derived from her best estimate of the cost of the fertility treatments that had been required to conceive the girl. Meredith's mother, Patricia, was a well-groomed, weary-faced woman in her late forties. Until the miraculous birth of her only child, Patricia Ripley had worked as an executive at an international consulting firm. She described motherhood as "the hardest multitasking job I've ever held."

Meredith gulped and sobbed while Patricia inspected a bump on the side of the girl's head. Even with a wet face and disarranged pigtails, Meredith looked as if she had just tumbled from a Victorian etching. Her mother dressed her in exquisite pinafores and ruffled blouses bought at a boutique that specialized in European clothing. Amanda had ventured into this store once, shortly before Ben was born. The shop's prices left her gasping, but she could not stop herself and paid seventy-five dollars for a tiny white linen sunsuit for Ben's ride home from the hospital. When the day arrived, Amanda unpacked the beautiful garment from its tissue wrapping and somehow wriggled his resisting body through the confusion of straps and buttons. Unfortunately, the nurse neglected to warn Amanda that her baby's first venture into the outside world would likely be accompanied by another colossal achievement: his first bowel movement. "Good God, it's leaking out the collar!" Bob gagged as he raced to their front door, thrusting Ben as far away from him as a proud father's arms could reach. That was the end of the sunsuit. It was also the last time Amanda bought clothing for her children that couldn't be washed or, for that matter, sterilized.

"Am I broken?" Meredith asked plaintively.

"There, there, you're not broken, darling, but it *is* a bad bump."

The other women exchanged awkward glances. Amanda murmured that she would go get Ben, but at that moment her son entered, pulling fiercely against the hand of Christine's nanny. In contrast to Meredith, Ben—dressed in sale-rack army shorts and a T-shirt emblazoned with a ferocious dinosaur—could not have appeared more guilty.

"Mommy!" he cried at the sight of his lone ally. He freed himself and charged head-on into Amanda's stomach. "I didn't do it!"

Ben's denial provoked a fresh round of outraged screams from Meredith. The mothers looked to the nanny, a slight, nervous woman from the Philippines, who addressed herself to her employer. "This boy hit little girl with truck, ma'am. I tell him to say sorry but he say no."

"I didn't!" came Ben's muffled voice as he buried his face deeper into Amanda's lap.

"Ben," Amanda said, gently tugging on him until she had gotten Ben to look up at her. "Tell Mommy what happened."

"Meredith's *head*," Ben insisted, "got in the way of my *truck*."

"Huh," Patricia sniffed. "I think a time-out is in order. At least, that's what I'd do."

"Ben," Amanda continued, "if you don't say sorry to Meredith right now, we are going home. Do you understand?"

"No!"

"*Ben!*"

The little boy walked sullenly over to Meredith. "Sor-*ry*," he spat out with as much contempt as a five-year-old can articulate. He shambled past her back to the playroom. The little girl looked helplessly to her mother.

"You stay away from that boy," Patricia warned her in a hushed, but not hushed enough, tone. "He's *violent*."

Meredith bit her lip and nodded, and was led away by the nanny.

"Well!" Christine declared. "Boys will be boys, won't they? Who needs some more wine?"

The mothers lapsed into an uncomfortable silence. Amanda stewed in mortification. Patricia would not look at her. The two other mothers, Kim and Ellen, offered her weak smiles. Every child in the play group had, at some point, launched a surprise assault against another, but Ben was thought to possess unique nuclear capability. Amanda knew that if it weren't for Christine, she would have been drummed out of the group long before. Amanda had tried to drop out herself, but Christine had been adamant that she remain. "I know Patricia can be rude—you know how ridiculous she is about Meredith—but really, Kim and Ellen would be *devastated*. And Victoria adores Sophie. So do all the girls."

Amanda yielded to the flattery but, even now, remained puzzled by Christine's interest in her. Christine once remarked that it was "so refreshing" to be in the company of someone "who is interested in *things*," but Amanda couldn't help but feel that Christine viewed her essentially as a new project, another room to redo or piece of furniture to refinish. It was in this spirit that Amanda had been introduced to the group—"Y'all are going to love Amanda. She's a bohemian"—but her novelty was clearly less appealing to the others. Kim and Ellen were polite and affable, but then, as Amanda had discovered, they were relentlessly polite and affable. Even the rounded tips of their manicured fingers and toes reminded Amanda of the shores of a coastline whose jagged edges and distinctive outcroppings had long been smoothed away. Amanda sometimes suspected that she could confess to murdering both her children and Kim and Ellen would nod sympathetically and say yes, they too had buried many infants in their basements, but if you placed open boxes of baking soda around the house it helped to absorb the smell. The first time Ellen and Kim had met Amanda, they greeted her with the feigned enthusiasm with which they accepted their children's "finds" from the backyard. Patricia, on the other hand, had immediately fired off a series of laserlike questions that might reveal Amanda's "point." What sort of work had she done before she quit? Was she on any of the committees at the school? What did her husband do? They all registered surprise when Amanda answered that her husband worked in government. Amanda could see the question marks in their faces—Government? How do they afford it?—followed by the conclusion: she must come from money. *So that's why Christine brought her.*

Amanda sank lower, if that were possible, into the chair cushions. She stared through the tall windows at a terrace framed by boxwoods and the flat glint of a swimming pool just beyond. Patricia kept glancing in the direction of the playroom and at one point disappeared for a few minutes "just to check." She reported that the nanny had plopped all the children in front of a video (*Thomas the Tank Engine,* she added, to the mothers' approval). This smoothed the atmosphere somewhat, and Amanda relaxed a little, knowing it was unlikely that Ben would launch any new assault so long as there was a television switched on.

Then it was Christine who startled them.

"I may as well tell you all," she said matter-of-factly. "You probably would have noticed anyway. I've chosen a very special present for my fortieth birthday. When Brian asked me what did I want—diamonds? a trip to Venice?—I told him, 'Honey, I want my thirty-year-old face back.'"

"That's fabulous, Christine!" Ellen exclaimed immediately. "You *deserve* it."

"What are you going to get done?" Kim asked eagerly. Kim was their resident scholar on beauty treatments. Every week she seemed to be undergoing some new treatment that promised to shave a year off her appearance. At their last gathering she had arrived with a swollen, blistered face. Amanda thought she must have had some terrible experience with a sunlamp, but Kim explained that she had received a "chemical peel"—a procedure that scorched away the top layer of her skin. Kim said the red blisters would fall off and expose the soft, youthful layer of skin below. The blisters disappeared as predicted, but Amanda could not detect any real difference: Kim's skin shone as any surface will, given regular and attentive polishing.

"Not a lot," Christine replied. "Eyes, forehead, chin. It won't be a full face-lift, not yet, just a general tweaking."

"Thank goodness I don't need anything," said Patricia, patting her sagging cheeks.

"Christine's not doing it because she *needs* to. She's doing it because she *wants* to—right, Christine?"

"You're nice to say that, Kim. I wish it were true." Christine arched her neck so the women could examine the sorry decline for themselves. "Look at these banjo strings," she said, strumming an imaginary surplus of skin below her chin. "And my eyes—these hoods make me look like a lizard." The women strained forward and shook their heads. "So what the hell? I think of this as an offensive rather than a defensive action. I don't want to turn into one of those old horrors you see at the club—you know, the kind who show up one day with their faces stretched tight as cellophane."

This last observation provoked protests all around—"Oh, Christine, you won't become one of them," "Really, you're beautiful the way you are"—but Amanda also detected a slight unease, as if Christine had just raised the ante among them. Ellen's hands rushed to check her own neck while Kim discreetly probed the skin around her eyes. Only Patricia seemed unperturbed. "It's all in the genes, you know. My mother is seventy and looks fantastic. Never had to do a thing."

Amanda didn't know, frankly, what to think. Part of her was too horrified to react. Why would Christine carve herself up to fit some male fantasy of how she should look? Wasn't this akin to other barbaric practices foisted upon women by patriarchal societies, a North American version of genital mutilation? Yet it was difficult to imagine Christine as being anybody's dupe when Amanda contrasted her indignant opinions with the composed figure of Christine herself—smiling, inviting them all to join in her plan to triumph over age and gravity.

At last Amanda found her voice. "Does Brian want you to do this? I mean, is he pushing you to do it?"

"Oh please." Christine waved away the very suggestion. "Brian supports whatever I do. He thinks I look great now. He'll be happy when I look even better. No, I'm doing this for *me*."

Christine's finality of tone hinted that it was time to move on to another topic, but Amanda couldn't let it go. "Because sometimes women, if they're insecure—"

"Oh, honey, I'm *secure*," Christine said, with a flash of irritation. "My fate doesn't rest on Brian's opinion of me. Look, I do the bookkeeping in the family, and let me tell you, if he left, I'd be more than secure. I've taken care of that."

"So have I." Kim giggled, and Ellen nodded.

"Heck, I've got an entire investment portfolio that Steve doesn't even know about," Patricia remarked lightly. "I built it up when I was working. I think of it as my 'disaster-relief fund.'"

"You know, a friend of mine gave me the name of a terrific lawyer—just in case. She just went through a hellish divorce."

"I have one, too, but quite frankly, Steve doesn't stand a chance if he walks out. Not that he would *want* to walk out, of course."

"No. But you've got to be prepared," Christine acknowledged. "We can't be like our mothers' generation. They went into marriage practically blind."

"You can say that again."

"A few months ago I walked into a Starbucks, and there was the mother of my best friend from high school—working behind the counter. Her husband left her after thirty years. *Thirty years!*"

Amanda, subdued by this turn of the conversation, took a

cracker from the untouched cheese plate and marveled at her own blindness. For all her professed independence, what steps had she taken to protect herself? When she gave up her job, the thought did cross her mind that she was surrendering what her feminist professors used to call "economic power." But somehow it hadn't felt that way. Amanda and Bob continued to divide the household tasks, viewing their new arrangement as simply a change in the form of their partnership. They were still equals, making different contributions to what remained a joint enterprise, the Bright-Clarke household. Or so Bob had characterized it in his typical attorney fashion, and she had agreed. It had seemed like an enlightened, egalitarian approach to a situation that was otherwise unthinkably traditional. Now it all struck Amanda as mad. Even Ellen and Kim had the wit to prepare themselves, while she, Amanda, had blithely thrown her lot in with Bob in every way, relying—so carelessly!—on the tenuous power of affection to carry her through these years of unemployment. Suddenly she felt like a tightrope walker who looks down and notices that she has been crossing without a net.

"Well, I think you're courageous, Christine," Kim was saying. "I've sort of been thinking of getting my eyes done."

"Gosh," exclaimed Ellen. "Maybe we should all go together. Make a field trip of it. I've always hated my nose."

Amanda struggled to pull herself up in her chair. "I don't know. It just seems a lot to put yourself through—surgery." She knew it was a retreat.

"Spoken like a thirty-five-year-old." Christine smiled. "You don't have to worry yet. You have great skin." She cast her eyes over Amanda appraisingly. "But have you ever thought about doing something with your hair?"

*   *   *

That evening, Amanda toweled herself off in front of the bathroom mirror and studied her body from every angle. She turned
sideways and backward. She raised her hair and let it tumble
down. She moved in so closely she could see the grayish pores of
her nose and then stepped back to judge the effect of her features
as a whole. She tried to do this all without flinching, in the
detached manner of an accountant logging assets and deficits.
Perhaps it was the lighting—the unflattering brightness of the
overhead light that cast some parts of her in high relief and others
in shadow. Or maybe it was because she was focusing upon herself all at once, instead of in pieces, as she usually did, so that
she could appreciate her nice calves and ignore her thighs. But
the longer she looked, the worse her body appeared. When she
finally turned away from the mirror Amanda wished she could
wrap herself in a chador rather than this thin towel.

Bob lay on their bed in his boxer shorts, reading legal briefs.
He was frowning slightly and marking passages with a highlighter pen. He did not look up when Amanda padded past him
to fetch her pajamas. Crouching self-consciously behind the
open closet door, Amanda pulled on her night uniform (an over-
sized T-shirt of Bob's, a pair of cotton sweatpants). What was
Bob's real opinion when she passed by him like she did just
now? Did he quietly revile the sight of her loose buttocks? How
often had his eyes traced the faint tributaries of stretch marks that
riddled her belly? And what did he think of her breasts? . . . During their courtship, when Bob had greeted every newly unveiled
attribute of hers with surprise and delight, he had been capti-
vated by her young breasts. Years of being put to utilitarian use
feeding babies had toughened her nipples and caused the breasts
themselves to hang charmlessly, like week-old party balloons.

She went to the bed and curled up uneasily beside him. Amanda waited for a single warm gesture that would banish her fears, that would make them seem hysterical and crazy. Bob continued marking his briefs. His bare chest rose methodically with his breathing; his gut, which had been firm when they met, rolled over the rim of his shorts. Occasionally Bob would announce that he needed to lose ten pounds, but he did nothing about it. Was Bob indifferent to the shape of his body—or indifferent to Amanda's opinion of it?

"Do I look okay?" she asked him.

"Hmm?"

"Do I look okay?"

He paused his highlighter pen. "Don't you feel well?"

"I don't mean that. I mean, do I look—do you still find me—attractive?"

Bob adjusted his expression to one of lawyerly inscrutability, as he always did when he suspected Amanda of asking him a trick question. "Of course. Why do you ask?"

"Really. I want to know."

The files were whizzing behind Bob's eyes as his brain searched for the correct answer.

"I think you look beautiful," he said, not altogether convincingly. "I always have. Really."

She laid her head upon his prickly chest. She heard him sigh and place his papers on the bedside table. He draped his arm across her.

"What's bothering you?"

"Nothing."

"Have I done something to make you think I don't think you're attractive?"

"No—"

"Then why do you ask?"

"Because—" It seemed too humiliating to explain.

"Because?"

"Because I just looked at myself in the mirror, and, I don't know, I look older."

"You are older. But then, so am I."

"With men it doesn't matter."

"With you it doesn't matter." Bob grasped her chin and forced her to look at him. "Christ, Amanda, you're still young. Your face looks the same as the day we met."

"And the rest of me?"

"So you've had two children. So you're a bit fuller. It doesn't make you less attractive."

But I will get older and less attractive. Then what?

She got up to brush her teeth.

"Are you coming to bed?" he asked. He sounded hopeful.

"In a minute."

In the mirror above the sink, Amanda saw a drab woman with blue ditches under her eyes, a brush listlessly marking time between bared lips. She spat and turned away.

Bob was waiting for her. She could sense his eagerness across the room. How long had it been? She couldn't remember exactly—a couple of weeks, maybe. Admittedly, making love to Bob these days felt like one more thing she had to cross off her to-do list.

On the dresser lay a candle and a book of matches. Her fingers moved toward them, hesitated, and then flicked off the lights instead. As she made her way to the bed in darkness, she experienced again that dizzying feeling of stepping upon a wire with nothing below to catch her if she fell.

Chapter Six

"I NEARLY FORGOT," Bob called out the next morning, while descending the stairs. "Are we free next Thursday?"

Amanda was nagging the children to put their shoes on.

"Gee, let me think." She placed her index finger on her chin. "Monday—you'll be working late. Tuesday—you'll be working late. Wednesday—you'll be working late. Thursday—I don't know. Are you planning on working late?"

"Okay, okay." Bob took a sip from a mug of tepid coffee waiting for him. "You won't be sarcastic when I tell you this. We're invited to a cocktail party at Jack Chasen's house. Do you want to go?"

Amanda blinked. "Jack Chasen?"

"Yes—you know, he's the CEO of TalkNet."

"Yes, I *know*. We're invited to Jack Chasen's house—*and you almost forgot to tell me?*"

"I'm sorry," he said sheepishly. "It was a busy day."

She sat down on the hall floor to help Ben with his sneakers. "Good God, Bob, how are we supposed to go to that? We won't know anyone there."

"We don't have to go. I thought it might be fun. Chasen's a

down-to-earth guy. I've been dealing with him a lot lately, and he just asked."

Amanda pounded at the heel of Ben's shoe until it slipped onto his right foot, and started on the second.

"I have nothing to wear."

"So go buy yourself something."

Amanda looked at him skeptically. "With what?"

"We can afford a dress, for God's sake."

"Not the kind those women wear."

"You're not those women. You don't have to compete with them. Anyway, it's just a cocktail party."

She raised herself, sighing, and said, "Ben, Sophie, get your backpacks. It's time to leave. You'll make Daddy late."

Bob handed Amanda his mug and hustled the children toward the front door.

"Look, think about it, okay?"

"Okay."

"What are you up to today?"

"I have that appointment with Ben's teacher."

"Oh yes." He kissed her quickly. "I'm sorry to miss it. Let me know how it goes."

Ben's teacher, Ms. Burley ("That's *Ms.* not Miss"), was the sort of person with whom it was impossible to have a light exchange of pleasantries. A quick hello might be greeted with, "Ben forgot to bring in his coins for math again yesterday." A fast dash into the classroom to deliver a forgotten lunchbox could provoke a five-minute discourse on personal responsibility. Amanda wasn't her only victim: Ms. Burley regarded parents generally as barriers to education. On the first parents' night, shortly after the term began in September, Ms. Burley had lectured the assembled adults on such matters as the correct tools for learning ("pencil cases must be twelve inches by four inches—nothing else will be considered acceptable") to instilling proper work habits in nursery students ("this year the children will receive a minimum of thirty minutes of homework per evening—this will prepare them for the increased workload they will face in kindergarten"). The ideal parent, Ms. Burley noted, perceived learning opportunities in every daily activity. Bath time offered "the perfect chance to demonstrate specific gravity, using simple toys that sink or float." A walk through the neighborhood could easily be turned into "an exercise for identifying grid patterns." Cooking dinner was, of course, basic chemistry. To prevent slacking, Ms. Burley would send a "suggested" exercise home every day for parents to complete with their children, such as counting all the clocks in the house or adding up the change at the bottom of Mommy's purse. Amanda was dubious of the benefit of these exercises to Ben, but she was certain they accomplished Ms. Burley's main objective, which was to make a mother feel that however much she was already doing for her children, it was still hopelessly inadequate.

Amanda entered Ms. Burley's classroom that morning at the agreed-upon time. The room was dark; the children had gone to recess and the lights were switched off. Amanda thought she might have made a mistake—maybe the appointment was the next day—but a rustle behind an open supply cabinet indicated the presence of Ms. Burley.

"Come in, come in," the teacher said, emerging with a sheaf of papers. "I'm here."

Physically, Ms. Burley was unprepossessing. She was slight

and short and dressed in the dowdy but practical clothing of a nursery school teacher—baggy blouse, leggings, and scuffed leather flats. Her personality expressed itself in the sharpness of her movements and the permanent expression of dismay pinched upon her face.

"The lights were off—I wasn't sure."

"I don't believe in wasting power. We can see well enough. Please sit down." Ms. Burley invited Amanda to pull up a child's chair that was three sizes too small for her. She settled herself in the upholstered swivel chair behind her desk.

"I want you to look at these." Ms. Burley handed Amanda a stack of Ben's crayon pictures.

"Oh yes, he loves drawing."

"I can see that. Just look at them closely."

The first picture showed some childishly scrawled airplanes with bright orange and yellow explosions bursting around them. Ben had labeled the drawing "WW1." Amanda turned to the next one, which was similar, except that it was labeled in the same uneven writing "WW2." Continuing through the stack, Amanda came across "WW3," "WW4," and "WW5." This last was especially bloody, with little stick figures strewn on the ground, red crayon spurting from them. Amanda placed the pictures back on Ms. Burley's desk.

"So, what do you think?" Ms. Burley asked her.

"Ben's an optimist?" Amanda said, hoping to elicit a smile from Ms. Burley.

"That's not what I think," the teacher replied sternly. "I think what we have here is a troubled boy showing early signs of an obsession with violence."

Amanda frowned. "I—I don't think that's right. I wouldn't say that Ben is 'obsessed' with violence—"

"Then how do you explain these drawings? And it's not just the drawings." Ms. Burley waved her hand in exasperation. "There is not an object in this room that Ben has not at some point turned into a weapon. Last week it was the blackboard eraser."

"I don't know. I can't explain it." Amanda picked up one of the drawings to study it again. "We certainly don't encourage violence at home."

And this was true. She and Bob did not allow what they called "war toys" in the house. The only exception to this rule was a plastic figure of General George Patton in his cavalry uniform, equipped with two miniature pearl-handled revolvers, a gift from Bob's father last Christmas. Amanda had immediately reproached her father-in-law for the present. "You know how we feel about guns," she had said. "We don't want Ben growing up to be a criminal." "Or a war hero," the old man had muttered under his breath. Ben, who understood at once that this was exactly the kind of toy his parents would never permit him to own, ripped it from its cardboard wrapping and kept constant watch over it, lest it "vanish" like the last Christmas present his grandparents had bought for him: a commando costume complete with a machine gun that lit up and made electronic zapping noises when fired.

"I'm not suggesting you encourage violence," Ms. Burley was saying. "What I'm wondering is, are there problems at home?"

"No—"

"Any changes recently? Upheavals?"

"Look, I really don't think Ben's behavior is that unusual—for a boy, I mean. Perhaps it's because his grandfather is a veteran; Ben likes to hear him tell stories, and maybe these

pictures just reflect a—a *historical interest* in war, like a lot of
boys have . . ."

"We needn't revert to sexist stereotypes to see that Ben has a
problem. The other boys don't engage in this obsession."

"Ben's best friend—Austen Saunders—likes that sort of play.
They're always shooting at each other! I put a stop to it, of
course—"

"It would be improper for me to comment on other children
in the class," the teacher replied stiffly. "But let me put it this
way: I haven't had to call in any other mother to discuss a similar problem. Other mothers, however, have called in to complain about Ben."

Amanda suddenly felt her gut shrivel up. Oh, why had Bob
not been able to join her at this meeting?

"I want this addressed before we promote Ben to kindergarten," Ms. Burley continued ominously. "It would be very
tough on him if he couldn't be promoted with his friends."

"I see." Amanda searched her brain for another line of defense but couldn't find one. "What do you suggest?"

"Well, before school ends for the summer, I'd like him to
attend a few sessions with our guidance counselor. With your
permission, of course. Dr. Koenig is excellent at dealing with
these kinds of problems."

"I think—"

They were interrupted by the yells and laughter of the class
returning from recess. Ben saw his mother from the hall. With a
whoop of excitement, he yelled, "Attack!" dived into the room,
and rolled across the floor to her feet.

"—that would be fine," Amanda finished.

Ms. Burley pursed her lips. "Good. I'll tell Dr. Koenig. She will
call you."

Amanda extricated herself from Ben's grasp and led him to his desk.

"I'll see you later," she whispered, ruffling his hair.

There was no time to get home before Sophie's dismissal so Amanda lingered in the lobby, brooding over this latest condemnation of Ben.

The front doors squeaked open and slammed. Their echo carried down the empty corridor. Only gradually did Amanda become aware of another presence. The "at-home dad" was hovering near her. His usually squalling toddler was fast asleep in his stroller.

"Hey, Amanda."

"Hey, Alan."

"What's up? You seem—kind of upset."

"Is it that obvious?"

"You look as if the Republicans have started drilling for oil in Rock Creek Park."

He sat down in his usual place on the floor, shifting to give her room beside him.

"I've just come from speaking to Ben's teacher."

"Oh. That's always fun."

"Yeah, like dental surgery, right? Especially with Burley. Wait till *you* get her. She thinks Ben is too—" Amanda couldn't bear to use the word *violent* so instead she said, "robust."

"Huh." The father's *huh* was not uttered with the astonishment Amanda expected; Ben's reputation had apparently extended into the lower reaches of the nursery school as well.

"I just don't understand it," Amanda went on. "At home Ben is so sweet. He plays for hours with his sister. They barely ever fight."

The father stretched out his legs and idly rocked the stroller with one foot. "That's one of the problems with this school," he said slowly. "They're always trying to put your kid into some sort of box. But I tell myself, that's the world, right? The world is always trying to put you into some sort of box, and you may as well learn early on how to fight your way out of it."

His burst of bitter profundity surprised Amanda, and she glanced at him sideways, uncertain how seriously he meant to be taken. He was still staring straight ahead, but his expression was not angry; it was bemused—as if life were always dealing him predictable blows. Her eyes lingered on him for a moment more—she hadn't ever really taken him in like this; they had always conversed hurriedly, among the other waiting mothers, their attention half focused on the stairwell—

"I suppose you must encounter that mentality all the time—being an 'at-home dad,'" Amanda suggested.

"Yeah. Actually, I'm a playwright, not that anyone ever bothers to find out. I work at home because it's more convenient and economical, and sure, I can watch Dylan while Lisa's at the office. But it's difficult—Nabokov warned of the perils of the pram in the hallway . . ."

"Are you able to get much writing done?"

"I work during Dylan's nap and again late at night. Right now I have a play being workshopped in Maryland. Fortunately they rehearse on weekends."

"That's great." It didn't sound promising, but still, it was something creative, something Amanda couldn't even imagine accomplishing herself. Guiltily, she recognized that she, too, had succumbed to boxlike thinking in regard to Alan. No matter how much she endorsed the idea of a father at home, when confronted with a fortyish unshaven man in tennis shoes and jeans pushing a stroller, Amanda could not help but think: *Loser.* She corrected her opinion now. Alan's scruffiness was his defiance of convention, his way of expressing his artistic integrity. For the first time she appreciated, in the sinews of his arms, in the sweat faintly spotting his T-shirt, that as well as being an attentive father, he was also very much a man.

"What's your play about?"

"You know, you're the first person here to ever ask me that?" Alan said, impressed. "I've sat here and chatted with dozens of mothers and we've never gotten beyond school stuff." He lowered his voice, for the mothers he referred to were beginning to arrive and collect around them.

"My play," he went on, almost whispering and causing Amanda to lean closer, "challenges exactly these kinds of stereotypes. My protagonist is a homeless man who is not really homeless. He's a young man who comes from inherited wealth and contracts AIDS. His family rejects him. He rejects them in return and everything they represent. He spends the last months of his life on a journey through the streets, defying the preconceived ideas we have about the homeless and people with AIDS."

"That sounds—really good."

"It's coming together okay," Alan replied modestly. "My last play was put on by the downtown Y. It was about—well, it's hard to sum it up in a nutshell, but basically it addressed gender issues through the eyes of a transsexual prostitute. The Warner was thinking about producing it for its 'New Playwrights' series but I think they found it too challenging."

"I'd love to see your play."

"I'll invite you to the opening."

The bell rang and they stood, smiling at each other.

"Sometime we should have a coffee together. It's good to get out and, you know, talk to other adults," Alan said, giving his sleeping baby an accusing look. "And you tell Ben to keep being—what was it?—robust. All he's doing is breaking out of the box."

Amanda touched his shoulder. "Thanks."

"Are you feeling okay now?"

"Yes—way better."

"That's good—although I like seeing you angry. There's fire in you, too."

Chapter Seven

THE HOUSE EVEN had a name: "Merrymount."

The car wheels crunched to a stop in the raked gravel. They were greeted by three valets in tuxedos.

"Good evening, sir," said the first, accepting Bob's keys. The second waited patiently for Amanda to unlock her door so he could open it, and bowed slightly as she emerged. The third handed Bob a claim ticket. None registered the slightest reaction to their car. It was driven a few feet away to join a line of BMWs, Porsches, and Mercedes parked in front of a six-door garage.

Bob and Amanda gazed up at the house. Its imposing facade of new orange brick was an opulent jumble of architectural styles, as if the owner had decided he could afford everything: Georgian roof, neoclassical pillars, Palladian windows. A row of perfectly symmetrical boxwoods stood sentry by the porch. All natural foliage seemed to have been banished to the rear of the house.

"Am I dressed okay?"

"You look *great.*"

A butler opened the door before they could ring the bell, and they entered a front hall crowded with guests. The house seemed to unfold in every direction. To the left of the stark white foyer was a curved staircase leading up to a similarly cavernous second-floor landing. To the right, a pair of lacquered doors had been thrown open to expose a suite of rooms that stretched farther than Amanda's eyes could see. Straight ahead a pair of tall, skinny columns framed a two-story window, showcasing a wooded view of the Potomac River.

A waiter stepped in front of them bearing a tray of white wine. Amanda and Bob each took a glass.

"Please, stay with me," Amanda whispered, grasping Bob's hand. "I don't know anyone at all."

They stood rigidly for a few seconds, uncertain how to proceed.

"Look, there's Sussman with Chasen," said Bob, pointing to the big window. Bob's boss was huddled in animated conversation with their host, Jack Chasen, founder, largest shareholder, and chief executive officer of TalkNet, the biggest Internet service provider in the world. "Do you want to say hi?"

"Oh God, no. We can't just go barge in on them."

"C'mon, don't be so frightened."

Bob gripped Amanda's arm and steered her through the crowd toward the two men. Sussman smiled when he saw them and waved them closer.

Amanda had met Frank Sussman a couple of times at Bob's office. He was a short, thin man with the waxy complexion and sunken cheeks of a cadaver. Chasen, by contrast, was tall and handsomely tanned, as if he spent most of his waking hours yachting or playing tennis rather than sitting in front of a computer screen plotting the downfall of his archrival, Mike Frith.

Sussman greeted Bob enthusiastically. "Do you know Bob Clarke?" he asked Chasen. "He's my most valuable soldier. He was on to Megabyte from the beginning."

Chasen circled an arm around Bob's shoulders. "Of course I know Bob. I've been working with him a lot these days. So glad you could come tonight."

Amanda stood behind Bob waiting to be introduced. Bob, flushed from Sussman's compliment, seemed momentarily to have forgotten her.

"You know, Frank," Chasen continued, turning back to Sussman. "If I had one guy as smart as Bob working for me, we'd have put Megabyte out of business a long time ago."

"Sorry, Jack, you can't have him."

The three men launched into a discussion of the looming Senate hearings on the Megabyte case. That very afternoon, apparently, the Judiciary committee had nerved itself to summon Mike Frith to testify in person.

Amanda sipped her wine and swiveled her head back and forth as if she were part of the conversation, her irritation gathering with each turn of her neck. Neither Sussman nor Chasen acknowledged her with so much as a glance.

Chasen appeared unusually interested in what Bob and Sussman had to say. He asked them questions solicitously, even humbly. And while Sussman answered with lawyerly evasiveness, Bob was soon expounding his views at length. He spoke in a manner entirely unfamiliar to Amanda, with the solemn, lowered voice of a panelist on one of the Sunday-morning political shows.

"See, Frith's so arrogant," Bob was saying, "I think he's going to come off badly no matter what the committee asks him. I think the best thing these hearings could do for us at this point is show the public what a vain jerk Mike Frith is. Right now the polls aren't great: people don't like Megabyte very much, but they like the idea of the government going after it even less. It's really critical we get popular support on our side—and Frith can help us do that."

"That's an excellent point, Bob," Chasen said.

Amanda discreetly prodded her husband in the back.

"Oh, excuse me, this is my wife, Amanda," Bob said.

"Amanda *Bright*," she added, extending her hand toward Chasen.

"Do you work at Justice as well?" Chasen asked.

The firmness drained from her grip.

"Um, no . . ." she stammered. "I used to be at the National Endowment for the Arts—but now I'm at home with my kids."

"Ah." Chasen dropped her hand. "Well, that's a very noble calling."

Sussman nodded perfunctorily, mumbled how nice it was to see her again, and turned back to Chasen. After several minutes of maintaining a frozen expression of interest, Amanda excused herself to find a bathroom.

Amanda supposed she should not feel so angry or hurt. She had grown accustomed to being treated at certain kinds of Washington parties as if she were invisible. But never before had she been invisible to her own husband. She edged her way back to the front hall, where she figured there would be a bathroom if she really needed one. She didn't, but it gave her a purpose: so long as she kept moving, she wouldn't appear stranded and alone.

A short, ridiculously foppish man stepped into her path. His hair was gathered in an elaborate comb-over. Over a sky-blue T-shirt, he wore a baggy white suit that looked as if it ought to belong to a gangster or a rap star. His eyes furtively scanned the room like two heat-seeking missiles locating their targets. She knew at once who he was.

"You must be Sherwood Pressman," Amanda said, with more warmth than she felt. "I'm Amanda Bright. We've spoken before on the phone."

The lawyer from Silicon Valley fixed his eyes upon her. He obviously could not decipher who she was.

"Bob Clarke's wife," she added, flushing.

"Yes, yes. I see." He nodded impatiently. "Is Bob here?" he asked, looking over her shoulder.

"I just left him. He's over by the window, talking to Frank Sussman and Jack Chasen."

"He is?" Pressman barged past her, leaving Amanda staring speechlessly into the empty space that he had so flamboyantly occupied a second before.

She drew herself up and continued walking. A waiter dipped by and exchanged her glass for a full one. There didn't appear to be a bathroom off the foyer, so she followed a corridor to a dining room where another big crowd surrounded a long table laden with hors d'oeuvres. Amanda noticed French doors leading to a flagstone terrace overlooking the Potomac. The terrace was empty; she wandered out and rested her elbows on a wrought-iron railing. In the winter the steep cliff might seem rocky and perilous, but at this time of year it was upholstered in green, and the river looked unimpressive, a muddy trickle taking its time to reach the Atlantic.

The early-evening heat cloaked Amanda's bare shoulders like a fur stole. Almost immediately circles of sweat began to form under her arms. Amanda was wearing a black silk camisole and a black linen skirt that she had found after much rummaging through department-store sale racks. She had bought the outfit on the advice of Christine, whom she had consulted in her pre-party panic. Christine warned her not to try to compete with the wealthy guests, but instead to choose something simple and black ("and spend your money on the shoes—those are what they always judge you by"). Christine, as usual, was bang on. Amanda stood out less starkly than she thought she would. A small minority, the very richest women, wore pale pantsuits that obviously cost thousands of dollars. But most of the women at the party were dressed in the familiar Washington cocktail outfit, what Amanda had come to think of as "the doorman suit": a big-shouldered synthetic blazer in a bright jewel color, with rows of shiny brass buttons. At the crushes she and Bob occasionally attended—events put on by organizations like the American Bar Association, in the stadium atmosphere of a downtown hotel ballroom—hundreds of these suits would bump up against each other, wearing plastic nametags in place of brooches.

Amanda retreated to the refrigerated comfort of the indoors. She saw, at a distance, Bob being buttonholed by Pressman, and decided to walk in the other direction. Amanda passed into a formal sitting room, painted lemon yellow and crammed with the brand-new "antiques"—Chippendale chairs, Colonial side tables, Ming vases—of office-tower boardrooms. Amanda recognized one of the combative hosts of *Left/Right* speaking to a tall silvery blonde, a right-wing regular on *Live from the Hill*. The two seemed to form their own eddy of Washington fabulousness, and Amanda instinctively steered wide of them. Between the sitting room and an equally commodious library was an arched antechamber, punctured by a small white door that Amanda guessed led to a powder room. She tried the handle and it opened into a tight, tomblike space encased in pink marble. Two walls were covered from waist to ceiling by mirrors, and in their reflections the tiny room redoubled itself into infinity.

Amanda locked the door behind her and sat down on the closed toilet seat. She removed her sandals—pretty, impractical, and expensive sandals that she had bought on impulse for her new outfit, which had rewarded her by carving red grooves in her feet. She dampened a linen towel and dabbed at the inflamed skin. She didn't mind the excuse to rest for a few minutes in a place where she wouldn't be seen. Not that she had been seen. The lines of Amandas in the mirrors assured her she existed, but out there, she would have to rattle the blinds to turn a head.

She ran more cool water from the tap—a brass rendering of a swan's neck—and wondered how much longer Bob would want to stay. Bob did much better than Amanda at these types of parties. Even before he had become important to the Megabyte case, he could walk up to a cluster of people and speak in a way suggesting they should know who he was. Indeed, it was at an anonymous party like this that she and Bob had first met. Susie had dragged her to that one—a keg party on Capitol Hill, in the row-house apartment of some junior-assistant-to-a-congressman, who put out some beer and welcomed anyone who cared to show up. The living room was jammed, but the crowd parted to admit Susie and, as an afterthought, Amanda. The two of them found their way back to the kitchen, where a group of young men wearing suit pants and open-necked dress shirts were standing around a plastic cooler, jocularly debating a health-care bill that was then making its way through Congress. Their joshing ceased the moment Susie entered. One pulled out a stool; another hunted through the cupboards for a glass for her beer. Susie accepted this all as her due—and then won even more admiration by refusing the glass and swigging her beer straight from the bottle.

Amanda had helped herself to a drink and stood by the doorway, turning her attention to the scene in the living room.

"Amanda," Susie called. "Tim here says he works for Congressman Weinblatt. Isn't he the one you know?"

Perched on her stool with her legs crossed, Susie reminded Amanda of a showgirl about to do her big number.

"Wein*berg*," Amanda corrected, turning away.

Amanda noticed a man approaching the kitchen. She reflexively stepped aside to allow him to pass. To her surprise, he stopped; he did not push through her to get to Susie. He did not push through her to get a beer. Nor was he seeking directions to the bathroom. Instead, amazingly, he seemed intent on striking up a conversation with her. Amanda.

"I'm Bob. You look as bored as I am."

She liked his face right away. She liked the way he looked at her—as if he had known her already for some time and was just reestablishing their acquaintance.

"I came here with a friend." Amanda nodded toward Susie in the kitchen. Bob glanced over her shoulder and appeared unimpressed. "I'm Amanda, by the way. And yes, I'm dead bored. How could you tell?"

"You seemed critical."

"Critical? That's different from being bored."

"Not really. When intelligent people are bored, their faces don't become all soggy and apathetic, like a fish's"—he paused to demonstrate, glazing his eyes and pouting stupidly—"they become critical. You were just thinking, *Hmm, how on earth did I wind up here? And who is this big galumphing guy coming toward me?*"

Amanda laughed. "I wasn't—not really."

Her laughter drew him closer to her. "Yes. You were."

"Not the *galumphing* part. I would never use a word like *galumphing*."

"Goofy?"

"Goofy yes. But not to describe you."

"That's a relief."

Bob leaned against the doorframe as he spoke to her, with one arm instinctively shielding Amanda from the jostle of people passing in and out of the kitchen. He craned forward to hear her every word. They talked and talked—at first, perfunctory details of where they worked and how they came to Washington, building to an almost urgent swapping of life stories, as if each of them could not get to know the other fast enough. Gradually every corner of the room filled up, and they moved outside to the front stoop of the house to carry on their conversation. Bob led her through the crowd clasping the tips of her fingers.

It was January, and Amanda had worn only a light leather jacket (vanity ruled against her more practical boiled-wool coat). They huddled together on the top step, the lit dome of the Capitol visible through the icy webbing of black trees.

"Cold?" Bob asked her.

"No," Amanda lied.

He shook off his heavy overcoat and wrapped it around her shoulders, refusing her pleas to take it back.

"You're freezing," he said reproachfully, as much to himself as to her. He arranged and tugged at the coat in the same way he might tuck a child into bed. "Do you want to go inside?"

"No. I like it out here with . . . all this quiet." She had nearly said *with you* but shied at the last moment from its honesty—although she sensed honesty was the right approach with this man.

Amanda nestled into the coat's heavy folds, relishing the unfamiliar yet newly intoxicating smell of him—a minty scent of shaving soap mingled with the faintest residue of sweat. She sensed, suddenly and keenly, that Bob's gesture offered more than a passing moment's comfort, and if she embraced it, this thrilling, all-enveloping feeling of warmth would never leave her.

"There you are!"

It was Susie, who had come up behind them. "I've been looking all over for you." She sounded irritated but also slightly amused.

Bob and Amanda scrambled to their feet, and Amanda introduced Bob to Susie.

Susie waited for the usual show of sycophancy and when it didn't come, she turned back to Amanda without showing any further interest in him.

"Are you ready to go?"

"I guess so." Amanda glanced at Bob with unconcealed disappointment.

He accompanied the two women to the curb, where he insisted upon hailing them a cab. He dashed into the street still wearing only a sweater and jeans, and frantically waved at taxis that were either occupied or off-duty until one finally slowed and pulled over. Other partygoers were starting to spill down the steps.

"What about you?" Amanda asked.

"Oh—I live nearby. Don't worry."

Reluctantly she surrendered his coat. Reluctantly he accepted it. Susie had already slid into the backseat. Bob touched Amanda's cheek.

"May I call you?"

"Yes."

"Soon?"

Amanda smiled. "Yes." She climbed into the taxi. "Tomorrow?"

"Yes."

He closed the door and it was only after they had pulled away that Amanda realized she had not given Bob her number.

Fortunately, there were not too many A. Brights at the National Endowment . . .

*   *   *

It had been quite some time since Amanda had experienced anything like a man's full attention. As a married woman, she no longer radiated sexual possibility. Without that whiff of promise, she felt like a rose stripped of its scent. At least when Amanda had held a job, men listened to what she had to say. Now, without sexual possibility, without a job title, who was she in the eyes of men but a house elf, a drone, a low-status person they had to endure only if she were seated next to them at a dinner party?

It was a harsh assessment, Amanda told herself, but true. What was going to happen when she put on her sandals again and smoothed her skirt and emerged through that bathroom door? To whom was she going to talk? Perhaps she would end up, as she so often did, seeking out another mother like herself. Amanda could always spot one: she was the woman standing slightly to the side of a group, laughing and nodding at whatever was being said, while wearing a vaguely distracted expression on her face, as if she were expected somewhere else.

Amanda mustered as much confidence as she could and opened the door. *I am not a drone!* she repeated to herself, determined to walk up to the first group she met and break in. But when Amanda reentered the living room, whom should she see chatting in the middle of it all but her friend Susie.

"Susie!"

"Amanda!"

The two women embraced, and Susie stepped back with some surprise to admire her.

"You look fabulous!"

"You think so?" For once, Amanda was greatly relieved by Susie's company.

"Hey, girls, what about me?" The man to whom Susie had been talking stepped forward to introduce himself. "I'm Jim Hochmayer, of Texas. Pleased to meet you."

"Jim, this is one of my dearest friends, Amanda Bright."

Hochmayer was a tall, well-groomed man who looked to be in his early sixties. His bearing, however, suggested a man much younger, and when he reached forward to take Amanda's hand, he moved as if all his joints were kept as well oiled and finely tuned as a race car. He greeted Amanda as if the whole point of attending the party had been to make her acquaintance.

Amanda beamed at him and then, turning to Susie, said, "I didn't know you were coming."

"I didn't know *you* were coming."

"Well, I'm glad you both did," said Hochmayer in his dry Texan drawl. "'Cause now I can stand here with the *two* most beautiful women in the room."

"Just ignore him." Susie laughed dismissively. "He's been making comments like that all evening."

Hochmayer grinned. "You can't blame a man for speaking the truth."

Amanda's usual reaction to the antiquated compliments of Southern gentlemen was to arch her eyebrows, as if to say, *Don't think that old sexist rot works on me.* This time the compliments seeped into her like water into a parched plant.

"Is Susie giving you a hard time?" she asked him playfully.

"Sure is. This woman's a *firecracker.* Just before you came up she was giving me both barrels about Megabyte. Now, can you believe she can stand here, in my friend's house, and *defend* Mike Frith?" Hochmayer sucked in his breath, pretending to take offense.

"I'm sorry to hear that," Amanda answered, joining in his mock disapproval of Susie. "But then, he does own her cable channel."

"Hey, I'm no cheerleader for Mike Frith," Susie interjected. "All I'm saying is that he has a right to market his product the way he wants." She frowned slightly the way she did on television. It was the pretty woman's equivalent of donning glasses and clearing her throat. "Suppose for a moment we weren't talking about computers. Suppose we were talking about—I don't know—let's say, cars. If Mike Frith was the biggest manufacturer of cars in the country, and he decided he wanted to put radios in every car he made, at *no extra cost to the consumer*, would you both still object?"

"Not if we had a choice of other cars to buy," Hochmayer replied cheerfully. "But we don't. Frith's got what amounts to a monopoly. And to further your analogy, what if Frith not only insisted that consumers buy his model with radios but then attempted to prevent them from buying and installing radios manufactured by different companies—*better* radios, with CD players and stereo speakers? Then what would you say?"

The Texan winked at Amanda.

"I'd say you had a point," Susie retorted, undaunted, "if those radio manufacturers were actually making better products. But the problem is, you folks aren't."

Amanda did not understand Susie's reference to "you folks," but she ventured a reply of her own. "How can they make better products, Susie, if Frith is always threatening to put them out of business? That's what he's doing, you know. He's terrorizing other companies so he can dominate the market."

"Well, bravo, Amanda," said Hochmayer, clapping her on the back and chalking up an invisible "point" in the air. "You and I make a good team. What makes you so knowledgeable about Megabyte, anyway?"

"Oh," said Amanda, her cheeks reddening. "My husband's leading the government's antitrust investigation."

"That so?" replied Hochmayer, impressed. "You're married to Frank Sussman?"

Susie chortled, and Amanda's face turned redder.

"Oh, no. My husband is Bob Clarke—he's the section chief for computers and finance at Justice. But he's organizing the investigation. Frank Sussman is his boss."

"Well, you shake your lucky husband's hand for me. You tell him that Jim Hochmayer is a big admirer—an even bigger one now that I've met you."

Amanda floated back toward the foyer. What a nice man! She hoped Susie wouldn't blow it this time. But who on earth was he?

Amanda returned to the spot where she had last seen Bob, but he wasn't there. The crowd was thicker now, and Amanda had to gingerly thread her way through without knocking into anyone's wineglass. She almost crashed into Jack Chasen, but fortunately his back was to her and he didn't notice. Finally she spied Bob over by the terrace doors deep in what appeared to be intimate conversation with a woman whom Amanda had not met before. The woman certainly seemed to have met Bob before. She pressed close to him and absently stroked his forearm as she spoke. Bob kept withdrawing his arm and taking small steps back, but every time he moved, the woman moved with him, until he had wedged himself into another cluster of people.

Amanda slowed her pace. It felt as if every one of her nerve endings were suddenly standing at attention. Her heart pounded in the hollow of her chest, and her eyes fixed on the scene the way a frightened animal stares at the tall grass in which it thinks it has heard a rustle.

Then Bob did something astonishing: he shook off his jacket and draped it over the woman's shoulders. The woman accepted it—rather coyly—and they continued talking.

Amanda was paralyzed, not knowing whether to bolt away or rush toward them. But the longer she stared, the more the sight of another woman in Bob's jacket filled her with possessive rage, and the rage soon eclipsed all other emotions, including fear. She pushed her way to his side.

"Hello, Bob."

Strangely, Bob seemed undismayed by her arrival.

"Hi, Amanda. Where have you been? I'd like you to meet Grace—what did you say your last name was?"

"Bertelli," the woman said in a soft, whispery voice.

She's not even pretty! Amanda thought indignantly, *and she's much older than Bob—forty-five maybe, or even forty-eight.* Her thick chestnut hair was cut bluntly below the chin, and she was dressed in the utilitarian skirt, blouse, and pumps of the think-tank world. Nonetheless, there was something insinuating about the woman, almost feline, that might be alluring if a man were dense enough not to know that cats purr and brush up against your leg only when they want something.

"I work at the Project for America's Future—Jack Chasen's think tank," Grace Bertelli said. She, too, seemed to find nothing odd in being introduced to a woman while wearing that woman's husband's jacket.

"I'm Amanda Bright."

Amanda turned abruptly to Bob. "I'd like to go now."

"Already?"

Amanda glared, making no reply.

"Okay—" He shrugged at Grace. "It was really nice meeting you—I'd like to hear more about your project."

"Another time."

"Hey, don't leave without this," Grace said, shaking off his jacket. "Your husband was so kind to lend it to me," she added to Amanda. "I always find myself *shivering* in these air-conditioned rooms—don't you?"

"No," Amanda said curtly. "I don't."

They made their way back to the front door. Amanda marched ahead of him.

"Frank asked me to appear on *Left/Right* next week for him," Bob said, catching up to her. "He's going to be out of town."

"Swell."

He handed Amanda the ticket for the car and excused himself to say good-bye to Jack Chasen. Amanda leaned against one of the porch pillars, feeling dizzy and confused. Was she going mad? Was she the only one aware of what had just happened? The valet startled her by leaping up the steps to hand her the keys to the Volvo. Another couple breezed by, shot a glance at the quivering and wheezing car, and slid off in their Mercedes. Amanda climbed into the passenger seat and waited.

She heard the driver's-side door slam and felt the car grind forward but she didn't raise her head from its resting position against the window.

"What kind of time did you have?" Bob asked as they turned onto the main road.

Amanda said nothing.

"C'mon, is something wrong? Why won't you talk to me?"

"'What kind of time did you have?'" she repeated sarcastically. "The question is, what kind of time were *you* having before I so inconveniently interrupted you?"

"What do you mean by that?"

They had come to a stop sign. There was no one behind them, and Bob kept his foot on the brake. "Amanda, speak to me. What did you mean by that?"

She snorted as if only an imbecile would not understand what she was talking about. "It was obvious. The whole room could see what was going on between you and that woman."

"Really? And what was going on between us?" A car tooted from behind. Bob rolled forward.

"For God's sake—do I have to spell it out?"

"I honestly don't know what you're getting at."

"You gave her your jacket!"

"What was I supposed to do? She *asked* for it. She was cold. I was just being polite."

When Amanda didn't answer, he went on, "You're being paranoid. It meant nothing—*nothing*."

"Did it mean 'nothing' when you gave me your coat that time, when we first met?" She looked directly at him now, her eyes filling up with tears. It was so embarrassing—she didn't ask to play the role of inquisitor.

"That was *completely* different."

"Why was it different?"

Bob kept his eyes on the road. It was that last moment of dusk when sky and earth meld together, and oncoming cars take on the gray camouflage of the pavement. This stretch of the route back to Washington twisted and turned dangerously, yet they flew along it, Bob distractedly pressing harder on the gas.

"Because I liked you, and was interested in you, and I wanted to—" He paused. "—protect you. You seemed so vulnerable."

A car lurched at them from around a curve, causing Bob to swerve. "Jesus, the drivers out here."

"And did you want to protect her, too?" Amanda asked bitterly. She thought of Grace Bertelli nestling into Bob's jacket, into his smell, his warmth. The audacity! And the insult! Did Amanda seem that easy a target? Had her value plunged so low?

Or was it that her husband's value had risen exponentially? *"You can't have him,"* *Sussman had said to Chasen.*

"No, I did not want to protect her. I just didn't want to be rude. Okay?"

"Then why did you let her stroke your arm? Was that about being polite, too?"

A shape dashed in front of their car and leaped away, eyes gleaming.

"Christ, a deer!"

"You didn't answer me."

"Forgive me. I was trying to prevent us from being killed."

"Why did you let her stroke your arm?"

"What are you, Amanda? The FBI? Did you have cameras set up in the room?" Bob gripped the wheel so hard his knuckles were white. He was grinding his teeth the way he did when he was enraged. That was fine. She was furious, too.

"I didn't 'let' her stroke my arm, as you put it. She just did it. I kept pulling away. She seemed like a very tactile person. What was her last name—Bertolucci? Maybe it's an Italian thing, I don't know.

"But what I do know," he insisted, "is that all she was interested in was antitrust law and that's what we were talking about. That's *all* we were talking about. Jesus."

"Sure." She mimicked him again: "'I'd like to know more about your project.'"

"Dammit, Amanda," he exploded. "Do you know what I think?"

He averted his eyes from the road to glare at her and accelerated at the same time.

"Watch what you're doing."

"I think this whole argument is about something else," he

continued. "I don't think you're really angry about Grace What's-her-name. I think you're mad about something else—something you've been mad about for weeks."

"Oh, so now you're going to change the subject."

"I'm not changing the subject because this *is* the subject. Face it. You're angry with everyone—me, the kids. You haven't been yourself at all. Every time I touch you, I can feel you practically recoiling from me."

Amanda was silent. It was dark now and there were no street-lamps. It was like being in the countryside except it wasn't the countryside. Every so often the headlights revealed the brick pillars at the end of a driveway and a huge house festooned with carriage lights would suddenly rise up from behind a screening of cypress, only to vanish into blackness until another identically lit house burst into their field of vision.

"So what is it?" he prodded. "Tell me."

"I—I don't know."

"You don't know." He had adopted her tone of sarcasm. "Well, that's just great. Because let me tell you something. I don't know why you're unhappy, either. Only six months ago you were telling me how happy you were. You told me how much you liked being at home, that it was the right choice, yadda yadda. Now, suddenly, you're telling me you're unhappy." Bob shook his head. "I give up, Amanda."

"Are you saying you don't care if I'm unhappy?"

"No. I'm saying I don't understand why you're unhappy. Because frankly, Amanda, if anyone should be unhappy, it's me."

"*You?*"

"Why not me? I've been working long hours. I come home and my house is a wreck. There's nothing to eat. You're, like, *Go read Ben a story* or *go give Sophie her bath*. Every night it's the same thing. You're pissed off about something; the kids are fighting. I can't even sort through the mail. And look at this car! It's filthy. It's breaking down, and I can't afford to replace it. You're asking me about summer camp for the kids, and I haven't bought a new pair of shoes in two goddamn years. And why? Because I thought you were happy. Because I thought this was what you wanted."

White light from a passing car flashed on Bob's face, illuminating an expression so cold, so inward, so detached from her, it frightened Amanda. She wanted to answer him. She *longed* to answer him. *You don't spend your afternoons cleaning out potties while another child is screaming he can't find his sock and the phone is ringing and the doorbell is going and you only got half of the living room vacuumed before you realized you'd forgotten milk at the store but now there won't be time to get it before supper and when are you going to find time anyway to deal with the little piles in every room that grow an inch every day like some magic beanstalk, and there's the laundry to catch up on too don't forget, and if you trip over someone's shoe on the staircase one more time you're damn well going to hurl it against a wall. But most of all, Bob, most of all, at least you exist in the eyes of other people. At least you exist.*

Instead she said, her voice trembling, "I guess I don't know what I want."

"Well, I don't know, either."

The rows of cypress gave way to power wires and streetlamps that marked their reentry into the city. When they got home, Amanda went straight upstairs, passing by the sitter wordlessly and forgetting that she hadn't yet eaten. Bob came up sometime after that, how long after she didn't know. She heard him lock the front door and switch off the lights; when she felt his weight settle in beside her, she pretended to be asleep.

Chapter Eight

THE PHONE rang and rang. Amanda was about to hang up until someone on the other end picked up, fumbled, and dropped the receiver. There was the sound of a brief scuffle, and a tiny voice said, "Huwwo?" Amanda could hear a baby crying. An adult voice scolded, "Give that to me *now*." After another scuffle, the adult voice answered, "Yes?"

"Liz? It's Amanda."

"Amanda!"

"Am I calling at a bad time?"

"Well, as you know, there is no *good* time. But I can talk for a few minutes, sure. Hang on."

Amanda waited through the muffled commotion of Liz trying to herd her children out of the vicinity of the phone. Amanda's old college friend, who now lived in Binghamton, New York, had given birth to her fourth child only six months ago. That fact alone made Liz's entry stand out in the Brown class of '87 bulletin. While other female graduates announced their promotions to "VP—marketing and sales" or "creative director for thelatestidea.com," and assured their classmates that they continued to enjoy cave rappelling, Himalayan treks, and hot-air ballooning, Liz proudly reported each one of her children's births and described herself as an "at-home mother."

"Even their wedding announcements read like corporate mergers," Liz once scoffed, as she read aloud from a recent bulletin. *"Melanie Saltzberger of Manhattan, associate at Phelps, Strong, Biddle & Throckmayer, was married in March to Yale graduate Peter Staunton, senior analyst for the First Equity Fund of Boston.* Their first child is going to be a stock offering. What these women don't realize, Amanda, is that *we* are the radicals—*we* are the pioneers on the new frontier."

Liz's philosophy on motherhood was bracing, if not always convincing, and certainly the opposite of what anyone who knew her at Brown would have expected. Back then Liz was a women's history major. She intended to devote her life to writing and teaching the next generation "the truth about how men have used domesticity as an excuse to subjugate women over the ages." Her first pregnancy was an accident—Liz mistrusted chemical methods of birth control—and to her friends' surprise Liz decided to have the baby. This was agreeable to her live-in boyfriend, Steve, a wiry and laid-back science major. He offered to do 50 percent of the child care, just as he already did 50 percent of the housework (his academic expertise gave him a flair for baking and laundry, although he had a tedious habit of pausing, midload, to explain exactly *why* borax brightened clothes). After graduation, the couple moved to Binghamton, where Steve had been offered a teaching position at the state university. Liz, who had previously disavowed any interest in "adding my spawn to an already over-populated world," proceeded to have babies two, three, and four. The spawn, apparently, turned out to be compelling little creatures when they were your own and not someone else's selfish indifference to the world's looming food and ozone shortages. Liz even succumbed to marriage between babies two and three. ("I got tired of Sarah asking to see my wedding pictures," she explained. "What can I say? Children are traditionalists.") Modern women, Liz took to lecturing to Amanda, have been misled into mimicking male definitions of success: it was typical male conceit to value the things men did—polluting the earth, waging wars, manufacturing pointless items of consumption—more than women's work. How could it be considered progress that their female classmates were now employed in the same boring jobs and enduring the same long, miserable hours as men in order to serve corporate America? Liz had gone so far as to publish an essay, titled "Motherhood Is a Feminist Issue," in *Jezebel*, a feminist literary journal. She was deluged with angry letters accusing her of betraying the women's movement, but she delighted in the reaction. Once, when Liz came to Washington for a visit, Susie asked what had become of her ambition to teach and write books. Liz cast her hand over her children, who were at that moment rolling about Amanda's living room floor, and said, solemnly, "These are my major works."

Liz returned to the phone, out of breath. "Got the kids settled with some crayons. Baby's here with me, eating a banana. What's up?"

"Gosh, Liz, it's kind of embarrassing, but I don't know who else to turn to."

"Out with it."

"I had a fight with Bob last night."

"A serious one?"

"Yeah—we were at a party—"

"Oh, hang on." Liz put her hand over the receiver. *(No, you may not watch TV. Finish your drawing or go play outside with your sister. Hey, who said you could have a marshmallow? Those are for our project! Okay, just one more. Now get out of here while Mommy is on the phone.)* "Sorry, a fight? With Bob?"

"Uh-huh. We were at a party, and a woman hit on Bob. Then—"

"A woman hit on Bob!"

"Well, sort of—she was all over him, stroking his arm and taking his jacket . . ."

"I'd say that's hitting on. What did you do?"

"I confronted him with it, of course."

"What did he say?" There was a wail on Liz's end. "Wait, hold that thought." *(No more marshmallows. No TV. And you're interrupting Mommy again. Go away!)*

"Continue," Liz said urgently.

"He said he was only being polite."

"Yeah, right."

"But that wasn't the worst of it. When we were driving home, he just exploded."

"*Bob* exploded?"

"Yes. He told me he was unhappy—how financially difficult it is for me to be at home. How upset he is that the house is always a mess . . . things like that . . ." Amanda stifled a sob, and groped around the kitchen counter for a tissue but saw she had forgotten to replace the last empty box.

"Is that so?"

"To be fair, I'm *not* keeping up with the housework," Amanda conceded. "And I don't cook dinner a lot of the time. I guess he wonders what it is exactly I'm doing around here all day, except being . . . overwhelmed."

"So that entitles him to flirt with another woman?"

"No. Or he claims he wasn't flirting, anyway."

There was a pause, and Amanda heard Liz offering the baby another banana. *(That's good, sweetie. You're a big, hungry girl! Shh, eat up.)* Her voice came back to Amanda.

"The problem here is that Bob doesn't value what you do."

"Liz, *I* don't value what I do."

"So you've got an even bigger problem. How do you expect him to value what you don't?"

"You're right. You're right."

"If you don't mind me saying so, hon, you sound in a bad way."

"I am." Amanda wiped her eyes with her fingers. "It was an awful fight. He barely spoke to me this morning. And he won't be back until late tonight—probably after I'm asleep. This damn Megabyte business."

"Okay, so you're just going to have to pull yourself out of this hole," Liz said firmly. "Get on top of things. What are you doing this week?"

Amanda glanced at the calendar taped to her fridge although she already knew what was on it: a series of blank days leading up to her children's summer vacation.

"It's almost the end of school! Good God, Liz, what am I going to do with the kids for two months? We can't afford camp—"

"Listen to you!" Liz interrupted. "Instead of letting it all get you down, why don't you use this bit of time to get the house organized, and then do some fun things with the kids? Do you want to know what my summer project is?"

Amanda hesitated to ask. Liz was capable of announcing that she was going to replumb the bathroom herself. She reminded Amanda of one of those unrattled hosts of a home-improvement program: "Coming up, we'll retile a backsplash and apply crown moldings to an old ceiling, all in the next hour."

"I'm going to redo my sunroom," Liz continued. "I've been researching female artisans from the Arts and Crafts movement, and I came across some beautiful embroidery patterns by Candace Wheeler, who—naturally—everyone has forgotten about. I'm going to use the patterns to teach the older kids sewing. They can work on some throw pillows while I get started on the valances. It's important to keep these crafts going—you know, recognize them as significant female contributions to the arts. Bastards like William Morris shouldn't get all the credit."

"You're amazing, Liz."

"No, I'm not. Just organized. You can be, too—but you're just going to have to learn to respect what you're doing. *Own* it, Amanda—own your time, your identity. It's yours and nobody else's." A sharp shriek from the baby cut Liz off. "Gotta run," she apologized.

Amanda hung up the phone. Well, she sure owned all this mess. Plates and crumbs on the table. A half-finished glass of orange juice and Bob's empty coffee cup. The dishwasher full of clean dishes, waiting to be unloaded and restacked. Upstairs, the beds unmade, pajamas on the floor, and Lord knows what sort of toy disaster left over from last night. Amanda picked up a sponge. This time, it was her phone that rang. It was the secretary of the school.

"Ben's here in the office. Ms. Phelps would like you to come pick him up."

Amanda checked her watch. It was only ten-thirty. "Is he sick?" she asked.

"No."

"Then why—"

"Ms. Phelps will explain," the secretary said, cutting her off. "Can you come?"

"Yes—yes, of course. I'll be there in fifteen minutes."

*   *   *

Amanda found Ben sitting on a long bench, fidgeting with the
zipper on his knapsack. The secretary, a young woman with
spiky red hair and fashionably thick-soled shoes, was photocopying some papers and ignoring him. He did not run to greet
his mother.

"Ben, sweetie?" Amanda said tentatively. "Are you okay?"

"I didn't mean it!" he cried, bursting into tears. "I didn't
mean it!"

"Didn't mean what, Ben?" Amanda asked worriedly. She
knelt down beside him and wrapped her arms around his heav-
ing body. "Tell me, honey, please."

Sheila Phelps poked her head out her office door. "Amanda,
can you come in please? Ben can stay there." And to her secretary, "Please tell Ms. Burley and Dr. Koenig that Ben's mother
is here."

The crispness of the director's tone told Amanda that whatever Ben had done, it was serious indeed. She continued to hold
him until the other two women arrived. They acknowledged
her, but not Ben.

"Shall we begin, Amanda?" Phelps asked, popping her head
out a second time.

"Don't go, Mommy!"

"I'll just be a minute, sweetie—"

"Gloria will keep an eye on him," Phelps said, waving at
the secretary. Gloria was speaking on the phone and nodded
indifferently.

"Mommy!"

"—right back, Ben, I promise, darling—"

Amanda took a seat in Phelps's office. The others had already
positioned themselves in a semicircle around the director's

desk. Dr. Koenig was a gaunt woman in her sixties with freeze-dried, upswept hair; she drummed her knee impatiently with a pen. Amanda mistrusted the expressions on their faces: they appeared to have reached a predetermined judgment and, like some star chamber tribunal, were merely going through the formality of informing Amanda what that judgment was. There was no suggestion that Amanda would actually have a say in Ben's defense. Amanda, who normally crumpled up before authority, felt a visceral surge of protectiveness toward her son, whose bawling could still be heard through the closed door.

"Ms. Burley, why don't you begin," said the director. "Explain what happened this morning."

"There is no explanation for it," Ms. Burley said tersely. "That's why we're here. Every child is well aware of the peanut rules."

"The peanut rules?" Amanda asked.

"I'm sure you're well aware of them too, Ms. Clarke—"

"—Bright," Amanda corrected.

Ms. Burley ignored her and reached into a bulging purse at her feet. After some rustling around she pulled out a cookie wrapped in a paper napkin. The cookie had a bite taken out of it.

"Do you recognize this?" said Ms. Burley, presenting the cookie to Amanda like an attorney for the prosecution. Amanda examined it.

"It looks like the cookie I put in Ben's lunch bag this morning."

"I see." The teacher took back the evidence and placed it upon Ms. Burley's desk. "So you are unaware of the peanut rules as well?" She said this with disbelief.

"Ms. Burley, I'm sorry, but I really don't understand what you're getting at." Amanda looked to Sheila Phelps for help.

"You know that we have a strict policy about bringing peanuts—or any peanut by-product—to school because of the allergy risk," Phelps explained. "We are a peanut-free school."

"Oh yes—if that's what you mean by the 'peanut rules,'" Amanda said. "But—forgive me—I'm still confused. What does this have to do with Ben?"

"This *cookie*," continued Ms. Burley, speaking slowly, as if to one of her five-year-old pupils, "is a *peanut butter* cookie. It is *infested* with *peanut butter chips*."

"It can't be," Amanda replied, stunned. "I'd never send Ben to school with a peanut butter cookie. I don't *buy* peanut butter cookies." She looked to the other two women, imploring them to believe her. "Honestly, I can't imagine how this happened!"

Could it have happened? Amanda asked herself. *Did I grab the wrong package by mistake—when we were in the snack aisle at Fresh Farms, and Ben was demanding yogurt-covered pretzels, and Sophie was screaming for fruit leather, and it was supposed to be the truce bag, carob-chip cookies?*

"Well it did happen," Ms. Burley said coldly. "And as a result—"

"Wait, you can't blame Ben for this," Amanda interrupted. "Surely it's not his fault if I, for whatever stupid reason, put the wrong cookie in his lunch bag . . ."

"There's a behavioral dimension as well," Dr. Koenig answered. "Please, let us move on to the behavioral dimension. Explain what Ben did with the cookie."

Ms. Burley cleared her throat. "Thank you, Dr. Koenig. I was getting to that. Ben took this *highly dangerous* cookie and *waved* it under another boy's nose."

The teacher sat back in her chair with a satisfied look of having rested her case.

"You understand the seriousness of his actions?" Dr. Koenig asked Amanda.

"Seriousness?" Amanda could not believe she had been called to the school—that they had caused Ben so much misery—because of this. "You're telling me all he did was *wave a cookie?*"

"It wasn't just a cookie!" Ms. Burley retorted. "It was a *peanut butter* cookie!"

"Oh please—"

"It's nothing to take lightly," Dr. Koenig insisted. "What worries me here is the way Ben *used* the cookie—pointing it at another child like a loaded gun."

"A loaded gun? Really, that's a bit strong—"

"I don't think so. To some children it can be as lethal as a loaded gun. Do you know how many peanut-related deaths occur every year? That's why we have this rule. All the children know it. The 'Just Say No to Nuts' curriculum starts the first year—"

Amanda was growing more outraged by the second. "But who was this boy? Was he allergic to peanuts? Were there any children with peanut allergies nearby? Tell me, *are there any allergic children in the class at all?*"

"That's not the point." Phelps flashed Amanda a look of warning not to argue the point further. "What we have to decide now is the best way to deal with Ben's behavior. And as we know, this is not Ben's first incident. I believe Ms. Burley has already spoken with you about Ben's tendencies to violence. He's met a couple of times with Dr. Koenig, but apparently these sessions have not resulted in the progress we hoped for. Dr. Koenig—why don't you continue."

Amanda backed down, but her whole body was tense with fury. She bit her cheeks and picked at her cuticles while Dr.

Koenig proceeded to outline the course of action. "What we're thinking now is that Ben should go home for the rest of today. Then, with the weekend, he'll have been away for nearly three days, which I think is an adequate period of suspension . . ."

Amanda could barely listen. Outside the door, Ben's sobs had subsided. She heard the secretary say sharply, "Stay on the bench please!"

". . . and as it's nearly the end of the school year, we think Ben should seek further treatment over the summer. He may require medication. I have the names of therapists who specialize in these types of behavioral issues. I'll write them down for you. I'm pretty sure they would be covered by your insurance."

Amanda opened her mouth to protest, but Sheila Phelps cut her off. "I'd urge you to seek help for Ben," she said. "We'd be very sorry if Ben was unable to return to the center next September."

The three women forced smiles in her direction, and the meeting was over.

"Let's go get your sister."

Ben had tied his shoelaces into knots.

"Are we going home?" he asked. His face brightened. "Can I watch TV?"

Amanda gathered up his knapsack. "Oh, maybe. Sure. What the hell."

Ben didn't ask if he was in any more trouble. That was the great thing about being five, Amanda thought. Back at the house, the children raced upstairs, arguing about which program they were going to watch, while Amanda paused outside. From her front porch, she had a fine view into her neighbors' adjoining one, uncluttered by tricycles, sand buckets, and strollers. Indeed, the only evidence of human occupation on the other side was a single flowerpot filled with dirt and the pointy brown stalks of a geranium that had died some months ago. Amanda rarely saw her neighbors. They were a young couple who left early in the morning and returned late at night. Amanda had gathered that he did something at the State Department, while she worked somewhere in Treasury. They wore government security passes but not wedding rings. The woman usually made a brief fuss over the children when she saw them; the young man seemed to regard them, when he noticed them at all, as weeds that needed pulling.

Upstairs, a fight had broken out. Amanda heard Sophie weeping piteously that it was her turn to pick a show. Ben insisted that "Mommy said *I* could watch TV—not you."

"Mommy will choose," Amanda said, striding into her bedroom and snatching the remote control away from Ben. "Oh look, it's time for Herman."

Herman was a friendly dragon on the public education channel who sang about safety rules and sharing.

"Not Herman!" groaned Ben. "He's so stupid!"

"Shh, Ben, don't use that word."

"I *like* Herman," Sophie sniffled, settling into the pyramid of pillows atop her parents' bed.

Amanda found the station; another show was just ending.

"It's on after this."

A cheerful woman wearing striped overalls was displaying shoe boxes that she had spent the past half hour decorating. One box was covered with sandpaper and patterned with tiny seashells. "I thought this would make a fun container for those memories from the beach," the woman explained. "And this one—" She held up another box elaborately pasted with cutout illustrations of Victorian dolls and trimmed with lace. "—is perfect for keeping a little girl's treasures safe." She waved her manicured hand across a group of boxes that, with construction paper, she had turned into a herd of wild animals. "These are terrific for storing all those little toys you never know what to do with. Kids love them."

What woman has *time* for that nonsense? Amanda thought scathingly. Look at all the brainpower and creativity that went into conceiving such ridiculous objects! God, she would rather be dead than spend her afternoons glue-gunning shoe boxes!

"Oh, Mommy, can we make them?" Sophie squealed excitedly. "I want the zebra!"

"I want the lion!"

Amanda switched the channel. "Where's Herman gone?"

On flashed a cartoon that Ben had only ever been allowed to watch at Christine's house.

"Yay! Space Rangers!" yelled Ben.

Sophie popped her thumb out of her mouth. "Herman!" she wailed.

Amanda looked back and forth between them. She remembered Ben's morning at school.

"Okay, Ben, just this once."

Amanda picked up the bawling Sophie and carried her downstairs. "You can help Mommy make lunch—"

"No!"

Amanda deposited Sophie on the kitchen floor, where she flailed around, crying. Amanda opened the dishwasher and began to tidy up the breakfast mess. The phone rang.

"Darling, why don't you put the knives and forks away for Mommy like a big girl," she pleaded. Sophie buried her face in her hands. Amanda answered the phone.

"I tried calling you half an hour ago," said Susie's voice, rather imperiously. "You weren't there."

"I do go out sometimes, you know."

"Guess who called me?" Susie did not want to waste time on Amanda's whereabouts. *"Jim Hochmayer."*

"Really?" Amanda's eyes were following Sophie's progress with the dishwasher. The little girl had pulled herself up and stomped over to the machine, but she wasn't putting the cutlery away; she was playing dolls with the spoons and forks.

"He didn't even wait the usual few days. He wants to see me right away—tonight, for dinner."

"That's not surprising. He did seem taken with you at the party." Amanda waved at Sophie to get her attention. "The drawer!" she whispered. "Put them in the drawer!"

"Amanda," said Susie impatiently, *"do you know how much money he has?"*

Amanda was taken aback. "No. I don't even know what he does."

"Jim Hochmayer? Hasn't Bob ever mentioned him? He's the founder of Texas CompSystems—he's worth *billions."*

"Oh," said Amanda, absorbing the information. She took the spoons from Sophie and began putting them away herself. ("Those are my princetheth!" Sophie protested.) "What's he doing in Washington?"

"He's up here all the time to lobby Congress. This week he's here to talk to Senator Benson about the Megabyte hearings. He's on Justice's side, for God's sake, I thought you'd know all about him."

"Bob and I don't really discuss—those things."

"Anyway, he's taking me to Sonoma," Susie continued, naming a chic restaurant of the moment. "Fabulous, huh?"

"Fabulous." Susie had dated rich men before, but Amanda believed this was her first billionaire. Also, possibly, her first date with a man nearly twice her age.

"How old is he by the way?"

"I'm not sure. Sixty, maybe sixty-one."

"That old?"

"He looks and acts about ten years younger," Susie said defensively. "Besides, his jet is young—brand-new in fact."

"Susie!"

"I'm joking."

"Well, he did seem nice."

"Yeah, a happy contrast to Brad. Jim liked you, too. He really admires what you're doing—being at home and all that. He said he knows how tough it can be. His own wife did it."

"What happened to her?" Amanda asked, with suspicion.

"I read somewhere that they split. A profile in some business magazine. She sounded like a real starter wife. You know—girl he met in college, raised the kids, ran the house, but couldn't keep up with him when he became a big success."

Starter wife! Amanda hung up the phone. At times Susie could have the opposite effect of an alchemist: she had a way of taking whatever humble piece of gold Amanda possessed and transforming it into cheap metal.

Amanda nearly tripped over Sophie, who had grown bored with her family of forks and was lying on the floor again, coloring Amanda's shopping list. Amanda finished unloading the dishwasher and leaned against the counter, looking around at what to do next. What had she been going to do today anyway? Put in some laundry, book dentist appointments, run to the grocery store. But it was nearly lunchtime, the kids were home early, and . . . it had all gotten away from her again. Maybe Bob was right—maybe she was getting hopeless.

Amanda wanted to call him at work and tell him about Ben. Normally it would have been the first thing she did when she got home. But given the friction between them, she didn't dare. Whenever they were at war with each other, Bob would treat her like a potential plaintiff at the scene of an accident. His manner grew stiff, hypercorrect, almost courtly, as if he were determined to say or do nothing that could further a claim against him. *Would you like me to take out the garbage or shall I leave it where it is? Will you be saving dinner for me or should I plan to pick up something at work? Thank you, but I'm happy to get coffee for myself.* His behavior would only provoke Amanda further, and that morning she had found herself slamming his coffee down on the table with a belligerent "It's Friday, so *obviously* you should take out the garbage." He took a sip from his mug and replied calmly, "Fine. I will."

Amanda sighed. She felt completely alone on her little island of problems. What had Liz said? Her friend's words came back like a mantra: *Own it, own it, just own it.*

Amanda left Sophie coloring to inspect her living room. God, how had she let it get this bad? The layers of toys, papers, pens, and books resembled geological strata, dating as far back as a year ago. How often had she passed by that half-clothed Barbie doll on the mantel or the monster puppet under the wicker chair and made a mental note to herself to put them away? The puppet's ghoulish grin seemed to mock her: *Ha! Ha! I'm still here!* Then there was the stack of magazines and catalogs she had been meaning to go through. Amanda checked the date of one at the bottom—a catalog selling, what else, useful containers to organize things. It dated from last summer. She flipped through its

pages—gorgeous photographs of exquisitely arranged rooms—
lingering over its descriptions of woven willow baskets "lined
with French cotton toile, perfect for fruit or soap," "stainless-steel
apothecary cabinets," and "heirloom-quality, hand-painted toy
chests." Amanda paused over a display of decorative brass hooks
in the shape of bees and sunflowers, upon which to hang "a straw
boater or perhaps a bouquet of dried lavender." Amanda had
never possessed a straw boater or bouquet of dried lavender, but
she felt suddenly that she ought to possess such things or at least
be the sort of person who would.

Was this what Liz meant? Surely not. Liz had been pushing her
to value the more mundane aspects of housekeeping. The catalog made tidying up seem like modern design work, while Liz
could lecture for a quarter hour on the lost "art" of scrubbing.
Amanda preferred the catalog's view, but sympathized with Liz—
the ability to "keep house" did seem as vanished a skill as candle
making or butter churning. Aside from spraying surfaces with
cleanser, Amanda did not actually know how to "clean." Her
mother knew: Amanda had occasionally overheard her directing
the housekeeper to use vinegar on the tile or instructing on how
to remove grape juice stains from one of Amanda's blouses. But
Ellie Bright had not passed this knowledge on to her daughter.
Indeed, it was knowledge her mother seemed vaguely embarrassed about possessing, something she once dismissed with the
comment, "Women of my generation were expected to know
these things, but that was all that was expected of us."

So long as Amanda had employed a housekeeper herself, her
ignorance didn't matter. The woman arrived every Friday morning while Amanda was at work. She brought her own tools and
colorful bottles of solutions with her, like some primitive
shaman. After she worked her magic upon the linoleum and

wood surfaces, they shone for days with a brilliance Amanda was never able to replicate. Amanda did not bother to find out how the woman did it. She treated chores as things to be "gotten through" in order to have time for more meaningful pursuits, such as taking the children to the park or teaching Ben to read. She took her mother's attitude that this kind of work held no value—its worth could not be calculated in dollars and cents. Its very nature was as evanescent as footprints along breaking surf: the progress she made one day was gone by the next. Floors needed mopping again, counters wiping, beds making. Every day dumped fresh flotsam at her feet—another load of dirty laundry, another basket of ironing, another child's knapsack full of papers to be sorted and filed.

Maybe, Amanda thought as she bundled up the magazines and catalogs, maybe the very value of housework lay in its seemingly pointless repetition. The ceaseless cycle of chores created the rhythmic tide of a home. The small act of making lunch every day for Sophie, as trivial as it might seem to Amanda, was for her daughter an event of ritualistic importance. The little girl carried the plates to the table. She set out two forks, "one for me, one for Mommy." She carefully folded the paper towels Amanda used as napkins into neat triangles.

The menu rarely changed: buttered pasta noodles with carrot or celery sticks on the side. Sometimes Sophie requested a sandwich, but she seemed to prefer eating the same meal day after day, not because she loved it especially, but because of its certainty. The noodles arrived as predictably as high tide. They were as essential in conveying to Sophie the fundamental stability of her world as Amanda's presence in her school lobby every noon or the lullaby Amanda had sung to her every bedtime since Sophie was born. When Amanda reflected upon her own childhood, her happiest memories settled on the bowl of tomato soup and the grilled cheese sandwich her mother had prepared for her at lunchtime for seven years—until Amanda's parents divorced and her mother decided that cooking regular meals was no longer part of her job description. The housekeeper took over, and the soup and grilled cheese never tasted quite the same again.

Amanda carried the papers to the recycling box and switched on a pot of water. She admired Sophie's finished picture, and called Ben down to lunch. After they had finished eating, Amanda proposed an idea—that the three of them tidy the whole house together.

"You can do your toys, Ben," she said before he could protest. "Pretend you're a general, and the toys are soldiers, and you have to ready them for battle. Sophie, you can help Mommy downstairs."

She put her daughter in charge of organizing the pot cupboards in the kitchen. Sophie took to the work with zeal, using a tea towel as an apron. Amanda, meanwhile, brought a box of green garbage bags into the living room and began ruthlessly dividing the junk into piles to be kept or thrown away. An hour later, she had amassed four bulging sacks of trash and created a reasonably civilized-looking sitting area. Ben had finished his task and begged to try the vacuum, which was now whirring overhead. Sophie was making soapy swirls with a sponge on the kitchen floor. Amanda moved on to the other rooms. As late afternoon approached and the bags collected outside by the trash, the house felt pounds lighter, as if it had gone on a superdiet, and Amanda's mood had improved as well. She realized how much the clutter had been preying upon her subconscious, how much it had lurked in the periphery of her vision, encroaching upon her mood. She might even have time to make a proper dinner.

"Come with Mommy," Amanda said, fetching Sophie, who had unspooled the paper towels and was using them to shine the front of the fridge. "We're all going to the store."

"I'm almost finithed," the little girl replied, brimming with self-importance. "We being mommieth today, right?"

"Oh, mommies do other things too, sweetie," Amanda said reflexively. "Great big important things like . . . fly airplanes, run for president, and . . ."

Sophie gazed up at her.

". . . clean the kitchen."

At the supermarket, Amanda bought chicken, broccoli, and a box of couscous—items she knew how to cook. Impulsively she threw in a package of scented candles and capitulated to Sophie's demand for some wilted, plastic-wrapped marigolds to make the table look "pwetty" and Ben's counterdemand for chocolate cupcakes for dessert.

Back home, Amanda found the recipe she had clipped from the Sunday *Times*—one that she'd been meaning to make for weeks. It was nothing fancy, just breasts of chicken marinated in lemon, oil, and oregano and baked in the oven. Amanda fished out the flowers from the shopping bag.

"Do you want to put these in a vase for Mommy, sweetie?"

The little girl eagerly arranged the marigolds in a small chipped vase that Bob and Amanda had been given as a wedding present. While the chicken soaked in its herbal bath, Amanda asked Sophie to set out mats on the dining room table and place the flowers in the center.

Amanda was just turning down the couscous when she heard Bob's key in the front door. His voice called out "Hello!" and then muttered, with surprise, "Jeez!" Amanda's anger had subsided, but she didn't rush to greet him.

The children came running downstairs.

"Do you like what we did, Daddy?"

"I thet the table!"

Bob's footsteps followed the children into the dining room. "Wow, look at this place! Are we eating in here tonight?"

"Mommy wanted to."

"Where is Mommy?"

"In the kitchen. Cooking dinner."

Bob poked his head through the dining room door.

"Hi," he said.

"Hi," she returned, checking the couscous.

He entered and poured himself a drink.

"Would you like one?"

"I don't like Scotch."

"I could open some wine."

"I'll have some with dinner, thanks. Not yet."

"What are we having?"

"Chicken."

"Mmm."

Bob busied himself with uncorking a bottle of wine and filling a bucket with ice. Amanda kept her back to him, ostensibly monitoring the pots on the stove. She was sick of fighting but felt Bob should be the first to make amends.

"You've been busy today, I see."

She didn't like the way he said that—with a hint of smugness, as if she had spent her day cleaning to atone to him for the night before.

"I had some extra time." She shrugged. "Ben came home early."

Amanda had not meant to introduce the topic of Ben yet—

not until they were on better terms—but there, it had slipped out, and frankly, she wasn't altogether sorry. *Don't think you're the only one who's had a long, tense day.*

"Ben? Why was Ben home early?"

"Because he was suspended." Amanda said this calmly but her hands were trembling. She switched off the pot of couscous and began hunting through the cupboards for a serving dish, studiously ignoring Bob's look of alarm.

"Suspended? Five-year-olds don't get suspended!"

"Apparently they do." Amanda found the bowl she was looking for and began emptying the couscous into it, spilling a few grains onto the counter.

"What happened? Amanda, please—talk to me!"

Sophie wandered in, followed by Ben. Amanda handed the bowl of couscous to Sophie and asked her to take it to the table. "You can carry in the salad, Ben," she said, adding, in a terse whisper to Bob, "I think we'd better discuss this later."

She reached into the oven and removed the chicken to the countertop.

"Here," Amanda said, thrusting the oven mitts at Bob. "Why don't you take in the chicken?"

At dinner, Bob reverted to defendant mode. Evidently the extent of his apology to her was the offer of a drink. Amanda served him his chicken with an air of defiance, as if daring him to compliment her about it. He didn't. The children, unaware, burbled on.

"Do you like the flowerth, Daddy? I picked them."

"I helped Mommy with the salad."

"We have a special dessert."

"I chose it."

"No you didn't—I did."

Bob lavished upon them the praise he withheld from Amanda and helped himself to seconds. Amanda, meanwhile, silently took in the spectacle of her tidy rooms, which had given her such a sense of satisfaction just an hour ago. She had dug up some old framed family photographs to line the mantel, and regrouped the furniture so it didn't look quite so much as if it had been dropped in place by the movers. Even their dirty sagging sofa, with its cushions plumped and straightened, looked vaguely respectable—like some small ruffian forced into a jacket and tie to await the arrival of company.

At the end of the meal, Bob rose to clear. The children ran off to play in their newly immaculate bedrooms, and Amanda followed Bob into the kitchen.

"Now are you willing to tell me about Ben?" he asked, pouring himself another Scotch.

"It's not about being willing—"

"Amanda—" Bob seemed as weary of fighting as she was. "Just tell me, okay? Let's stop making a federal case out of everything."

She wanted to challenge that last remark, too, but restrained herself; instead she described what had happened to Ben that morning with the matter-of-factness of a reporter. She saw Bob growing outraged.

"So they suspended him over a *cookie?*"

"The way he *used* the cookie," she corrected. "You know, they think Ben is violent."

"How is Ben taking it?"

"It's hard to say. He seems fine—or at least, he did when we got home and I let him watch TV."

Amanda began scraping and rinsing the plates.

"It's just so ridiculous!" Bob fumed. "I did those things as a boy. We all did those things!"

"We did a lot of things that are now considered wrong."

"Do you think we ought to get him out of there? Change schools, maybe?"

"You're always saying yourself we can't afford a different school."

"I don't mean private school. Won't he be old enough for public school next year?"

Amanda stopped what she was doing and looked at him incredulously. "Is that what you really want for him?"

"We may not have much choice from the sounds of it."

"But you saw the public school!" Amanda was now stacking the dishwasher, but with such force that Bob edged in and took over the job. "We were both there! The syringe in the playground . . . all those kids crammed into one class . . . the teacher who couldn't spell . . ."

Amanda filled a pot with warm soapy water and started to scrub at it angrily.

"Then what do you think we should do?" Bob said with rising exasperation. "I'm not getting your point. You know our finances as well as I do. I'm happy to go over them again—"

"No—"

"So what are you saying?"

"Just that I don't want to put him in public school."

"So you want to keep him at the center?"

"No." She placed the pot on the rack to dry, and started in on another. "Maybe. I don't know."

"Yes, yes you do—you seem to be suggesting there's another choice. What choice are you suggesting?" He closed the dishwasher and switched it on. "Because the only other choice is for me to leave government and find a job that will pay for private school. Is that what you're suggesting?"

"That's *not* the only choice." In her hotness, Amanda realized that she had backed herself into a corner.

"So tell me another." Bob was waiting for her answer, patiently drying the second pot she had smacked down on the counter.

"*I* could get a job."

To her surprise, Bob did not treat this as an absurd proposition.

"That would work," he agreed, putting the pot away. "If that's what you want to do, then yes, you're right, we do have another choice."

"I don't know if it's what I want—" she said helplessly.

"Oh boy. Let's not go back to that again. I think we covered that ground fairly extensively last night."

"Well, you obviously don't appreciate anything I do here," she shot back. And as she marched off, leaving him with the rest of the dishes, Bob called after her, "Hey, *you* were the one not speaking to *me*."

Chapter Nine

SHE FOUND CHRISTINE sitting peacefully in the backyard, paperback and glass of white wine in hand, enjoying the lazy passage of Sunday afternoon.

"So remind me," Christine said, glancing up with a wry smile. "What were our mothers complaining about?"

This was, Amanda had learned, Christine's long-running joke with herself. At age forty Christine had become "everything my twenty-year-old self would have considered my worst nightmare."

"So Tuesday's my big day," she said as Amanda pulled up a chair beside her. "Wine?"

"Sure, thanks."

To one side of the terrace, the mottled blue surface of a rectangular pool sparkled invitingly; to the other was an elaborate jungle gym, partially hidden by a tall hedge. A slight breeze nudged the empty swings back and forth. The children were inside, watching television.

"You're really going to go through with it?"

"Quit acting so shocked. You'll be doing it, too, before you know it."

Amanda's sunglasses concealed her look of doubt. "How long will it take you to recover?"

"Not long—but I'll be in hiding for about three weeks, until the bruising disappears. Then I plan to reemerge—like a butterfly from its chrysalis. You wait. You'll be so jealous you'll be begging me for the name of my plastic surgeon."

Amanda smiled. "I may well need one. After Friday I don't know that I actually want to show my real face around the school again."

"So I heard."

"You did? From who?"

"Austen told me Ben got in trouble and didn't come back from the office. I was going to call you—then Kim phoned with the whole story."

"How did *she* know?"

"She heard it from Ellen. Ellen's on the rules committee, so she would be informed right away."

"And she took it upon herself to inform everyone else?" Amanda was aghast.

"They take the peanut policy very seriously. It's a warning to the whole school not to be careless."

"And you agree with it?"

"Of course not. I think it's ridiculous." Christine lifted the bottle of wine from its plastic bucket to check how much was left—about half—and placed it back. "Cheer up, Amanda. It's nothing to be embarrassed about. Everyone thinks it's stupid. But it's the rule."

"Ben may have to leave because of it."

"Really?" Amanda thought she detected more prurience than sympathy in Christine's surprise.

"I might be wrong," Amanda said, attempting to backpedal.

"It's just that Burley and Phelps and Dr. Koenig—well, they seemed so angry. I don't know . . ."

"Oh, they can overreact. I wouldn't worry about it. I'm sure, given your family connections, that Ben will be protected."

Amanda's eyes darted at Christine's. Did Christine know? *How* did she know? Christine, like some private eye, was in the habit of asking dogged questions to which Amanda had always been deliberately vague in her answers. She had not discouraged Christine's emerging theory that she was the estranged, bohemian child of a rich father. (What business was it of Christine's, after all, that Amanda's real father—whom she rarely heard from—was the bohemian? He had long ago given up practicing psychiatry in Manhattan and moved with his second family to a cottage in Maine.)

She could feel Christine scrutinizing her. "I don't know what you mean," Amanda replied evenly, keeping her gaze on the pool.

"Isn't Phelps a good friend of your mother's?"

"They were activists together in the seventies."

"Uh-huh." Christine apparently already knew this, and Amanda worried that she would push further. "The whole sisterhood thing. I think you're safe."

She poured more wine, and to Amanda's relief the conversation seemed to have ended.

"Do you mind if I take a dip? I'm getting hot sitting here."

"Go ahead."

Amanda stripped down to her bathing suit and descended the half-moon steps, slowly immersing herself in the lukewarm water. Aware of Christine's critical gaze upon her, Amanda duck-dived to the bottom, following the slope of the pool to its deepest point, and resurfacing at the far end. She pulled herself up on the edge and waved across to Christine, who was still watching her. Water trickled off her thighs and seeped into the sun-baked bluestone.

"It's gorgeous," Amanda called out. "You should come in."

"I don't really like swimming."

Amanda toweled herself off and rejoined Christine.

"I've been thinking," Christine said. "You should probably join a committee. It's the best way of protecting Ben—Sophie, too. You're going to need a good reference from the center if you want to send them to a really top elementary school. Where is Ben going to go, by the way? I've already sent in Austen's forms to Beauvoir and Maret, although of course I hope he'll eventually go to St. Alban's."

"But it's still a year away!"

"You mean you haven't applied anywhere yet?" Christine removed her sunglasses to underscore her astonishment.

"I hadn't realized—" The truth was, Amanda had not yet figured out how Ben was going to avoid public school. It seemed pointless to start up with private schools where tuition began at fourteen thousand dollars a year.

"Oh, Amanda." Christine seemed truly anxious on her behalf. "Laura Crabbe actually took a *job* at Beauvoir—in the library, part time—to improve Sam's chances at getting in."

"I don't know—"

"You *must* apply for a committee—right away. The auction committee is pretty easy to get on—I'm on that one—and they like people who raise money for the school."

Amanda stared down at her wavy, unvarnished toenails. (She had declined Christine's invitation to join her for a pedicure.)

"I don't know that I'd be very good at that."

"Sure you would. It's easy. Besides, you're creative, and a lot of the work is planning the items to be auctioned. Trips and that sort of thing."

"How does one get on a committee?" Amanda asked reluctantly.

"Depends. How much money did you give to the school last year?" Christine was staring at her intently now, the private eye about to expose the false alibi.

"Um, probably not enough."

"I'll look into it if you like. Recommend you to Phelps. Not that you *need* my recommendation—" Christine raised an eyebrow.

"Thanks. Let me think about it."

On Monday Amanda arrived at the school deliberately late for noon dismissal. She had planned to fly into the front hall, grab Sophie, and fly out again, praying she would not bump into anyone she knew. But as Amanda raced up the steps, there, leaning against one of the columns of the veranda, was Alan. Amanda could not pass by him without at least nodding hello.

"Hey, Alan."

"Hey, Amanda." As she rushed on, he said, "You're late today. I was looking for you."

Amanda whirled around. She was running against the tide of dismissal, and her abrupt stop created a bottleneck of children and mothers.

"Why?" Had word about Ben trickled down to Alan?

He eased his way to her, using the stroller to create a path, and guided them both out of the way of the doors.

"I just wanted to let you know I can get you tickets to the opening of my play—it's starting its run at the end of the month."

"Oh. Great."

"How many tickets will you need?"

"Gee—I'm not sure—"

"Do you think Bob will want to come?"

Distracted, Amanda scanned the stream of children, concerned that Sophie might pass by without seeing her.

"Bob? No."

Alan seemed affronted by her bluntness.

"I mean, he's pretty busy with the Megabyte case," she explained quickly. "He's not going out to anything these days. But I would love to come, sure."

Alan looked pleased. "Good. I'll arrange it and give you the exact date."

"Okay." She made a move to leave but Alan stopped her again.

"I heard about Ben," he said. "Outrageous."

Amanda wilted slightly; so it *was* everywhere. Alan perceived her dismay and grasped her shoulder.

"Amanda, I didn't tell you to upset you. I just wanted to let you know I'm on your side. Anything I can do to help . . ." His eyes sought hers.

"Thanks, Alan. I really appreciate it."

She hugged him lightly, and he hugged her back.

"Remember—it's hard being outside the box," he said, giving her an extra squeeze. His arms felt thin and ropy yet strong, like tough cords; not soft and enveloping like Bob's.

"Better find Sophie," Amanda murmured, pulling away.

All that afternoon, Amanda thought about Alan. At first he came to her in glimpses—his solicitous words, the touch of his hand, the kind expression of his eyes. She was grateful to him, she really was. He was the only other parent at the school with whom she felt she could be honest, herself. She even thought about phoning him at home, to seek out his advice further on what to do about the situation with Ben. Should she join a committee? What would Alan say to that? *(Don't let them force you into the box.)*

But as she flipped through the school directory, seeking his number, other thoughts began intruding themselves, thoughts that caused Amanda to pause. Did she seriously want Alan's advice—or was she calling him for another reason? Her conscience resisted the idea that there could be anything wrong in making this call—hadn't she phoned him many times to arrange play dates?—but the more it resisted, the more strongly the other thoughts rallied for her attention. She shut the directory and put on the kettle and walked into the hallway to listen for Sophie, who was napping upstairs; all was silent, except for the gradual whine of the kettle.

What would it be like—with Alan?

The question posed itself starkly, as Amanda stirred her cup of tea. She continued stirring, almost hypnotically. The question, realizing it finally had the floor, posed itself again.

What would it be like?

She carried the cup to the table and sat down, the sight of the newspaper that she'd intended to read dissolving in the dam burst of images suddenly flooding her brain . . .

Minutes passed, until Amanda drew herself up, trying to snap out of the fantasy, but one image lingered, and she clung to it—the thought of the two of them atop a duvet twisted from passion, their hot bodies cooled by the manufactured breezes of an air conditioner. Where were they? In his bedroom. Yes— his bedroom, on a weekday morning. The thrill of it lay in the hour of the day, when the children were at school and the sun forced its way through the blinds no matter which way you angled them. The rest of the world was working while they traced the soft hair on each other's bodies . . .

Stop it! Amanda told herself. *This is ridiculous. I don't want an affair!*

What *did* she want then?

She got up and rinsed her cup in the sink. *Christ,* she thought, *even my fantasies now accommodate my children's schedules.* And that was it, wasn't it? Here's what she wanted: she wanted an entire afternoon to pass without being asked to fetch a glass of juice. She wanted to lie in one morning, sipping coffee and reading the newspaper. She wanted to make love without having to lock a door or wait until children were asleep, to make love without feeling there was something else she ought to be doing. The last time Amanda had felt so free was six years ago. She could chart it to the day. She and Bob had traveled to Rome for what turned out to be their last holiday without children. One morning they decided simply not to get out of bed. They made love, they napped, they read, they talked. Food arrived on silver trays, the sheets remained unmade; through the tall windows, they followed the arc of a Roman day. When they finally stepped out at nightfall, Amanda leaned on Bob's arm, her limbs exhausted by pleasure. The young men had begun to crowd outside tables; passersby hurried home, packages clutched under their arms; here and there a shop remained open, selling highball glasses and key rings to the evening surge of tourists. Bob led her down cobbled alleyways and through squares with the confidence of a man who had mastered his new surroundings in less than a week. They ended up in a little restaurant where a waiter persuaded them to try raw fresh fava beans with olive oil and a scraping of pecorino. They drank cold red wine. It was impossible to feel any happier.

Amanda and Bob tried once to recapture this trip a few months after Sophie was born. Amanda's mother volunteered to baby-sit the children over a winter weekend. Amanda and Bob didn't go far—just a ninety-minute drive to the Eastern Shore of Maryland. They stayed at a bed-and-breakfast Amanda had read about in a travel magazine. Its charming description as an eighteenth-century whaler's cottage turned out to be miserably apt: eighteenth-century whalers did not expect much in the way of comfort or privacy. Amanda and Bob were assigned a drafty attic room furnished with a spindly bed with noisy springs. The bathroom was across the hall. The owners of the house urged Amanda and Bob to join them by the fire in the gloomy parlor for "afternoon tea." It was too bitterly cold to go outside, most of the nearby town was shut down, and she and Bob had not gone away to listen for hours to the innkeeping aspirations of their genial but relentless hosts. They left early Sunday morning— luckily so, as it turned out, since Amanda's mother had decided after a hellish weekend of her own that she was "not the sort of grandmother to play mommy" and wouldn't be offering her services again. When Amanda looked back on this disastrous little trip, she liked to think it might have gone otherwise—if only they had chosen a different inn, a different season—but she knew, really, that it couldn't have gone otherwise. Had she and Bob been dropped into that hotel room in Rome again, there would not have been a moment in which she wasn't waiting for the phone to ring, not a moment in which her children weren't hovering near her conscience, banging to get in.

Thoughts of Alan continued to intrude upon her, despite her efforts to banish them; by the time Amanda readied herself for bed, she felt uneasy with desire—and the uneasiness of being desired. What was it that he had said to her?—"There's fire in you, too." His words played through her head as she fell asleep; she wasn't dead, no, not yet, the embers glowed still . . .

Amanda was awakened by the noise of a drawer being closed. She had left a bedside lamp on for Bob, and its glare blinded her when she opened her eyes. It took her a moment or two to adjust to the light; Bob was sitting on a chair unrolling his socks from his feet.

"What time is it?"

"Close to midnight," he answered. "I'm sorry—I didn't mean to wake you."

"It's okay." Amanda propped herself up on her pillow. "What time did you get in?"

"About half an hour ago. Thanks for leaving me some of that spaghetti."

"I figured you might be hungry."

"I was. Ravenous. Worked right through dinner again."

Relations between Amanda and Bob had thawed to the point that they were speaking, but without intimacy, like two military officers exchanging situation reports at the end of a shift: "Anything happen?" "No, not much. You?" This was fine. Amanda was certainly not eager to tell him what had been on her mind for most of the day. She watched quietly as Bob put his clothes away, except for his blue suit, which he left out to wear again tomorrow.

The jacket looked as tired as she felt. It was hunched over the rack. There were creases in its arms, and the buttons had worn circles in the fabric. She remembered Bob's complaint that he had not bought a new pair of shoes in two years. It struck her now that he had not bought a new suit, either. Her mind reeled back to another memory from their trip to Rome, when Bob had tried on a beautiful cashmere blazer. It was handmade by a tailor who fussed and pulled at the shoulders as Bob admired his reflection in the mirror. The tailor had gotten as far as making chalk marks on the seams before Bob decided against buying it. Amanda urged him to change his mind but, as he explained as they walked away from the store, while he could afford it, he could only *just* afford it, and they had much better uses for their money than blowing it on a blazer for him. A day later, in another shop, Amanda paraded before him in a pair of purple suede jeans. He insisted upon getting them for her even though they cost nearly as much as the blazer. She gave in, pleased, and wore them throughout the rest of the trip. When they got home, she unpacked the pants lovingly, folded them over a hanger, and never wore them again.

Bob's suit came back into focus; Amanda felt sickened by guilt. She rolled over and clutched his pillow, her fantasies chased away by the footsteps of Bob returning from the bathroom, the man who was not Alan. Why had she permitted herself to think about him so much?

Bob pulled back the covers and settled in next to her. He did not shut the light but opened a magazine. He turned the pages delicately, in a way that suggested he thought she had fallen back to sleep.

Amanda burrowed in closer to him, wide awake with remorse.

"Did you have a rough day?" Her tone was more solicitous than it had been in weeks.

He folded up the magazine and gathered her tightly in his arms. "I thought you were out cold."

"I was. Now I'm not."

He strained to reach for the light without disturbing her position. When he spoke again it was dark, and she couldn't see his face although it was only a few inches away. His freshly rinsed breath still smelled faintly of Scotch.

"It wasn't bad," he said. "Just a lot of trench work, trying to line up companies to testify against Frith."

"Are they coming along?"

"Uh-huh."

There was a long pause, in which Amanda realized Bob was drifting off to sleep. She didn't want him to, not yet—not until she was certain things were normal between them again.

"Are you speaking to Jim Hochmayer?" Amanda remembered that she had not told Bob about the Texan's dinner invitation to Susie.

"Yeah," he said sluggishly.

"He's dating Susie."

"Huh?" This roused him slightly.

"She met him at Chasen's. I did too. He asked her out. He seems like a nice guy. For once."

"Wow. That's impressive." Bob's voice started to fade again. "Good for her." He yawned. "I didn't think she still had it."

"I beg your pardon?"

"What?"

"What did you mean by that?"

"Oh, Amanda." Bob disentangled his arm from her and rolled over, as if to end the conversation. "I'm whacked. Do we have to discuss Susie now?"

Amanda sat up. "Explain what you meant—about her not 'having it'?"

The dark lump next to her groaned. "I meant exactly what I said—that I didn't think she still had it. Now can I go to sleep?"

"No!" she exclaimed, and then, accusingly, "How can you say such a cruel thing? Susie's young, she's beautiful—and in any case, Hochmayer's so old—!"

Bob switched on the light, squinting at its brightness. "I wasn't trying to be cruel, okay?" He rubbed his eyes. "I was merely *observing* that Susie is not what she was five, even three years ago. She's what the folks at Treasury would label a good consumer, but not a good producer."

"Excuse me?"

"What I mean is that she demands a lot and doesn't expect to give anything in return. That may work when you're twenty-five. But a man—especially the kind of man she wants—eventually tires of the privilege of escorting her to parties, paying for her dinners, taking her on expensive vacations. And there will come a moment when all the Botox treatments and mud peels and whatever the hell else she does to herself will cease to work their magic and she'll be left with the fact that she's a rather dull, self-absorbed middle-aged woman with no husband.

"Now may I go to sleep?" He switched off the light again. Amanda simmered for a few minutes in silence. Finally she summoned the courage to ask him, "So is that what you think of me? That I'm a 'consumer,' not a 'producer'?"

"Oh, Amanda. Why do you take everything I say as a statement about you?" He tried to reel her back into his arms but she resisted.

"That's what you were trying to tell me—in the car. Wasn't it?" The shock of the light was still playing patterns with her eyes; the room was a jumble of black shapes that made no sense.

Bob sighed heavily. "No, I wasn't saying that. I was saying—I *said* some pretty harsh things, which I regret. You just made me angry with your jealousy and all. We'd had such a great evening."

"*You* had a great evening."

"Okay, so I had a great evening, and I thought you did, too. Sussman and Chasen—did you see the way they were talking to me? It's taken me ten years at Justice to get to the point where people speak to me as if I matter. Sussman wants me to appear on *Left/Right* on behalf of the whole department—he's grooming me to be the spokesman for this case . . ."

Bob's hand fumbled for hers in the darkness and settled for her forearm. "I know it's been hard on you. I know—" he paused and continued, "I know if I left government I could earn more, a whole lot more. But I thought you supported what I do. You've always said you'd hate to see me sell out to the private sector."

"I *do* support you. It's just that—"

"It's just that my idealism imposes a lot on you. I know. I feel really guilty about that. But God, Amanda, I can't leave now. This Megabyte case is historic. It's going to be argued in classrooms a generation from now. I would never get a chance at a case like this at some law firm. That's why I came to Justice. It may even lead to me being appointed assistant attorney general one day, who knows?"

"I understand that—"

"So I guess what I was trying to say is this: all I want for you is to be happy—in whatever you're doing. As happy as I am right now."

She didn't reply right away but lay there thinking about what he had said. When she next checked, the glowing red digits of the alarm clock indicated nearly an hour had passed. Bob's breath was steady—he had fallen asleep. She had just begun to sink into sleep herself when a tiny voice jerked her back awake.

"Mommy!" it whispered. "I wet the bed."

Chapter Ten

"THAT'LL BE EIGHTEEN dollars."

The cashier tapped his fingers on the countertop to some silent rhythm in his head while staring blankly into the mall behind Amanda. Nothing, apparently, bored him more than accepting her money. His flat expression contrasted with the cheery colors of his striped uniform and the overhead banner of a happy clown riding a choo-choo, welcoming one and all to PlayZone.

"Eighteen dollars?" Amanda replied incredulously. "For *two* children?"

"Uh-huh."

Amanda fished through her wallet and saw that she was down to her last twenty. She hastily counted her single bills: after paying the entrance fee she would be left with only twelve dollars to last her until Friday. Today was Tuesday. Her credit card had reached its limit, and Amanda was reluctant to borrow from Bob—it would be the third time in two weeks.

"C'mon, Mommy." Ben was pushing against the turnstile. A line was building behind them.

Amanda surrendered her twenty and accepted two creased bills in return. A few feet in, they were stopped by another attendant who ordered them to remove their shoes and checked their pockets for "sharp objects" as thoroughly as if they were entering a prison. Once cleared, Ben and Sophie plunged into a vast play area. Straight ahead of them was a tangled mass of climbing equipment and bright plastic sliding chutes; off to one side was a little carnival setup with flashing arcade machines and a miniature train ride. The chatter and screeches of children echoed around them like a jungle coming alive at dawn.

"We need to buy tokens," Ben told her.

"Tokens? But I just paid for our tickets!"

"For the *games*," Ben said, as if it were obvious. This was his second visit to PlayZone; the first time was for a classmate's birthday party that Amanda had been spared from attending.

Sophie clapped her hands with excitement. "I want to ride the twain!"

Ben led his mother to a small booth beside a counter selling pizza and soft drinks. The token attendant was engaged in a lively personal conversation with the girl at the pizza register. It took Amanda two theatrical coughs to catch the attendant's attention. Slowly he redirected his neck in her direction and adopted the same dead stare as his colleague at the entrance.

"How many?"

"How much are they?"

"Twenty-five cents each. Five for a dollar."

"I'll take ten." Amanda unhappily handed him her two dollar bills.

"That won't be enough," Ben complained.

"It will be plenty. Thanks."

Amanda divided the tokens between the children, and they

approached the arcade. Sophie repeated her desire to ride the train, while Ben pointed to what looked like a glass aquarium of stuffed animals.

"It's easy, Mommy. You just have to use this big crane to pick one up. I'm good at cranes."

The game cost five tokens. Amanda glanced around and saw that all the signs posted on the games indicated a minimum of five tokens each.

"Well, I guess you'll both be allowed just one," she tried to say brightly.

Ben wasn't paying attention to her; he was too consumed with the possibility of winning a garish plush dog. He fed his tokens into the slot and placed his hand on the stick that controlled the crane. The machine jolted to life, lights blinked, the crane lurched and buzzed, and before Ben had even the wit to move the stick, the crane returned empty. The machine switched off.

"I want to do it again," Ben said, stunned.

"No. That's it. It's Sophie's turn."

"I wanna do it again!"

"No, Ben. I told you—that's it. Only one game each."

Ben hurled himself upon the machine and pounded his fist against the inanimate toy faces. Amanda led Sophie away to the little train. It was dark and out of order. They returned to Ben.

"I want a puppy," Sophie announced.

"Why don't we try a different game, sweetie?"

"No. I want a *puppy.*"

Ben lit up at the prospect of another try and edged Sophie aside, saying sweetly, "Here, let me help you."

Sophie fumbled with her tokens, pushing them one by one into the slot, and the two fixed their eyes on the crane. The machine repeated its performance—the crane dipped and lifted without grasping the coveted puppy—and when it rattled to a stop, the children stared in disbelief that the game could betray them a second time.

"Well!" Amanda exclaimed, as if surprised herself. "Let's go see if we can find the others."

The others were Amanda's play group, which was meeting for the last time before the start of summer holidays. Ben and Sophie followed her silently, too seared by their loss to show much enthusiasm for the rat's maze of tunnels and slides. A boy shot through a tube and rolled into Sophie's feet, knocking her down. Before Amanda could say anything, he had vanished down another plastic hole. Ben whined that he wanted to go home.

Amanda found the mothers seated on stubby stools around a table shaped like a flower. Patricia looked the most out of place: she was wearing a navy-and-white linen suit with a silk scarf patterned in gold horseshoes, as if she had been deceived into dressing for a charity luncheon. Kim and Ellen were slightly less conspicuous in their sherbet-colored capris and slides. Amanda, in a pair of old jeans and a T-shirt, fit in only too well. Christine had not come—she was having her "before" photos taken by her plastic surgeon.

"Whose idea was this again?" Amanda grimaced as she pulled up a stool.

"Meredith's," Patricia sighed. "Sometimes I have to indulge her in ordinary children's tastes."

"Where are Ben and Sophie?" Kim asked.

Amanda turned and saw that she had lost her children. She scanned the play equipment and after a moment pointed them out crawling across a net.

"I think my head is going to explode from the noise," moaned Ellen.

"We don't have to stay long. We could all go to my house afterward," Kim suggested. "I'm not far from here."

"When is your renovation starting?" Patricia asked.

"Not until the end of July. I'm taking the kids to Nantucket for August, so we'll miss the worst of it, thank God. David has to stay and work, so he can deal with the contractors."

Faces, houses—what did these women *not* renovate? Amanda wondered.

"You're lucky you *have* contractors," Patricia remarked. "I had to wait two months just to get my painter to repair a patch on my ceiling. Two months! And even then, he insisted on coming by on a Saturday evening when we were having a dinner party, if you can believe it. But what was I going to tell him—no?"

"A friend of mine was fired by her painter."

"How do you get fired by your painter?"

"She told him she didn't like the job he was doing on some trim, and he walked out on her, right there, leaving the paint bucket and brushes behind. She and her husband had to finish the job themselves. It was pretty funny, actually—her husband makes four hundred dollars an hour, and there he was, up on a ladder rolling the walls."

"We need a recession," observed Patricia, adjusting herself uncomfortably on her stool, "otherwise I'm never going to get my new addition built."

It was Amanda's habit to let her mind wander when the mothers' conversation turned to decoration. She rarely had anything useful to contribute on the debate over bullion versus tasseled fringe, or whether chintz can be paired with toile, but today she followed the discussion with interest. One of the reasons she was so short of money this week was that, having cleaned her house, she had decided to buy some things to fix it up—not much, just a few baskets for the magazines and toys, a couple of table lamps for her living room, and some throw pillows to enliven the sorry sofa. While everything had been bought on sale, even sale items added up, and they cumulatively exceeded the limit of her credit card. The sting, however, was that the expenditure did not purchase any improvement. To Amanda's dismay, the new objects only drew attention to their tattered surroundings. Many times Patricia had noted that Amanda's house had "such good bones" and could be "a real little jewel" if only her decorator could be given the chance to "do it over." Amanda had dismissed her comments just as she had learned to dismiss the other mothers' pitying glances at her old furniture, or the way they let their children rampage through her rooms, as if to say, *Go ahead. It's all broken anyway.*

But as Kim burbled on about "maple cabinets" and Ellen, fresh from a kitchen renovation of her own, mused about turning her bedroom into a "master suite," Amanda asked herself: how had it happened that these women could redo entire houses while her credit card could not cope with some pillows and lamps?

"What are your plans for the summer, Amanda?"

Ellen's voice cut into her thoughts.

"Me? Oh—" Amanda cast around for a suitable answer. Patricia, she knew, would be off next week to her family's estate in the Algarve; Kim, as mentioned, went to Nantucket; and Ellen owned a converted mill house on one of the fashionable rivers of the Eastern Shore.

Their faces looked politely expectant; Amanda felt a surge of resentment. Where did they think she was going to go?

"Actually, I'm going to spend the summer redecorating my house." Amanda could not quite believe that she had put it that way, but now that she had said it, she enjoyed watching the women's reactions.

"How wonderful!" Kim exclaimed.

"What a great idea," said Ellen.

"Who are you getting to do it?" Patricia asked suspiciously.

Again they looked to her expectantly, and Amanda hesitated, a smile frozen on her lips. Who, indeed?

"Well," she said slowly, "I thought I'd do it myself."

The interest immediately drained from the women's expressions but Amanda barreled on, having learned from her friend Liz that you could make any domestic task sound less dreary by describing it as if it were a hobby. "I've always enjoyed painting, so I thought I'd experiment with the walls a little . . ."

"Please God, no sponging—it's so overdone," Patricia interjected.

". . . and I came across an easy way to do curtains, you know, on one of those home shows when I was flipping through the channels . . ."

"Martha Stewart needs a good dose of Ativan," chortled Ellen.

"In any case," Amanda continued, trying to keep up a breezy tone, "Bob's going to be so busy this summer with Megabyte that we simply won't be able to get away.

"Did any of you see his press conference?" she added hopefully.

The women shook their heads, except for Patricia, who glowered. "I do hope this Megabyte nonsense is going to end soon. We've taken a beating on the stock."

They were interrupted by Meredith Ripley, who dumped a handful of prizes on the table. The little girl looked as triumphant as a gambler who had just cleaned up at the baccarat tables.

"Where did you get these?" Patricia asked, glancing with distaste at the pile of cheap novelties—whistles, fake teeth, rubber balls, an elastic bracelet.

"I won them," Meredith answered proudly. "I need more money."

At that moment Ben and Sophie arrived, trailed by the other children. Ben immediately fixed his eyes on the prizes and, looking wildly at his mother as if he had missed out on some benevolent fairy's generosity, demanded to know, "Where did these come from?"

"They're Meredith's," Amanda replied calmly. "She won them."

Ben cast a surly glance at Meredith, but to Amanda's relief, he did not further contest the girl's ownership.

"I'm hungry," Sophie said, tugging at Amanda's sleeve. "I want pizza."

"Pizza!" the others agreed in chorus.

The mothers immediately reached for their purses and dispensed bills to the eldest children. Amanda didn't open her purse but instead said in a low voice to Ben and Sophie, "You just had lunch. You don't need pizza. We'll have a snack later."

Ben looked horrified by this latest injustice.

"I'm *hungry,*" he insisted. "I want *pizza.*"

"No," Amanda repeated. She was aware of the eyes of the other mothers upon her; it was unusual for her to resist her children's demands.

"Really, they just ate," she explained.

"No we *didn't.* We haven't eaten for *hours.* I'm *starving.*"

Amanda made no motion to open her purse. The rest of the children bolted impatiently in the direction of the pizza counter. Ben and Sophie continued their standoff.

"Could I have a thoda?"

"Yeah, I'm thirsty, too."

"Why not let them have something?" said Patricia with irritation; it was obvious she wanted the children just to go away.

"Okay," Amanda said, rising and taking their hands. "I'll go with you."

She found the other children sitting at the counter, slurping from plates of microwaved pizza and gigantic tumblers of cola. Amanda asked the clerk for two glasses of water. The clerk deposited two bottles in front of her.

"That'll be three dollars."

"No, not *bottled* water. Tap water will be fine."

"I don't want water!"

"Shut up, Ben," Amanda hissed.

"Mommy said shut up!" cried Sophie, shocked.

"We don't give out tap water. You want tap water, you have to use the fountain by the bathrooms." The clerk clucked with disgust and put the bottles back in the fridge.

Amanda pulled her children back toward the playground. "Look, we're only going to be here for a few more minutes," she pleaded. "Why don't you enjoy yourselves and Mommy will make a nice treat for you when we get home?"

"I *can't* enjoy myself without pizza," Ben retorted.

"Then I guess you're going to have a lousy time."

Amanda strode off toward the mothers while Ben and Sophie wandered back to the counter to watch the other children eat pizza, like two park pigeons hoping some of the crumbs might fall to them.

"Everything's fine," Amanda remarked when she sat down again. The women nodded; by now they were engrossed in a conversation about schools.

"I've applied to Beauvoir for Meredith," said Patricia, attempting to pronounce the tony school's name with the proper French inflection but succeeding only in producing the noise of a Parisian welling up to spit: *Boh-vwach!* "I wanted her in a nurturing environment."

"Beauvoir's fabulous," agreed Ellen. "I'd like Jonathan to attend the International School for a few years—they have a tremendous French immersion program. Of course eventually he'll have to go to St. Alban's. That's where his father went."

"Charlotte's going to go to Beauvoir, too," said Kim, and then corrected herself. "I should say we've *applied*, but I'd be surprised if she wasn't accepted. I attended Beauvoir and Lord knows we've given them enough money over the years."

Once more their faces turned expectantly to Amanda.

"I hadn't really thought about it yet—I've just assumed he's going to go to Oliver Wendell Holmes," Amanda said, naming the public school three blocks from their house. "Bob and I believe in the public school system," she added, without conviction. "And Holmes is a national merit school . . ."

Patricia offered her a consoling smile. "I think that sounds like the perfect environment for Ben."

Amanda turned into the snarl of Connecticut Avenue. Most of the cars struggled north, like salmon beating upstream; Amanda headed south toward the city. Ben and Sophie sat glumly in the backseat. Their disappointment at PlayZone manifested itself in alternating moods of self-pity and quarrelsomeness. Amanda wondered wearily why she had bothered to take them at all.

Amanda slowed for a red light. They were passing through Chevy Chase. On either side gracious mansions obscured their faces behind tall hedges like demure ladies holding emerald

fans. Heat and exhaust billowed in through Amanda's open car
windows. The air-conditioning system had mysteriously failed
the day before. Who knew when she would be able to afford to
get it fixed? She tried turning up the vents but that only blew the
hot air more intensely into her face. The heat made Amanda feel
sleepy, dreamy. She glanced sidelong at the car next to her, a
gleaming black sedan whose occupant was tightly sealed inside
a climate-controlled compartment. Beyond him was the stone
fence demarking the Chevy Chase Country Club; from somewhere she heard the sharp thwack of a tennis serve.

The traffic picked up again and soon they had crossed the District line and entered the familiar reaches of Woodley Park.
There was the transient woman shaking a cup for change outside the drugstore. Perspiring mothers in string T-shirts pushed
strollers over sidewalks that glittered with broken glass. A waiter
mopped down the plastic tables of an outdoor café.

To Amanda, the shabbiness of her neighborhood was its
badge of urbanity; it felt hip and comfortable, like a worn pair
of bell-bottoms. But now, as she paused behind a car blinking
left, Amanda saw her life stretching out like the motley blocks
ahead. Where would she end up if she persisted in going on like
this? She watched as an elderly woman climbed the stoop of a
depression-era apartment building, its dirty beige bricks streaked
with rusty drips from gasping air conditioners. A sign advertised
GARDEN UNITS with KITCHENETTES and all the modern conve-
niences of a bygone era. There were many of these buildings
along this strip of Connecticut—buildings that had missed
gentrification during the great boom, buildings in which the
hallways reeked of someone else's cauliflower.

Amanda's car lurched forward and cut over a lane; they were
nearing their street. She glimpsed, in the rearview mirror, the
reflection of two sleeping heads: Sophie's mouth was parted,

her eyelids dappled with sweat; all the anger had drained from Ben's face and with it, three or four years of age. He looked again as he had in his crib, during those soft hours of nap time, when she would brush her lips across his forehead and be amused that so forceful a creature could appear so benign when asleep. Soon he would be in kindergarten; next fall Sophie would be in school for a full day. Last summer, every single one of Amanda's movements had been constrained by a diaper-clad free weight. She had been unprepared for the extraordinary sensation of lightness she experienced on Sophie's first day of school, when her daughter toddled into Ms. Fishbein's class and assured her anxious mother, with a wave of her tiny hand, that she would be fine and to please go home. As Amanda walked back down the hallway, with no tearful child clutching at her leg, she asked herself if she felt bereft or sentimental over her daughter's sudden independence. No, came the immediate answer. Not one bit.

As she pulled into the driveway of their little house, Amanda admitted a thought she had long resisted—a thought she had blurted out to Bob the other night and then almost as quickly suppressed again.

Why not go back to work?

Why not?

Chapter Eleven

TAPA-TAPA-TAP-TAP. Tapa-tapa-tap-tap.

The show opened with a drumbeat, followed by heraldic blasts of trumpets and the obligatory shot of the Capitol dome. The panel appeared, seated around a wood-grain tabletop. The camera settled briefly upon Bob. He looked petrified.

"Why is Daddy orange?" Ben asked.

"I think it's the TV makeup. Shh."

"Daddy ith wearing makeup?" said Sophie.

"*Shh!*"

The image of the host, Fred Fallow, in his trademark red vest, filled the screen. His fat jowls, mesmerizing comb-over, and belligerent why-is-everyone-but-me-so-stupid attitude would have disqualified him from any other on-air job in the country, but Fallow thrived in the elite hothouse of Washington television like one of those rare snapping plants gardeners prize for their oddity and ugliness.

"Tonight on *Left/Right*," Fallow shouted at the camera, "Megabyte faces the biggest corporate fine in history for flouting its deal with the Justice department. Meanwhile, the Senate will begin hearings next week on competition in the software industry. Megabyte: is it a Mega monster? Or is it—as billionaire founder Mike Frith insists—merely Mega Misunderstood?

"Joining us are Chris Kachinski, legal counsel for Megabyte, and Bob Clarke, head of the computers and technology division at the Justice department. My cohost, Jane Henshaw, is on vacation. Sitting in for the right is Cathy O'Toole of the *National Standard* magazine. Welcome back, Cathy."

"Thanks, Fred." The camera panned to a blond woman in a crisp red blazer, the woman Amanda had seen at Jack Chasen's party. O'Toole greeted the lens with a wry, crooked smile that seemed to imply she knew more than she was letting on. Amanda grimaced and immediately felt sorry for Bob. Cathy O'Toole was like a bull terrier—once she had sunk her teeth into a guest's pant leg, it was hard to dislodge her.

"Well, Fred, we'd all like to be on vacation in this weather," O'Toole was saying with false bonhomie. "Washington is filled with hot air all year round but right now it's as hot as it gets. Or maybe not. I suspect the Senate hearings are going to generate even more heat—especially for Mike Frith. Chris, how is your client preparing for his much-awaited appearance before the Judiciary committee?"

Chris Kachinski was bland, reassuring—like a family doctor.

"Cathy, he reminds me of a professional athlete before a big match," Kachinski replied smoothly. "He's pumped, he's confident. He feels the government has no case against him, and that's going to become very apparent during these hearings. Frankly, he's looking forward to the chance to tell his side of the story."

Fallow jumped in. "C'mon, Chris, everyone knows the public can't stand Mike Frith. He's arrogant and defiant. I understand the Justice department is rubbing its hands together in glee at the prospect of having Frith take the stand. Isn't that right, Bob?"

"Uh, not exactly, Fred," Bob said, clearing his throat.

"Daddy!" the children cheered in unison.

Bob paused—for a heart-stopping second, he appeared to have forgotten what he meant to say. As he shifted and leaned forward on his elbows, his fellow panelists stared at him like hungry crocodiles, waiting for the baby gazelle to stray near the edge of the water.

"The government's position is this," Bob began, his voice fluttering. "Megabyte, er, flagrantly violated the consent decree it had with the Justice department with the launch of its new software, MB-98. Basically, you see"—he shifted again—"Megabyte bundled its Internet navigator with MB-98 after promising us it wouldn't, and that's why the company got fined. Now we have reason to believe that Megabyte is, uh, threatening its competitors and distributors who won't play the game their way. We're currently investigating whether these actions violate the Sherman Anti-Trust Act—"

Amanda winced at Bob's technical verbiage. She could almost feel the loyalties of the viewers shifting to Kachinski.

"What's Daddy saying?"

"Quiet—I'll tell you after."

"Bob," interjected O'Toole, her grin widening, "my understanding is that the antitrust laws were not designed to protect competitors from competition. They are supposed to protect consumers from dangerous monopolies. What evidence, if any, does the government have that the consumer is being hurt by Megabyte?"

"As I said, we're collecting that evidence right now," Bob said, his voice no steadier. "But in any case, Cathy, from our point of view, it's more about the *potential* threat that Megabyte poses to consumers."

"Well, folks, now you have it directly from the government's mouth," Kachinski retorted, shaking his head in mock astonishment. "The Justice department has no evidence that Megabyte has done anything wrong. Instead it's on a fishing expedition at the behest of our competitors. It's a dangerous legal precedent to accuse a company of wrongdoing based on a 'potential' threat. Either the threat is real or it's not."

"Is that man bad, Mommy?" Ben asked as the show went to a commercial.

"Uh no, not bad exactly."

"Doesn't he like Daddy?"

"He *disagrees* with Daddy."

"Who is Mike Frith?"

"He's the person that man is representing. He's like—" Amanda sought an analogy a child might understand. "He's like Mike Frith's friend. He's defending Mike Frith."

"Is Mike Frith bad?" Ben persisted.

"Yes," Amanda replied without hesitation. "Mike Frith is very bad. He wants to control all the computers in the world."

"Like Lord Zordon?" Ben said, referring to the alien villain in his beloved Space Rangers.

"Yes—I guess so. Like Lord Zordon."

"And Daddy's fighting him?"

"Uh-huh. Daddy—and the United States government."

Ben looked dazzled. "Cool!"

Not so Sophie. "Will Daddy win?" she asked worriedly.

"Oh, honey, yes, I'm sure he will," Amanda said, regretting the nightmare she had inadvertently dropped into her daughter's head. "He's not fighting him with swords or weapons, sweetie. He's fighting him with the law. He's going to court—you know, with judges and people like that. No one is going to get hurt."

Sophie did not seem reassured; she raised her thumb to her mouth and directed her attention back to the television. The show resumed, with no letup in the hammering of Bob.

"Why can't you just admit, Bob," O'Toole lit in, "that Megabyte produced a better product than its competitors, and now its competitors are acting like sore losers and using the Justice department to get back at Megabyte?"

"Exactly," agreed Kachinski while Bob stammered, "Cathy, uh, Cathy, if you could just let me respond," but failed to inject himself into the debate. "What's more, you've got guys like Jim Hochmayer and other honchos lobbying the government. These guys contributed a lot to the president's campaign and, by the way, a lot to Senator Benson's election—and he's going to be chairing the hearings!"

"Wait, wait, wait!" Fallow said in his loud, dismissive voice. "You make it sound like Megabyte is some poor little company, when in fact it's been crushing to death any competitor that's dared to get in its way!"

"I think—" Bob began, but was immediately cut off by O'Toole.

"Yeah, like who? I'm finding it hard over here to shed a tear for billionaires like Hochmayer—and let's not forget Jack Chasen and TalkNet. They're hardly getting 'crushed to death.'"

"I think what's important to remember," Bob managed to say, "is that the government is not seeking justice for Jack Chasen or Jim Hochmayer." He pulled himself up in his chair. "We're not seeking justice for Megabyte—"

"I'll say—" Kachinski murmured.

"We're seeking justice for the consumer. That's our job and we're going to do it."

O'Toole snorted.

"With those words, let's take a break," said Fallow. "When we come back, we'll be joined by Congressman Smathers, who'll give us the dirt on his controversial sanitation bill.

"Thank you, gentlemen."

"You're sure I did okay?"

"Yes. Positive. Really, you were fine."

It was the next morning, and Bob and Amanda were pushing through the weekend crowds at the National Zoo. Minutes would pass without him speaking to her, and when he did, it would be to return to the subject of the show.

"I still think O'Toole came off as really biased."

"She did."

Bob nodded to himself and slipped back into thought. Amanda had to remind him to pause at the giraffe pavilion, where a reticulated giant was straining to reach some of the last unstripped leaves from a buffet of trees. Bob had been distracted since he woke up: Saturday was his morning to make breakfast for the children, but Frank Sussman had telephoned just as Bob was about to pour their cereal. He took Frank's call instead, and the children retaliated by banging their empty bowls. Bob stormed up to the bedroom where Amanda was reading the paper and, while clutching the portable phone in one hand, pantomimed angrily with the other for her to get downstairs and quell the rebellion. By the time he reentered the kitchen, Amanda was rinsing the dishes and the children had fled to watch television. He fixed himself a cup of coffee and, without any acknowledgment of the favor she had just performed, launched into Sussman's reaction to the show.

"He thought it went great, really great. He said the important thing was to look strong while telling them nothing. It's easy to get trapped into saying more than you want to on these types of programs, but you can't let that happen. You've gotta stay on message, gotta repeat yourself if necessary. He feels I did that . . . They didn't land a blow on me . . . The department was pleased . . ."

"That's good," Amanda said, without raising her eyes from the sink. She noticed, though, that Bob seemed more anxious than he had been the previous evening, when any doubts he might have harbored about his performance were eclipsed by the sheer triumph of having survived his first brush with combat television. He returned home flushed and high-strung, burbling about how he "really landed one" on Kachinski and "did you see the look on O'Toole's face when I said—?" He was no calmer in bed where, in what felt more like a relief exercise than an act of affection, he groped and thrust himself upon her. Amanda acquiesced—even though she was tired, even though it was late, even though she would normally have protested at serving as sexual paramedic.

Today, however, all mood of victory had drained from Bob, and he was consumed with doubts about how the battle had looked to his generals. He had wanted to go into the office straightaway, but Amanda reminded him that Saturday was their one family day together and he had promised to take the children to the zoo.

Now, as Bob stood before the giraffes, perspiration forming damp continents on his CAMPAIGN FOR TOBACCO-FREE CHILDREN T-shirt, she saw that he was glancing around impatiently and calculating how soon he could leave.

"Jesus, don't they have an Arctic pavilion? Where the hell do they put the polar bears in this weather?"

Amanda unfolded the map she had picked up at the entrance. "They don't have polar bears. They have an *Amazonia* exhibit. That's the tropical rain forest—"

"Yeah, well, we don't need an exhibit for that. We're living it. What else?"

"There's something called *Animales de Latinoamerica*. I think that's where they have the tropical birds, if I remember correctly."

"Christ, why the obsession with hot places? You'd think, in this climate, they'd do the Himalayas. Or Antarctica. What's wrong with Antarctica? Doesn't anyone like penguins? They're cute. They're educational."

"Bob," Amanda said, trying to control her own exasperation, "there's no need to be so irritable. What about the Ape House?"

"Gorillas!" Ben exclaimed, turning away from the giraffes. "I want to see the gorillas!"

"Gowillath!" seconded Sophie from her stroller.

"Fabulous," muttered Bob. "I wonder if they use deodorant in this weather."

"It's all the way toward the bottom," said Amanda, still study-ing the map. "It's going to be a hike."

"Who wants to see the elephants?" Bob said with sudden enthusiasm. "Big huge elephants! Like Babar and Queen Celeste! And look—they're *right over here!*"

Ben squeezed through the onlookers to a spot by the fence and Bob hoisted Sophie to his shoulders. They gazed at the dusty, desultory creatures, and after a few minutes, Sophie said, "Now gowillath."

"You're sure you're not ready to go home?" Bob asked as he lowered her. "The elephants are the best part."

She scrambled back into the shade of her stroller, a small prin-cess in her palanquin. "No," she said imperiously. "Gowillath."

Bob pushed the stroller forward with a sigh. Ben trotted on a few feet ahead of them. The morning heat felt as if it were rising with every pace they took. The sun was not yet overhead, but already the temperature hovered near ninety degrees. Amanda felt guilty that she had dragged Bob outside on a day like this, and resentful that she should feel guilty. He barely saw the children these days, and she could hardly be held responsible for the weather.

Nonetheless, he was behaving as if it were somehow her fault. He was no longer preoccupied but openly annoyed at having to walk to the Ape House. He grunted rudely when they were halted by a group of Japanese tourists photographing each other in the middle of the path. Amanda wondered what she might say to placate him but then decided it wasn't her job.

"What a day to come here!" he exclaimed, as the Japanese dispersed. "How much farther are the damn gorillas?"

"They're just beyond the white tiger."

"Tiger!" Sophie called out. "Want to see tiger, too!"

Bob wiped the sweat from his forehead. "Of course you do."

"Bob—" Amanda said warningly.

He resumed pushing. They followed the path around a bend and came upon a heavily fortified concrete pen. The tiger was splayed out on a rocky ledge, with all the ferocity of a tabby cat dozing on a windowsill. Sophie and Ben clutched the fence and growled at it. Bob and Amanda parked the stroller and sat down on a low wall a few feet away. Amanda fanned herself with the map.

She had been wanting to speak to Bob about her decision to return to work, but there had been no opportunity. Judging from his mood, this would not be the best opportunity either, but she did not know when else she might have his attention, and Amanda urgently needed to know what he thought. When she had first blurted out the idea, Bob had seemed supportive, but Amanda did not know if that had simply been a bluff. She didn't think that he had given the idea any further consideration; she had done little else but. Yet now that she was on the verge of confiding her decision, she hesitated, as if exposing it to the air might cause it to shrivel up like a seedling that has not yet taken root. Amanda urged herself on—to seize the chance while the children remained distracted by the tiger.

"Were you serious the other day—when you said you didn't think it would be a bad idea if I returned to work?"

The abruptness of her question flustered Bob. For a moment he looked defensive, as if she had just lobbed an accusation.

"*Did* I say that?"

"You said—you *agreed*—that it was an option."

"*You* raised it as a way we could afford to send Ben to another school. And I said, yes, that would be a way to do it. But I wasn't *urging* you to do it—"

"I understand," Amanda said patiently. "And I'm raising it again, as a real possibility. I've been thinking hard about it— about returning to work in the fall, when the kids start school again."

Bob seemed reassured that she was not returning to their old argument, but he didn't immediately offer her an opinion. She expected him to launch into a debate over the negative and positive consequences of such a decision—that was his usual way of discussing big family issues—but instead he remained silent and, if possible, appeared even more preoccupied. He fluttered the front of his T-shirt while his gaze wandered over to the children, where it found Ben sticking his arms through the fence.

"Don't do that, Ben."

"What do you think?" Amanda pressed.

"You know what I think," he replied, his eyes still on the children. "You should do what you think is right."

"But is it right? Sophie will be in school next year for a full day, but I'll have less time to take care of things at home . . ." *C'mon*, she thought, *I can't decide this entirely for myself. I need you to tell me it will be okay.*

Bob exhaled wearily and placed his hands on his knees. He seemed to want to make it very clear that it was Amanda's idea to discuss the issue again, and that he was going to remain a neutral party to it.

"Are you thinking of working full or part time?" he asked.

"It would only make sense financially to work full time, don't you think?"

"It depends." He shrugged. "We can get by, obviously, on what I earn now. So the question is, are you returning to work so we can have more money, or are you doing it because you want to get out of the house?"

"Both," she said honestly.

"Well then, you're right—a full-time job would bring in real money. If it were just a matter of getting out of the house, there are a lot of other things you could do."

Amanda was not finding this Socratic back-and-forth helpful. She could think through for herself what sort of work she would like to do—she *had* thought it through, down to the outfit she would wear on her first day back at the National Endowment, if it would have her. What she needed to hear from Bob was that her family would be fine—that returning to her old job would not impinge upon them.

"It's just that—" Amanda faltered. "It's just that—well, you talked about making us suffer for your idealism, and I've been thinking maybe I've been making everyone suffer for mine. Maybe it was idealistic of me to quit my job and stay home. Maybe it was even selfish of me. I can't ask you to go to work at a firm you don't want to, just because we could use the money. You've been carrying the load for three years. And the children—they're older and don't need me as much, and my income could be a real help—we could send Ben to a school where he might be happier, where they don't want to send him to a therapist—give them both some of the things other kids have . . ."

"I've never thought of you as selfish."

"I know—I'm not saying you have. But it amounts to a kind of selfishness, doesn't it? Demanding that you support us all?"

"No, Amanda, I've never seen it that way." Bob cautiously put his arm around her shoulder; the heat of his body was stifling but she did not pull away.

"Maybe you just weren't cut out to be at home."

"Maybe not."

They got up and beckoned the children to follow. Sophie raced into the stroller and Ben clambered on the back, complaining that he was too tired to walk any farther.

Amanda told herself that Bob had given an answer to her question, but she wished he had given her something more—approval, disapproval, that sane army of pros and cons he could march out at will and that always brought logic and coherence to her feelings. Admittedly, she had dwelt very little upon the cons, whether out of fear or guilt—though it amounted to pretty much the same thing. Maybe Bob could be so agnostic on the matter because she wasn't asking so much of him, really—just a nod of approval and a higher tolerance for a messier house. No, the people of whom she would be asking a great deal would be the very people whose opinions would not be solicited. Sophie's little head was bobbing in the stroller in front of her, looking this way and that, trusting that she was being pushed in the right direction. Children, like ancient tribes, accept that their fate lies at the mercy of forces beyond their comprehension. One day Ben and Sophie would have their mother. The next they would find themselves among the children who arrived at school at seven forty-five in the morning for "Early-Bird Care" and who remained long past three o'clock for "Extended Day." Instead of rushing to the embrace of Amanda at dismissal time, Ben and Sophie would join the daily shuffle of children into unused classrooms, where they would spend the next several hours gluing Popsicle sticks, waiting for their mother to pick them up. This image, above all others, was the one that most wobbled Amanda's resolve to return to work.

"How do you think the kids will take it?" she asked Bob in a low voice.

"They'll get used to it."

Perhaps a similar image came to his mind, because the comment seemed to effect a change in his mood. As they came upon the Ape House he cheered up considerably—or at least enough to convince the children he was enjoying the visit to the zoo. He accompanied Ben and Sophie inside the smelly enclosure, and afterward consented to a round of ice cream cones; he did not lose his patience even when Ben immediately dropped his on the pavement, and had to be bought another.

When they returned home, everyone was filthy and hot. Bob showered and left for the office—"Got some calls to make and I'll see if there's any more fallout from the show"—but he promised not to be home too late. Amanda filled up the kiddie pool and, sipping iced tea, watched the children through the back window. It all came upon her in a rush—the return to a chaotic household, the pressure that would build up inside her like a steam kettle, the sudden preciousness of weekends, the smell of warm bananas in a child's lunch box at the end of a long day.

What was she about to do to them? she wondered, as Sophie, squealing with delight, turned the hose upon Ben. The little girl was naked, completely and unselfconsciously so. She had not yet left Eden; there were still puppy wrinkles in her thighs. Amanda went to fetch a towel, and as she went, triggered another question: what was she in danger of doing to herself?

She left the towel by the back door and returned to her post by the window, vigilant but detached. Maybe this was the mother's role: to make sure her children were in no danger but otherwise to allow them to find their own way. And how were they going to find their own way if she was always waiting nearby, towel at the ready?

Amanda knew this much: she had to do something. There would be no more excuses, no more second thoughts, she told herself firmly. They needed the money, but even more urgently, Amanda needed to be able to open her fists years from now and see that they held something of value; something that proved she had not let life run through her fingers like sand.

Chapter Twelve

"HEY."

Alan was sitting in his usual place with the stroller. It was the last week of school, and Amanda had entered the lobby feeling exhilarated about her impending liberation. Suddenly the looming summer holidays did not seem so much like a prison sentence as a last chance to enjoy, and even savor, her final weeks as a full-time mother. Amanda had heeded Liz's advice and planned excursions and projects for the children. By September her house, and life, would be in order. The sight of Alan momentarily threw her. Amanda had locked away her fantasy of him. But as the memory of it escaped, flooding her body with pleasant, tingling associations, she could not lie to herself, either: she was not unhappy to see Alan.

"Hey."

He was obviously pleased to see her.

"I have the tickets with me," he said eagerly.

"Tickets?"

"To my play. It's opening this Friday. Can you still come?"

Amanda remembered promising to go to his play, but at the time the promise had felt like little more than a friendly gesture. Amanda wondered at the implications of saying yes now. The fantasy seemed manageable so long as it stayed in her head.

Alan was aware of her hesitation for he said quickly, "I understand if you can't. I mean it's short notice—"

"No, no, I want to come to the play—I just don't know if I can get a baby-sitter."

"Sure," he said, with a trace of disappointment.

Amanda became impatient with herself. Why was she always so afraid of taking risks? What on earth was she afraid of with Alan? It had been her fantasy, not his. They were both responsible grown-ups. She was keen to see his play.

"It probably won't be a problem though. My neighbor's kid is usually free. I'll check. Assume yes," she said.

Alan's face lightened. "Fabulous. Do you need a ticket for Bob or is he still going to be working?"

Amanda sensed, but could not be certain, that Alan was rather hoping for the latter.

"I'm pretty sure he'll be working. Besides, he's not a big fan of experimental theater. Not that he wouldn't be interested in your play . . ."

"I'm not offended. Many people find my work too challenging." He smiled in a way that included her in the better-knowing audience.

"Yes. Well—" The bell rang and Amanda made a motion to leave.

"I can pick you up if you like," Alan offered. "It's playing in Rockville. If you've never been out there before, it's easy to get lost."

"Rockville? Why Rockville?"

"It's where they had space."

"Oh."

"They workshop a lot of serious plays there. It's sort of the off-Broadway of Washington. Anyway, did you want me to pick you up?"

Again Amanda hesitated, not sure what to answer, but as if reading her thoughts, he added, "A bunch of us are going—"

This relieved her a little, although why it should, she asked herself, she didn't know. *Stop being so fearful!*

"Thanks. I'd appreciate it."

"Good. We'll pick you up around six then, if that's okay. I have to get there a little early—you know, as playwright and all."

"Fine."

Amanda nearly crashed into Dr. Koenig, who had just emerged from the office, carrying files.

"There you are, Amanda," she said accusingly, as if Amanda had been in hiding for the past week. "I was going to call you today. Did you find a therapist for Ben?"

Dr. Koenig made no effort to keep her voice down, and Amanda cast an awkward glance around the lobby to see how many of the other mothers had overheard. Fortunately, not many had arrived yet; only Alan seemed to be listening closely.

"Um, yes," she lied. "I've been looking into it."

"Many go away for July so I wouldn't dawdle. Ben needs assessment *immediately.*"

"I understand."

"Good." Dr. Koenig marched off down the hallway. Amanda bit her lip and shrugged at Alan, who raised his eyebrows in sympathy.

By the time Friday arrived, Amanda was almost breathless with excitement. She stood in front of her wardrobe, trying to decide what to wear. Everything she pulled out was wrong. She found herself reaching deeper and deeper into the back of the closet and pulling down shirts from high shelves.

Amanda couldn't remember going out for an evening without Bob; and while she was guiltily aware of the spark of attraction between her and Alan, what excited Amanda more was her rediscovered sense of independence. Some years after she and Bob were married, they were in a restaurant, and Amanda noticed a couple at the next table who were obviously on their first date: the man and woman were recounting their life stories to each other with the earnestness of candidates at a job interview. Amanda had felt so pleased that she was married and not dating anymore—how awful it would be to have to keep offering yourself up on a plate to a different person every week!—and instinctively she had gripped Bob's hand. Tonight, however, Amanda was looking forward to describing herself to someone new. This evening would be an opening of sorts for her, the official launch of herself as an individual with a life and interests outside the house.

(Bob had encouraged Amanda to go, although she could tell he was glad to have an excuse not to join her, especially after she repeated Alan's description of his play. "*Workshop* is not a verb," he corrected her. "Besides, why is it playing out in Rockville? Why isn't it downtown?"

"Apparently a lot of important plays are workshopped—get their start—in Rockville. At least that's what Alan told me. He says it's the off-Broadway of Washington."

"Or maybe the New Jersey of Washington."

"Look, you don't have to go, okay? I'm really just going to show Alan support. It's a big deal for him. He's a nice guy and he's been at home, you know, like me. He doesn't always get the respect that he deserves.")

Yet what to wear? There were her mommy clothes, and her old office suits, and the cocktail outfit she had worn to Jack Chasen's, which was too dressy. Amanda dug around some more and came up with a black T-shirt she used to wear to clubs, before she had met Bob. She pulled it over her head and found that it fit her more tightly than before, but not unattractively so. With jeans it would work—she would look arty, youthful, her old self again, especially if she loosened her hair—

Sophie entered the bedroom, dragging a stuffed dog on a makeshift leash.

"Where are you going?" she asked her mother.

"Mommy's going out tonight."

"With Daddy?"

Yeesh, Amanda thought.

"No. With some friends. We're going to see a play. How do I look?" Amanda turned around, modeling her T-shirt and jeans.

"Not pwetty." The little girl went over to the closet and pointed to a long creamy lace dress that Amanda had worn to a wedding. "You should wear thith."

"I don't think that would be right, sweetie. It's too fancy. Now run along and play with your brother." Amanda ushered her out of the room.

She brushed her hair and made one last check of herself in the mirror. She asked herself if the T-shirt really was too tight. No—she liked it. It made her feel good. She would wear it.

The baby-sitter rang the doorbell, and Amanda hurried to find her sandals. They were where she had last kicked them off, beside the bed. As she slid them on, she noticed the pad of paper and pen she kept on her night table. Amanda tore off a sheet and wrote, impulsively, "Having a great time—sorry

you're not with me. Hope your work went well. Love you. A."
She placed the note on Bob's pillow.

Alan drove up in a silver Lexus sedan.

"Nice car."

Alan patted the dashboard fondly. "It's Lisa's," he said, referring to his wife.

Amanda kissed him lightly on both cheeks and noticed him
taking in the effect of her T-shirt. She turned and reached for her
shoulder belt.

"Where is Lisa, by the way?"

"Working on a big case." He put the car into gear and pulled
out from her driveway. As he reversed, he rested his arm over the
back of her seat, and Amanda shifted uneasily. Admittedly, Lisa
had not loomed large in any of Amanda's thoughts, but now
that she was sitting in the woman's car, she became vividly
aware of her existence—the lipstick in the cupholder, the hair-
brush shoved between the two front seats, strands of unfamiliar
reddish hair caught in its bristles—

"Lisa couldn't come to your opening?"

"Nope."

Amanda waited for him to elaborate, but Alan seemed suddenly distracted with figuring out the best way to avoid rush-hour
traffic on Connecticut Avenue. They drove without speaking
through a maze of side streets that led them north of the worst of
it. She glanced sidelong at Alan, who was frowning in concentra-
tion. Somehow he looked different in this context, less appealing,
and she realized it was partially due to his clothes: there was defi-
nitely an "author's-photo" quality to the black blazer he had
thrown over his jeans. She was struck, too, by how odd she felt sit-

ting in the front seat of a car with a man who wasn't her husband, and she wondered if Alan felt similarly. When the quiet between them grew awkward, she asked, "Who else are we picking up?"

Her question seemed to take Alan by surprise, for he replied immediately, "No one"—and then, as if suddenly remembering their conversation from earlier that week, he added, "A couple people from my book group are coming, but they decided to take their own cars. It wasn't that convenient to go together."

His answer increased Amanda's awkwardness, but she fought against it, trying hard to summon that sense of ease that she had always imagined would exist between them if they were alone together. Alan, too, seemed to notice her discomfort; once traffic began to flow more easily as they reached the wider, suburban boulevards, he said, "I'm sorry if I seem a bit tense. I always am before an opening."

"Oh—that's okay. I understand."

"I just can't tell you how much I appreciate it that you could come. It's a big night for me. Lisa—well . . ." He let the sentence trail off as if it were too much to explain. When he resumed, an edge of bitterness had crept into his voice. "I suppose I should feel lucky in my position. I mean, a lot of artists would appreciate the support of someone like her. It's just that—" He shook his head, dismissing the remainder of his thought.

"It's just what?"

He paused. "It's just that I never feel she takes my work as seriously as I take hers. There—I said it. The law, *that's* a career, but writing plays—that's a hobby."

"I know exactly what you mean."

"I know you do."

Alan slowed as they came abreast of a driveway leading to what looked like an apartment complex set back from the busy road. There were three or four stumpy gray buildings that jutted into the flat skyline like broken teeth. Alan turned into a vast parking lot and began driving up and down the rows, hunting for a spot.

"Where are we?" Amanda asked.

"A seniors' home."

"Where's the theater?"

"Inside the main building. There's an auditorium." Alan seemed slightly embarrassed.

"But is it open to the public?"

"Yeah. The home allows us to sell tickets to outsiders—basically to cover our production costs—but the residents watch it for free."

"I don't get it," Amanda said. "How does the play . . . find a wider audience?"

"We book the play wherever we can at this phase. Then, when word gets out, you hope for one of the bigger stages to take it—the Virginia Repertory Theater in Chantilly or the Outer Circle at Gaithersburg—that one's very highly regarded."

"We open next month at the Bethesda JCC."

"There's one." Amanda pointed to a gap between cars.

"No—it says residents only. We have to use the visitors'."

Alan continued to drive up and down like a farmer plowing a field; finally a car signaled it was pulling out. The spot was a long walk from the entrance to the main building. By the time they reached the double set of glass doors, which swung open automatically to allow the passage of wheelchairs, Amanda's hair was sticking to the back of her neck. Inside, the air was at least cooler, but it felt stagnant and recycled; the odor of whatever they were cooking in the cafeteria—boiled potatoes, to Amanda's nose—was laden with a heavy dose of disinfectant.

Alan approached a surly-looking receptionist who sat behind a fortified pane of glass.

"We're here for the production of *American Stigmata*."

The receptionist leaned forward to speak into a microphone. "Who?" her voice echoed.

"It's not a person, it's a *play*. *American Stigmata*. I'm the playwright."

The receptionist scanned a clipboard although she did not appear certain of what she was looking for. After a few moments she shoved the clipboard through a slot under the glass and asked Alan if he could find what he wanted. He found it quickly and pointed it out to her.

"You see here? *American Stigmata*, a play. It's in the 'MacArthur Room.'"

She nodded, uninterested, and took the clipboard back.

"You'll be getting more people coming through here asking for it. You can just send them there, okay?"

"Uh-huh."

"Jesus," he muttered as they walked away. "I hope we're the first ones."

There was no worry on that front. When they arrived, the room was empty, except for about a hundred or so banquet chairs lined up to face an accordion wall. It was not the auditorium Amanda had expected, but a large reception room the residents might use for birthday parties and other types of social events. The walls were covered in a worn pink paper with patterns of raised velvet that reminded Amanda vaguely of eczema; coffee cups and an unplugged electric urn had been set out on a long banquet table to one side. Amanda could not see where the production would take place, unless the accordion wall was going to double as a curtain. That hypothesis seemed to be correct, for shortly after they entered they heard the sound of voices coming from behind the partition.

"That should be the cast," Alan said, looking about. "I better go check."

Amanda sat down in one of the chairs toward the back of the room and glanced at her watch. The play was due to start in less than half an hour. They had passed a sign in the corridor listing the evening's events—aside from Alan's play, there was bingo and a ballroom-dancing lesson.

Alan returned to report that the actors were all assembled and changing into their costumes. He was twittery with anxiety, like a dinner party hostess. He paced back and forth at the front of the room, running his fingers through his hair and pausing every few minutes to check the corridor.

"They said there would be someone here to take tickets," he muttered at one point.

"Do the residents need tickets?"

"No, but outsiders do. My impression was that they had sold quite a number of them . . ."

One of the actors poked his head out. He was a tall, stocky man of about forty made up to look much older, with white powder sprinkled in his brown hair and lines on his face sketched a little too darkly in greasepaint.

"When do you think we'll start, Alan? We're all ready to go back here . . ."

"I know, I know. Let's hold off a bit, shall we?"

The actor scanned the room and absorbed the lone sight of Amanda.

She gave a shy wave. "Hi."

"I'll inform the others," he said worriedly.

At about five minutes before curtain time—when Alan,

nearly hysterical, was threatening to hunt down a building supervisor—they heard clattering in the hall, and a nurse pushed in an ancient man in a wheelchair. He was wearing a blue hospital gown and did not appear entirely certain about his whereabouts. He seemed to be protesting something to the nurse, but his words were slurred and inaudible. The nurse, unruffled, ignored him and wheeled him to a place in the front row. An equally ancient woman followed behind with a walker. Alan gaped but didn't move. It was Amanda who came to the nurse's aid, helping to move a banquet chair to accommodate the wheelchair and then showing the elderly lady into a seat. More people began to enter the room: a pair of lively, white-haired women who noisily reminisced about a bus trip to Broadway to see *Cats*; a dapper gentleman in jacket and tie with dyed red hair slicked straight back; a sour-looking woman in bathrobe and paper slippers, who asked Alan if he had any idea "how long this damn thing was going to last"; a frail, silver-haired man, complete with Quasimodo hump, who made several attempts to pour himself a cup of coffee from the unplugged urn. Alan retreated backstage, leaving Amanda to perform usher duty. By ten past the hour, a good thirty or forty residents had filled the front seats and were looking restlessly toward the partition.

Alan returned to the room and switched on a single spotlight that had been set in the corner and trained on the center of the accordion wall. All the other lights were switched off. He walked into the spotlight and greeted the residents.

"My name is Alan Fielding, and I am the writer and director of tonight's play, *American Stigmata . . .*"

"Speak up!" shouted the woman in the bathrobe, and the rest of the audience mumbled its assent.

"Sorry." Alan cleared his throat and began speaking again in a slightly louder voice. "The play you will see tonight, *American Stigmata*, which I wrote and directed—"

"Still can't hear you at the back!" yelled the woman in the bathrobe.

This time Alan did not pause. "IS A CHALLENGING NEW PERSPECTIVE ON WEALTH, HOMELESSNESS, AND AIDS. IT IS NOT LIKE OTHER PLAYS YOU MAY HAVE SEEN IN THAT THERE IS NO SET OR SCENERY. THE PLAY'S POWER DERIVES SOLELY FROM THE TALENT OF THE ACTORS AND THEIR ABILITY TO MAKE YOU BELIEVE IN THEM."

"Did he say it was a musical?" Amanda overheard the man with red hair whispering to one of the *Cats* ladies next to him.

"Yes," she replied. "A make-believe musical."

"Oh good."

"BECAUSE OF THE INTENSE NATURE OF THE PLAY, I ASK THAT YOU HOLD YOUR APPLAUSE UNTIL THE VERY END. THERE WILL BE TWO ACTS AND ONE BRIEF INTERMISSION. THANK YOU."

The man leaned over to the woman again. "A nature play?"

"I guess." She shrugged. "Maybe he means it's like *Lion King*."

Alan found Amanda, who had moved up several rows, and sat down beside her. His eyes searched the faces around them.

"Frieda and Neil aren't here."

"Who are they?"

"The people from my book club."

The partition rolled back, exposing the other half of the reception room. Three actors and two actresses squatted in the shadows to the side of the single spotlit microphone. The actor Amanda had seen earlier stepped up to the microphone and announced, "My name is John Barrington the Third. I am a

retired industrialist and father of John Barrington the Fourth."
He sat down and one of the actresses took his place at the
microphone. She, too, had powdered hair and greasepaint
wrinkles, but clutched a shawl around her shoulders. Amanda
noticed that aside from makeup and one distinguishing accessory—the first actor had worn a bright scarlet tie—the cast
members were dressed identically in black T-shirts and jeans.
"I am Abigail Barrington, wife of John Barrington the Third and
mother of John Barrington the Fourth." She sat down and the
next actor took her place—and so on, until the entire cast had
introduced itself in some relation to John Barrington the
Fourth, who came last, and whose accessory was a red lesion on
his face.

"I wanted it to begin like an AA meeting," Alan whispered,
"with each person revealing their identity as if it were an
addiction."

"I guess they couldn't afford costumes," observed the old
gentleman in front of them.

The actors then performed a series of swift tableaux, grouping
and ungrouping themselves around the microphone. The son
announced to his parents that he had been diagnosed with
AIDS. The parents argued over the distressing news, the father
expressing his horror, the mother pleading for sympathy. The
son then argued with the parents, accusing them of insensitivity
and blaming them for the double life he had been forced to lead
as a homosexual. The other actress played an activist, who urged
him to embrace his true identity as a gay man. Then, after a
tableau in which the son denounced his family, the cast changed
their roles. They adopted new accessories that identified them as

the homeless people John Barrington the Fourth encounters on his journey through the streets. The actor who played the father now shook a cup, the mother huddled with shopping bags, the activist dipped a ladle in an imaginary soup kitchen.

Alan watched the play critically, sitting forward in his seat with his chin propped in his hands. Amanda could tell he was making notes to himself about lines he wanted to change, scenes he wished to adjust—and this fortunately had the effect of making him impervious to the mutiny gathering around him.

The bathrobe lady was the first to rebel. Barely a quarter hour had passed when she stood up and, with an exasperated sigh that even the deafest among them could not have missed, shuffled out of the room. Her behavior seemed to elicit more disapproval than agreement from the audience, most of whom were still watching the play as if they hoped that dancing lions might yet appear, except for the man in the wheelchair, who kept up his angry mumble. During the son's confrontation with his parents, John Barrington the Fourth knocked the microphone with his elbow, and the actors had to break character for a few seconds to adjust it. Alan crept up to the performance area to ensure the microphone was solidly back in place, and the man with the hump called out, "Could you turn up the volume while you're at it?" There was more fumbling and a few nasty electronic screeches as Alan played with the controls. The play resumed. Ten minutes later, three more residents rose to leave, more quietly—but not less visibly—than the woman in the bathrobe. The man with the dyed hair had nodded off, while the two *Cats* women continued to watch the play with weakening smiles.

Amanda wished she felt more indignation on Alan's behalf, but the truth was, she was enjoying the play about as much as the residents were. The first act lasted nearly a full hour. When the lights were turned back on for intermission, only about twenty members of the audience remained. Amanda's mind had wandered so completely that for a moment she mistook the intermission for the end of the play.

"What now?" she asked Alan.

"Coffee, I think," he said, giving her a strange look.

As the residents milled about sipping their coffee, Amanda wondered what she should say to console Alan. He insisted on standing off to the side—out of aloofness or disappointment, Amanda couldn't tell. She managed to cobble together a few words of reasonably plausible praise, but just as she opened her mouth to speak, one of the *Cats* women approached. The woman was of a type Amanda recognized from New York theater lobbies twenty-five years ago who arrived in gaggles at the Sunday matinee, pantsuited and stiff-haired, as reliable in their attendance as Catholic churchgoers in Bay Ridge, *Playbills* clutched under their arms in lieu of Bibles. For a moment Alan looked as if he might try to bolt, but the woman—clearly an old pro in the art of cornering—had already caught his eye and stretched out her hand while her arthritic legs struggled to keep up.

"You're our playwright!"

"I'm afraid so."

The woman grasped Alan's arm to steady herself and introduced herself as Judy Mansing. Amanda saw that she had gone to a great deal of trouble to dress up for the evening, even if the outcome was not perfectly successful—she was wearing an unseasonal tweed suit and her coral lipstick had overshot her mouth by a quarter inch.

"Is this your first play?"

"No. I've written several."

"Really? Good for you. I *love* the theater. Always used to go when I lived in New York, until my daughter moved down here, and then, when the grandchildren arrived—"

The other *Cats* woman joined them.

"Eleanor," said Judy, "this is the playwright. What did you say your name was?"

"Alan," he said. "Alan Fielding."

"This is Mr. Fielding," Judy said, as if her friend had not heard Alan.

"I know, I know."

"He says he has written other plays."

"Has he?"

"He has."

"Fancy that." The women looked to Amanda for the first time. "Are you Mrs. Fielding?"

"No, I'm Amanda—Amanda Bright. I'm just a friend."

"Oh." Whatever conclusion Judy Mansing drew from this remark, it was not to Amanda's advantage, for she resumed her conversation with Alan.

"You're so young, I thought it had to be your first play."

"Forty-three is hardly young!" Alan objected.

"It's young to us. Thirty—forty. It all runs together."

"Tell me, have you had any plays on Broadway?" Judy asked.

"No," Alan said. "I think my work may be a little too—innovative—for Broadway."

"Too what?"

"He said 'innovative,'" Judy repeated. "We enjoyed *Cats*. I guess that was considered innovative at the time."

"Same with *Chorus Line*."

"And *West Side Story*. My gosh, do you remember how none of our friends wanted to see it?"

"I adored *West Side Story*."

"I think the play may be resuming," Alan interrupted, as one of the actors began flicking the overhead lights off and on.

"It was a pleasure meeting you."

The two women wandered away, with Eleanor guiding Judy by the arm.

"God," said Alan in despair. "What an audience."

"They aren't that bad. At least they're enthusiastic about the theater—"

"Oh really? Look."

The women were now walking out the door. They were not the only ones. Other residents were streaming out as well, including the man in the wheelchair, pushed by his nurse. Amanda heard one person say, "I can't last much past eight o'clock," while another said, "I don't know—I might have some energy left for bingo."

By the time the partition rolled back for the second act, three members of the audience remained—Amanda, Alan, and the man with the dyed hair, snoring loudly in his chair.

Only John Barrington the Fourth pressed for the show to go on; the others began packing up the equipment. Amanda awoke the sleeping man and told him the play was over. He thanked her kindly and assured the cast that he had greatly enjoyed their "little production."

"I'm going to the bathroom to get this makeup off," said the actress who played Mrs. Barrington. "Anyone feel like going for a drink after? There's a Friday's across the street."

Alan was trying to force a buckle closed on the microphone case. "I could use a drink. How about you, Amanda?"

Yes, she could use a drink—for sure she could use a drink—but she did not want a drink with Alan. Amanda decided right then that she did not want anything with Alan. What she wanted was to get the hell out, to bolt home, like a horse to its barn.

"I don't know. My sitter's a teenager—"

"It's only nine-thirty." Alan snapped the buckle closed and stood up, facing her.

"Count me in for a double," said John Barrington the Third.

"She's probably not expecting you home until at least eleven."

"I know, but—"

"But?" He raised his hands, as if to say, *So what?*

John Barrington the Fourth took the microphone case. "I'll put this in the car and meet you over there."

Alan was looking at her meaningfully now. Amanda averted her eyes and said, "Look, you go, okay?"

"I'd really like you to come." He drew her aside. "Is something wrong?"

Amanda resented the intimate scene he was creating in front of the others. One of the actresses—the activist—had returned from the bathroom in her street clothes and was watching them with interest.

"No, nothing's wrong. I'm tired and—"

"We don't have to stay late. I don't want to stay late. Would you rather go somewhere—*just the two of us?*"

"No!" Amanda jerked away so sharply that Alan could no longer be uncertain of her intent. A flash of hurt crossed his face, but he got rid of it quickly. When he spoke again, his voice was sulky and defiant.

"Fine. *I'm* going for a drink. Let's go, Theresa," he said.

Only then did Amanda realize that she had trapped herself. Evidently, she no longer had a ride home. A taxi from out here would cost at least thirty dollars. She had brought just a few dollars with her and a credit card.

"Alan," she said, trying to sound as friendly as she could manage, "I came in your car, remember? If you go for a drink, how will I get home?"

"I'm sure the front desk could call you a cab."

"Are you going to the District?" asked Theresa, slinging her bag over her shoulder.

"Uh-huh." Amanda was still staring after Alan, not quite believing he was prepared to treat her so casually.

"I can give you a lift. I'd like to get home, too."

"Thanks."

Amanda collected her purse from her chair. Alan preoccupied himself with the lighting equipment.

Amanda closed her front door gratefully, the smallness of her house for once enveloping her like a tight embrace. The babysitter appeared on the upstairs landing, carrying an empty bowl of popcorn. Hannah was the fourteen-year-old daughter of their neighbor. She had, in the past year, developed the habit of answering adult questions like an unhelpful bureaucrat: usually when Amanda asked how everything had gone, Hannah would look at her feet and answer in a monosyllable. But tonight Hannah greeted Amanda excitedly.

"You got a phone call from Susie Morris," she said, clomping down the stairs. "She's, like, that person from TV?"

"Uh-huh."

"Cool."

Amanda waited for Hannah to reveal what the message was, but Hannah flipped her short, oily brown hair and continued,

"She was, like, totally nice to me. Asked me about my school. She's doing, like, a show with that guy from MTV?"

"Uh-huh."

"Cool."

Amanda took the empty bowl from Hannah and carried it to the kitchen. "Did she want me to call her back?"

"Oh yeah—she said it was, like, really urgent. It's about dinner Sunday night."

"Dinner?"

"She says she has a friend in from out of town and wants to bring him over." Hannah seemed to find this improbable—that Susie Morris would wish to dine with the likes of Amanda. Only one thought occurred to Amanda—Susie wanted to bring over Jim Hochmayer? This struck her as equally improbable.

"Okay. I'll call her."

"How do you, like, know Susie Morris?"

"We went to college together."

"Wow. She doesn't seem—" Hannah stopped herself.

"That old?" Amanda finished for her.

Amanda noticed a scrap of paper beside the telephone with Hannah's loopy scrawl upon it.

"What's this?"

"Oh—sorry. That's another message. For Bob."

Amanda read the name: Grace Bertelli.

"I don't know if I spelled it right."

Amanda felt her insides seize up, as if she had been bitten by something poisonous.

Chapter Thirteen

EVERYTHING ABOUT JIM HOCHMAYER seemed to spill over the sides. His long arms and legs splayed beyond the canvas deck chair; his great, booming voice reverberated into the neighboring gardens. Each time Amanda returned from the kitchen—first bearing hors d'oeuvres, then drinks ("A beer will do fine and don't bother with a glass—I'll drink it the way God meant it to be drunk"), she was jolted by the sight of a billionaire in her backyard. Hochmayer, however, seemed fully at ease. He was a man who gave the impression that he would be fully at ease anywhere, whether it was eating beans out of a can on the Texas range or escorting the queen of England in to dinner. If he was uncomfortable in his rickety chair, he didn't show it. If the sedentary heat of the evening was causing sweat to appear in the creases of his shirt and pants, he said nothing about it. He helped himself to the mozzarella balls and slightly stale French bread as eagerly as if they were delicacies from Fauchon. Every so often he would pause in his conversation or interrupt someone else to offer Amanda a compliment—and not some all-purpose compliment but a custom-made one.

"Did you put rosemary in the oil?" he'd exclaim. "Damn if it isn't delicious."

Susie sat only a few inches away from Hochmayer and gazed at him so rapturously that Amanda worried Hochmayer might wilt under the klieg lights of her affection. But Hochmayer took Susie in stride the way he did everything else, and now and then he would direct one of his bespoke compliments to her: "Tell me, has anyone ever seen eyelashes as long as this lady's? How long are they anyway? 'Bout two feet?"

Bob, meanwhile, struggled to light the charcoal grill. Small puffs of smoke rose like Indian signals, hovered for a few seconds, then died away. After a few minutes, Hochmayer lifted his tall frame from his seat and excused himself to join his host.

"Bob, my man," he said good-naturedly, inspecting the bag of charcoal, "I applaud you for going for the real stuff and not caving into those sissy, self-starting briquettes . . ."

"I thought they *were* self-starting." Bob examined the bag for himself.

". . . but if you don't mind a word of advice from a Texan who's been around a few barbecues, you're going to need some kindling."

"Kindling?"

"Uh-huh."

Hochmayer began hunting under the straggly bushes that lined the fence. Amanda now confronted the extraordinary spectacle of her guest—in his khaki linen pants and shirt that probably cost more than one of Bob's suits—down on his knees, pawing through the dirt. Susie shrugged and smiled as if to say, *Isn't he the most incredible man you've ever met?*

"Now, where I come from," Hochmayer was explaining from beneath a shrub, "we use something called mesquite. It's basically a weed that grows like brushfire. Until a few years ago no one knew what to do with it. Then some guy gets this bright idea to sell it to easterners. It's no longer a weed, you understand, it's a 'gourmet' grilling wood. Huge industry now, shipping our weeds to you folks. Whoa, what's this?"

Hochmayer held up a mud-encrusted toy stock car. "Bet someone was mighty upset to lose that." He handed it to Amanda and continued his search. She prayed he would not reach the corner bushes where she had concealed the children's plastic yard junk. Soon Hochmayer seemed satisfied with the handfuls of dried mulch, broken twigs, and old Popsicle sticks he had managed to amass, and after requesting some newspaper from Bob, he covered the rubbish with coals and stoked them into a steady flame.

"Give it forty minutes or so, and you'll have a good cooking fire," Hochmayer said, patting Bob on the back and guiding him back to the circle of chairs.

Amanda replenished everyone's drinks and went to take the seat next to Hochmayer. He leaped to his feet and remained standing until Amanda had sat down before he took his own chair again. Amanda was so surprised that she could not help glancing at Bob, who was chatting with Susie and had not noticed.

Hochmayer caught Amanda's faint look of disapproval and immediately sought to dispel it. "Your Bob's a real good fellow," Hochmayer said, sotto voce but not so sotto that Bob's ears missed it. "Clever. Honest. Solid. A fine lawyer."

Amanda was not much in the mood to hear Bob's praises sung, but she acknowledged Hochmayer's observation, and allowed herself to believe, for the first time since Susie had asked to bring Hochmayer to dinner, that the evening was not going to be a total disaster. Darkness had begun to coat the tips of the trees, and the fireflies commenced their doomed, incendiary courtship. Their twinkling against the deepening black-green foliage veiled the garden's ugliness, and as the light dwindled to the glowing pools cast by two citronella candles, Amanda's astonishment and anxiety at having Hochmayer in her house gradually subsided, too. Susie had brought boy-friends to dinner many times before: she claimed that she liked to audition potential mates in a familial atmosphere. Amanda doubted that this was true: the domestic scene at their house resembled less a Norman Rockwell painting of family life than it did an advertisement for birth control. More likely (Amanda suspected), Susie used Amanda's family as a flattering backdrop to her own beauty, just as florists will showcase the exotic loveliness of their orchids against an arrangement of ordinary ferns.

Still, this theory did not explain why Susie would want to bring Hochmayer to dinner. He clearly needed no inferior setting to be persuaded of Susie's uniqueness. And if this was a test of some sort, Amanda could not see what was being tested—unless it was Hochmayer's tolerance for bad food, which, come to think of it, might not be a bad qualification for matrimony. Yet if Hochmayer truly wished to visit with Susie's "oldest and dearest friends"—the excuse Susie had given her—why had they not simply gone out somewhere? Susie insisted that a home-cooked meal would be a real treat for a man like Hochmayer, who was always traveling. And Bob—who was, if anything, even more nervous about entertaining Hochmayer than Amanda—thought it would be wiser not to be seen in public dining with a man who would be one of Justice's star witnesses at the next day's Megabyte hearings in the Senate.

"I'm not saying there's anything wrong with it," Bob had said. "It's just that it might be taken the wrong way—you know, the Justice department getting cozy with Megabyte's enemies."

"It's purely social," Amanda countered.

"Yes, but appearances in Washington often matter more than facts, and I don't want to take the risk."

"Well, I don't want to take the risk of entertaining a billion-aire—good God, what are we going to serve him?"

Yet within twenty minutes of Hochmayer's arrival, his easy nature had convinced Amanda that having him to their house had been an inspired idea. The children had been unusually cooperative, agreeing to go to bed before the guests arrived in exchange for an extra half hour of cartoons the next morning. Amanda had planned a simple dinner on the assumption that Hochmayer would see through any attempts to impress him with fussy food. The swell of the cicadas' overture relaxed her nerves, and Amanda sipped her wine and followed along as the conversation took pleasant, meandering turns. Bob and Hochmayer seemed to have come to some silent agreement not to raise the Megabyte case before dinner; instead they discussed Susie's new television show, which had debuted just a few days before. Dis-tressingly, the debut had garnered few reviews, and those that had appeared were dismissive—TALKING AIRHEADS was the subhead in the *Post*'s brief notice—but Hochmayer expounded so ardently on the show's certain success that for the moment they were all swept up by his confidence and enthusiasm.

"I tell you there is a market for this sort of program. And Susie here's got enough charisma to launch an entire network," he said, with a fond look at Susie.

As Amanda rose to check one last time on the rice, the screen of the back door squeaked open and a sleepy Sophie padded out onto the terrace, clutching a small blanket. The little girl hesitated to draw too near, but stood shyly a few feet away, her eyes darting from adult to adult.

"I can't thleep."

"Sophie!" Amanda was about to scoop the child up and carry her back to bed when she noticed Hochmayer's enchanted expression.

"Get a load of those curls! Come here, my princess!"

It was not like Sophie to take to strangers, especially strange men, but she rushed into Hochmayer's outstretched arms, and he pulled her up onto his knee.

"Sophie," Bob said sternly. "It's way past your bedtime."

"I was thcared," she told Hochmayer.

"Scared? Well you better stay here with Uncle Jim for a few minutes," he cooed, jiggling her up and down on his knee and whinnying like a horse. Susie fastened a melting gaze on the two of them and, to Amanda's utter amazement, began praising Sophie's hitherto unremarked-upon virtues.

"Sophie's smart as a whip, too, aren't you, sweetie? Not just cute, but brainy!"

"Got that from your mommy, didn't you, princess?" Hochmayer said, winking at Bob.

Hochmayer only agreed to relinquish the little girl when Amanda announced that dinner was ready.

"They're just magical at that age, aren't they?" he marveled as Amanda led Sophie away. "I missed my own children's growing up. Curse myself every day for it. Worked too damn hard. I look at them now—why, my boy practically towers over his old man. He's got feet the size of school buses. I think of him back when he was all chubby cheeks and"—he chuckled—"so filthy that you could smell him coming from a mile away. Thought his daddy was the greatest hero who ever walked God's earth."

He smiled sadly. "You can't have them back that way again for one minute. Not for one damn minute."

"How old are your children now?" Amanda asked, pausing at the screen door.

"Jim Junior's just graduated from college. My daughter Katie's a sophomore—stunning girl. A regular spitfire, like this one." He nodded his head toward Susie, who wriggled with pleasure.

Bob carried in a platter of smoking kabobs and set it down in the center of the dining room table.

"I think I may have overcooked them a little. It was hard to tell out there."

The preassembled kabobs, which had looked so plump and appetizing on the "ready-to-grill" counter at Fresh Farms, had shriveled to half their original size.

"There's plenty of salad and rice." Amanda indicated two bowls that, a few seconds ago, had seemed ample.

"Can't be too well done for me." Hochmayer jabbed his fork into the pyre of burned beef and managed to extricate three for himself. "I'm forgetting my manners—Susie, would you like one?"

"No, thanks. I'm not that hungry."

"C'mon, you could use something to fatten you up."

"No, thank you."

He shook his head. "Amanda?"

"Yes, thanks."

They sawed away at the meat and chewed in silence while Susie picked at some salad. Amanda ransacked her mind for a conversational gambit that might distract attention from the food. Devising a compliment for the meal seemed beyond even the skill of Hochmayer, whose eyes were roaming the small

room and examining the family photos arranged on the side-
board. Bob was struggling to detach a piece of blackened pepper
from his skewer. Amanda swallowed her mouthful with effort
and was about to ask Hochmayer about his home in Texas when
Hochmayer, still chewing, broke the silence first.

"You know, Bob," he said, his tongue dislodging the remain-
ing bits of food from the back of his teeth, "I was just thinking
what a damn lucky man you are."

His abruptness caught them all off-guard. Bob, who was
rarely flustered, stared at Hochmayer, his fork half poised
between plate and mouth.

"You got yourself a real nice setup here—a lovely family, a
lovely home. Let me tell you, a man gets bored of restaurant
food and lying alone in a hotel room night after night, hoping
there's something new on Spectravision.

"And you," he said, turning to Amanda, "I understand it's not
fashionable to say so, but I truly honor what you're doing. People
today don't appreciate the hard work and sacrifices a mother
makes for her family. An educated woman like you could be making a killing out there in the workforce—dammit, you're *expected*
to be out there—and instead you've chosen to do something that
is, frankly, much more difficult . . . and much more worthwhile.
You've gone to a lot of fuss and bother for me tonight and I appreciate it. I think we should all toast you."

And with those words, Hochmayer raised his wineglass.
Amanda glanced down at her plate while the rest of the table
murmured approvingly, "To Amanda."

After a pause, Bob put down his knife and fork, apparently
surrendering his battle with the meat. He dabbed his mouth
with his napkin and said, "If Amanda and Susie don't mind, I'd
like to speak with Jim about his strategy for tomorrow."

"Fine with me if it's okay with you all," Hochmayer replied amiably.

Amanda nodded her assent as did Susie, who did not usually agree so readily to being shunted from a conversation. She followed Amanda into the kitchen and offered to help serve dessert.

"So what do you think?" Susie asked when they were alone together. "Isn't he fantastic?"

"Susie, he's *wonderful*." Amanda wiped her hands on a dish towel and came around the counter to embrace her friend. "Is it going to work out?"

"Oh, I hope so." Susie squeezed Amanda in return. "I don't know—I'm so giddy. I've never felt this way about anyone."

"Tell me one thing. Does he drink coffee?"

Susie laughed. "Yes, we'd both like decaffeinated, please."

Susie left to fetch more plates. Upon one point, at least, Amanda's mind had been set at ease: Hochmayer's ring finger was bare, although deeply imprinted with the mark of a wide band; it could not have been very long since he removed it.

And yet Amanda could not help harboring misgivings. Much as she was taken by Hochmayer's charm, marrying a man in his sixties—even a vigorous man—would demand sacrifices of Susie for which money would not compensate. Would he consent to more children? How long could Susie enjoy being his wife before she became his nurse?

But Susie appeared so happy, so thrilled at her good fortune, as she bore the last of the dinner plates into the kitchen, that Amanda tried to put aside her doubts. What a relief Hochmayer was after the long "parade of horribles," as Bob called Susie's succession of suitors. Hochmayer was so sensitive, so thoughtful, so obviously proud of Susie. And really, what was the alternative?

Every year Amanda had grown more worried on her friend's behalf, fearful that by the time Susie actually met the right person, she would no longer be able to recognize that he *was* the right person. How could anyone sustain faith in love when every affair ended in a cold exchange of house keys, borrowed books, and spent passion? How much of herself would Susie still have to give after she had bestowed so much upon other people? The problem with Susie—Amanda thought, arranging four mugs on a tray—was that she used her beauty the way an increasingly desperate gambler plays his dwindling stack of chips. The longer Susie stayed at the table, the greater her need for a big payoff. Susie spoke confidently of still "being young," but she only *felt* young because she was living exactly as she had lived in her twenties. Susie did not realize how old she would suddenly feel when she had children. That was the thing about children. They rise up next to you like new buildings: there they are, sparkling and gleaming in the sunlight—and there you are, your joints starting to settle at odd angles and fresh coats of paint failing to conceal the flaws on the surface . . .

"What else?" Susie asked as Amanda counted out dishes for dessert.

"Just pecan pie and ice cream—but the coffee's not quite ready." Amanda unboxed the pie and handed Susie a scoop.

"Tell me more about Jim," Amanda said, making a hash of the first slice and trying to neaten it on the plate. "How serious is he?"

When the women emerged from the kitchen, Amanda's manner toward Hochmayer had completely changed. All friendliness was gone. She set out the mugs and poured the coffee with the detachment of a waitress, and took longer than might have been expected to return with cream and sugar. The men were still deeply engrossed in conversation about the Senate hearings.

"I believe Senator Benson, even though he's a Republican, is friendly to our point of view," Hochmayer was saying. "Frith, being the arrogant sonofabitch he is, hasn't bothered to make any friends on Capitol Hill—and being the stingy sonofabitch he is, hasn't bought himself any political influence, either."

Susie passed around the dessert and silently took her seat opposite Hochmayer. He appeared to sense the drop of temperature in the room and looked for a clue in the women's faces. Failing to find one, he returned to his discussion with Bob.

"The thing is, we've got to be able to count on you folks. You can't let us down. Your boss has come a long way, but I get the impression he's still a bit squeamish about the whole thing."

"He is," Bob acknowledged. "I can't blame him. I mean, Megabyte's stock has plunged, and there could be huge political fallout. The *Wall Street Journal* is screaming that Megabyte will pull the whole economy down with it. So before Sussman goes for Frith's jugular, he's got to feel damn sure we have a good case."

"I understand, I understand. You don't try to bag the snake before the bag's in position. I just hope Sussman has the guts to go through with it. He's not like you, Bob. You've got stuffing. I can see that. You've been gung-ho from the beginning. You're an idealist like I am, and you don't like to see bad guys like Frith getting away with what they shouldn't be getting away with. That's why you're in Justice, and not piling up the hours at some corporate law firm. I just wish . . ."

Hochmayer's voice trailed off and he sipped his coffee.

"Wish what?" asked Bob.

"Well, I shouldn't say. Let me put it this way: we could use more of that sort of idealism outside the government. The private sector—well, it doesn't always have to be about just making money."

With this, Hochmayer flashed one of his winning smiles at Amanda. Amanda did not react. Bob gave her a questioning look, but she stood up and began collecting the mugs.

"I realize that, Jim, but I have to say it's pretty exciting right now at Justice," Bob replied, his eyes still on Amanda.

"Sure is. And there's nothing like being a young man with his first big game walking square into his crosshairs. I know exactly how you feel, Bob. Same as when I bagged my first big deal."

Hochmayer finished off his coffee, patted his thighs, and stood up.

"Let's not keep these nice folks up all night, Susie. We've got a big day tomorrow."

Bob showed them to the door. Amanda followed a few feet behind. Hochmayer made one last attempt to engage Amanda—"Honestly, best time I've had in a while . . . such fine people . . ." —but she just nodded and pressed her lips into something like a smile. Susie kissed her cheek and whispered, "We'll talk tomorrow." Hochmayer shook Bob's hand and, after thanking them graciously again for their hospitality, accompanied Susie down the front walk toward an idling black sedan.

"What was that all about?" Bob asked the moment after Amanda closed the door. She was leaning her body against it, as if afraid Hochmayer and Susie might barge back in.

"He's married."

"Separated, you mean."

"No—I mean married."

"Really married?"

"Yes. Susie told me. When we were in the kitchen."

"Gee," said Bob, as he absorbed the news himself. "I guess I can't say I'm surprised. I told you I thought he was married."

Amanda wandered into the living room and dropped down on the sofa. "I didn't know. I can't believe Susie didn't warn me."

"Warn you?" Bob seemed amused. "Since when does Susie ever warn anyone about anything? And what was she going to say? *Hey, Amanda, just wanted you to meet the man I'm having an affair with.*"

"You're right." Amanda dully surveyed the shards of their evening, Hochmayer's coffee cup, the scrunched-up napkins, the stubby candles.

"I just don't think Susie should have brought him here, that's all. No wonder they insisted on coming to our house—they didn't want to be seen together in public."

"I'm not sorry she did though."

"How can you say that?"

Bob was perched on the arm of a chair opposite her, his face cast half in shadow by a lamp. "Think about it—to have an opportunity to spend an evening with Jim Hochmayer? How many people get to do that? It's almost like having Mike Frith to dinner. I learned a hell of a lot from him—and it was great to be able to talk strategy—"

"For God's sake," Amanda interrupted. "Couldn't you for once look at a situation outside of its relationship to the Megabyte case? Susie, whatever you think of her, is still my friend. Now she's gone and got herself involved with a married billionaire—"

"Yeah. And . . . ?"

"And . . . well, for starters she's going to get hurt."

"Oh please. Susie knows what she's doing."

"No, I don't think she does, actually—not this time. I think she's really in love with him. I think she truly believes he's going to get a divorce and marry her."

"Then she's in for a rude shock."

"Why are you so sure? Maybe he *will* leave his wife. Susie's much younger. She's pretty, smart—a celebrity."

"A billionaire like Jim doesn't just 'get divorced.' Look, maybe his marriage is miserable. For all we know he's had affairs for years. Maybe his wife knows about them. Maybe she's even comfortable with the arrangement. It happens, you know—especially in those circles."

Amanda weighed this unsavory possibility. She was struck by the equally unsavory way Bob described it—so lightly, as if it were nothing more than a weather report from a distant city. Foul weather in Seattle. Yet the foul weather had blown right through their front door. What was he suggesting? That it was a woman's job to put up with whatever arrangement suited the man? Susie, the wife, they were all the same? Amanda studied his face intently. She had not asked Bob about the phone call from Grace Bertelli. She had left the message on the counter, and it was gone when she had come down the next morning. Amanda did not dare raise her name again, but the pressure inside her to know, right now, as he so casually discoursed upon the etiquette of adultery—

"Perhaps that does happen in 'those circles.' I wouldn't know. Anyway, since when did 'all the rich people are doing it' become your idea of a good defense?"

"I'm *not* defending it. I'm saying we don't know all the facts." Bob rose and stretched. "In any event, it's none of our business. Susie is a big girl and can take care of herself."

He began switching off lights.

"I'll be up in a minute," she said quietly.

*   *   *

For a long time Amanda stared at the black shapes of the living room. She felt that she could not make sense of anything. Bob's words had been reasonable enough. Susie *was* a big girl, the affair was none of their business, and who knew what Hochmayer was up to? Maybe his wife was a shrew. Maybe he had good reasons for tiring of her, for seeking happiness elsewhere.

And how could Amanda of all people condemn him for it? Hadn't she had . . . thoughts . . . herself? Nothing had happened—nothing would have happened—right? *Right?* Well, what would she have done if the evening with Alan had not turned out so badly? Would she have . . . ?

The thought sickened her. Her feelings for Alan, for all their explosive intensity, had spent themselves quickly; all that was left behind were the empty casings—embarrassment, shame even, and surprise at her own audacity. (Recklessness, her conscience asserted, but for now she would stick with audacity.) The whole episode had been just another dodge, just another way of looking to someone else to make the decisions she needed to make on her own. Or so she had been telling herself. But Hochmayer and Susie . . . that was different, surely. Everything about it felt wrong. What if Hochmayer and his wife had been reasonably happy until Susie had come along? What if the wife's crime was simply doing what it was Hochmayer claimed to honor: spending her life taking care of him, raising his children, losing her gloss?

Amanda shuddered. She felt behind the sofa for an old afghan that had slipped off. There it was. Despite the night's heat, she pulled the dirty cloth up around her throat. It prickled with dust and old cookie crumbs, but she clung to it, her gaze resting upon a wedding photo she had set upon the mantel the day she had reorganized the house. The room was too dark for Amanda to make out anything except the white gleam of her dress, but she could see every detail in her mind's eye, not just as it was in the photo, but as it had been on the steps at New York City Hall. Bob draped his arm around her shoulders confidently, as if getting married were the most natural occurrence in the world. Amanda was smiling with forced cheer, depending upon his light grasp to hold her upright. She had loved Bob for his confidence and he had loved her despite her lack of it. Indeed, she had been so self-conscious about getting married that they had not even had a formal wedding—they invited just their parents and a few good friends to a civil ceremony and a wedding feast afterward at a Chinese restaurant on the Lower East Side.

Of course Bob was confident—*his* parents had just celebrated their thirty-fifth wedding anniversary. At the time Amanda had insisted that she would have been just as happy living together. She told Bob that she did not need a "piece of paper" to prove their love. Now, as her gaze drew back from the portrait, she realized that the "piece of paper" was much less flimsy than it had seemed. Everything in their life rested upon it. Their contract existed regardless of Bob's love for her, or her love for Bob. It turned feelings into words, and promises into facts. It ratified, in the dry language of the law, the emotions in their eyes and hearts that humid June afternoon so many years ago—before Ben and Sophie, before this house, before they knew each other's minds as intimately and instinctively as Amanda knew this dark room. Yet all that would come later had been implicit then; it was wrapped up in their vows like the DNA of an embryonic cell, already dividing and developing into what would become this life. These lives. *Their* life, together.

Somewhere, Amanda imagined, a Mrs. Hochmayer was drawing the curtains in her bedroom, turning down the sheets on her side of the bed, glancing over at the empty spot that was not truly empty because for so long it had belonged to her husband. On his nightstand would be the stack of books he planned to read; in his closet, a row of suits still bearing the shape of his elbows. And on his dressing table would be the collection of personal artifacts—cuff links, collar stays, loose change—so familiar that you cease to see them, yet so essential to the harmony of the room that were they to vanish it would have the shock of a robbery.

Did Mrs. Hochmayer know that some thousand miles away another woman was wrapping herself around her husband's naked body? That this woman had set her own, unfamiliar artifacts—face cream, earrings, cosmetics case—alongside his on the marble ledge of a hotel bathroom?

Amanda could picture it no more; the image left her gasping. She stood and walked slowly upstairs.

Other thoughts were flying at her now—distressing thoughts. *It happens, you know.* Was it happening to her?

Through the half-closed door of their bedroom, Amanda could see the long figure of Bob asleep; his shoes and socks lay scattered on the floor, illuminated by a quadrangle of light from the hallway.

Desperately Amanda wanted to wake him. But as she paused at the door, gathering up the words she would use to confront him, her nerve fell away. What could she say? What cause for doubt did she have except a phone message? Amanda found herself simply, almost childishly, grateful for the sight of him, there, in their bed. She changed quickly and joined him, burying her face into his back. He half roused at her touch, rolled over, and pulled her toward him. Gradually, the rhythm of her breath joined his.

Chapter Fourteen

A BEEP ON Amanda's line signaled that a second call was trying to get through.

"Hang on a sec," she said to Liz. "Hello?"

"Is this Mrs. Clarke?" It was a male voice Amanda didn't recognize.

"Who's calling?"

"Grover Mudd, of the *Washington Post*."

"Thanks but we already subscribe."

"It's not a sales call! I'm a reporter—I write 'The Ear' column," he said, before Amanda could click off.

"Could you hold on a moment?"

"Sure."

Amanda returned to Liz. "It's a reporter. I don't know what it's about."

"Call me back—it sounds interesting."

Amanda hesitated before picking up the other line. "The Ear"—that was the daily gossip column. Why on earth was Mudd calling her?

"Mrs. Clarke?"

"Amanda—Amanda *Bright*."

"Hi. I'm friends with Susie Morris. She suggested I call you."

"Susie? Why?"

"I just bumped into her at the studio. I was doing the noon-hour show," he explained, with a touch of self-importance. "She told me she had dinner at your house last night . . ."

"She did?"

"Don't worry, I know all about her and Jim Hochmayer. She told me herself. That's not why I'm calling."

Amanda was staggered by Susie's indiscretion. She knew her friend was a blurter, but to blurt about Hochmayer to a gossip columnist!

"Then why are you calling?"

"I'm doing an item on her new show. It's starting to generate buzz. Susie tells me you've known her longer than anyone else in Washington."

"That's true," Amanda allowed. "I don't mind talking about that—if Susie said it was okay."

"She did."

Amanda, who had spoken to the press on several occasions when she worked at the NEA, tried to recall the little "rules" she had observed when dealing with reporters. Chief among them was, "Don't say anything interesting." It was hard to apply this rule to the topic of Susie. That's okay, Amanda told herself. Just be positive—blandly positive.

Mudd fired off a few questions about Susie's career: Had Susie always aspired to work in television? Did Amanda think her friend found it difficult, as a beautiful woman, to be taken seriously as a journalist? Amanda answered cautiously, saying her friend had always been ambitious and agreeing, yes, she imagined it was tough sometimes for Susie to be taken seriously in Washington but Susie wouldn't have come so far if she didn't have talent . . . the new show was a perfect vehicle for Susie . . . certain to be a great success . . . blah blah blah . . .

"What I find funny about it, between you and me," Mudd confided, "is how she could date Hochmayer and work for Mike Frith's cable station."

"Look, I don't want to comment on anything to do with her personal life—"

"Yes, but don't you think it's awkward?"

Mudd's presumption discomfited Amanda. She could see the story line he was taking—"Sleeping with the Enemy"—and Amanda grew worried on Susie's behalf. Perhaps she could deflect it—without entering into the Hochmayer business?

"I know that Susie agrees with Mike Frith. She strongly opposes the Megabyte case."

"So how is it possible that she gets along with Hochmayer?"

"Look, I really don't want to talk about her relationship with him—"

"No, no, no, of course," Mudd reassured her. "I'm just thinking aloud, as her friend. We go back a long way, too, you know. It's a kind of strange dynamic, don't you think?"

"I assume they just don't talk about it."

"But how is that possible? I mean, when she told me they were at your house—with your husband, Bob—right? He works for the DOJ?—I would've imagined the four of you having a big argument about it. Susie's pretty feisty in her opinions."

At that moment there was a bang from upstairs where Amanda had left the children to play. She heard Sophie cry out.

"Look, it didn't come up, okay?" Amanda half listened for further noise. "At least not in that context," she added, realizing Susie might contradict what she had just said.

"I find it hard to believe that the night before the Senate hearings, the topic simply didn't 'come up'—"

Sophie materialized at Amanda's side sobbing. She pushed her wet face onto her mother's bare leg, but the gesture did little to muffle her squalls.

"I'm not saying it didn't come up. I'm saying—" Oh God, what was she saying? "I'm saying there was no disagreement. The men may have talked about the case a little—strategy and stuff—but it was really just a dinner between friends, all right? A private dinner. Please, let's just leave it at that. I really don't want to talk about it anymore, and I can't see why it's relevant to your story. Frankly, I'd appreciate you not mentioning it."

"Fine. Just one more question—"

"Look, my children. I better go—"

"I'm sorry, I don't want to keep you. Your husband spells Clarke with an *e*, correct?"

"Yes—" Amanda crouched down and put a consoling arm around Sophie. "But why do you need the spelling of my *husband's* name?"

"Just in case the editor asks. I'll let you go. Thanks." *Click.*

Amanda stared at the dead receiver for a second before hanging it up. She pulled Sophie close and stroked her hair.

"There, there, sweetie, it's all right. You go back upstairs and play."

"Ben's a bad boy!"

"I'll make him say sorry. Go on, I'll be up in a minute."

The little girl heaved a few more sobs. Amanda kissed the top of her head and prodded her in the direction of the stairs. When she was gone, Amanda immediately phoned Bob.

"I know you're busy but . . ."

"I'm just about to walk over to the Hill to watch the hearings but I have a minute. What's going on?"

Bob sounded cheerful; Amanda knew he was up about the hearings.

"I just got the weirdest call. Do you know Grover Mudd? He writes 'The Ear' column for the *Post*."

"Yeah—what would he want?"

"Well, at first I thought he was trying to find out about Susie and Jim."

"Jesus," said Bob, suddenly alarmed. "What did you tell him?"

"Nothing—nothing at all. He already knew all about it. He's a friend of hers—or so he said. I think I remember vaguely Susie telling me that she had once dated him."

"God, she can't keep anything secret, can she? But why did he want to talk to you?"

"He said he was writing an item on Susie's show, and since I know Susie so well, he just wanted a bit of background—you know, was Susie ambitious in college, that sort of thing."

"That seems okay."

"Yes, I thought so, too."

"Was that all he wanted?"

"Um, there was a little more—he said he couldn't understand how Susie could work for Frith when she was dating Hochmayer, and asked me what I thought about it."

"You didn't answer that, did you?"

"No—not really. I told him I didn't want to talk about her personal life, but I did say that Susie had always been pro-Megabyte."

"Good, good—that was exactly the right thing to say."

"I'd better call Susie—"

"Yes, you should. And ask her why she's such a blabber-mouth. Christ, Hochmayer. Why would she tell 'The Ear' that?"

"Don't ask me."

Susie was in a story meeting with her producers, and Amanda left a message. By the time her friend called back, Amanda was halfway through a floor puzzle with the children. She took the phone into the bathroom for privacy and seated herself upon the toilet.

"Susie, I just got a call from Grover Mudd."

"I know. He told me he was going to call you. I was going to warn you, but I got called into a meeting."

"I wish you had warned me."

"I didn't think he'd phone so quickly. It must be for tomorrow's column." Susie sounded pleased.

"Susie! This is serious—he knows about you and Hochmayer. He asked me about it."

"And what did you say?"

"I didn't say anything! Why would *you* talk to him about it?"

"Oh, Grover's an old friend. We dated years ago and—"

"Susie, I can't believe you told him," Amanda interrupted. "What would *possess* you to tell him?"

"Grover asked me," she said calmly. "I bumped into him and he asked if I was seeing anyone these days, and I said yes, Jim Hochmayer. It's not a secret. A lot of people know."

"And so you decided to announce it to the newspaper?"

"No, I told *Grover*. It's different—he's a friend. He's doing an item about the show. That's why I told him to call you."

Amanda was speechless—was Susie being deliberately stupid with her?

"Well, I can tell you that's not what he's interested in—he's interested in you and Jim."

"Oh?" Susie sounded remarkably unruffled.

"You're not worried? What if his wife finds out?"

"Gee, that would be too bad," Susie replied with heavy irony.

Ah, it was she, Amanda, who was being stupid—at last it dawned upon her what Susie was up to. "You did this—*on purpose?*"

"Look," said Susie, lowering her voice, "it wouldn't be the worst thing in the world if a little heat were put on Jim. I told Grover because I can trust him to do it right. I'm sure he's going to do one of those blind items, you know, like 'What married computer executive is seeing a well-known TV pundette?' It won't cause Jim any problems—who reads 'The Ear' in Texas?—but he'll get the idea that word is slowly leaking out, and he can't keep sitting on the fence.

"I'm not going to be anyone's goddamn mistress."

Amanda decided not to challenge the glaring falseness of this assertion, but she remained staggered by Susie's recklessness.

"What if it backfires?"

"It can't. Jim's been saying how much he loves me, so let's just put him to the test."

"I wish you hadn't dragged me into it."

"I didn't mean to—he asked me for the names of some friends, and how could I not give yours? Ostensibly his interest is in the show. I'm sure you handled it well."

"I told him I didn't want to be quoted about that stuff."

"Then he won't quote you. Grover's a good guy."

"Are you *certain* he won't quote me? Maybe you should call him—because, Susie, I don't want to be involved in this, okay?"

"I'll let him know how you feel." Susie sounded slightly affronted by Amanda's mistrust. "Grover wouldn't do anything to hurt me."

"Yes, but my God, Susie—"

"Grover will listen to me," Susie repeated. "I'll call him. Stop panicking."

Ben began banging on the locked door. "I need to pee!"

"Let me know what you find out," Amanda said, before hanging up.

*   *   *

But Susie did not let her know. Bob did. He came storming into the bedroom the next morning before Amanda was fully awake and threw the newspaper down on the bed.

"I thought you told me you said nothing!"

Amanda sat up on her elbow. She glanced back and forth between the newspaper—opened to "The Ear" column—and Bob's furious face. She picked up the newspaper and, squinting, read the following:

Strange Bedfellows

On the night before the Senate began grilling Megabyte executives, guess where one of the Justice department's key witnesses was dining? The Ear hears that **Jim Hochmayer**, billionaire owner of Texas CompSystems, was chowing down at the Woodley Park home of **Bob Clarke**, who is spearheading the DOJ's antitrust case against Megabyte. Clarke's wife **Amanda** confirmed in an interview yesterday that the two men talked "strategy and stuff" and that there was "no disagreement" between them—"it was really a dinner between friends." This intimate tête-à-tête certainly lends credence to the "paranoid" rantings of Megabyte's **Mike Frith**, who has accused the DOJ of cozying up to his competitors in order to destroy his company. But wait, Mike, the story gets better. The Ear has learned that Hochmayer's date that evening was none other than beautiful TV pundette **Susie Morris**, whose new political affairs show, *Morris & Johns*, airs on Megabyte's cable station, MBTV. Hmm, do we sense a conflict of interest here? If this news doesn't keep Frith up at night, then it ought to worry Hochmayer's missus, who is back on the ranch in Texas. Hochmayer himself was unavailable for comment but Morris claims the two are "just good friends." Frith, meanwhile, is scheduled to testify before the hearings later this week.

"Bob," Amanda whispered, letting the paper fall, "I didn't say it like that. I swear to you, that wasn't what I said."

"Then why did he quote it?"

"I—I don't know," she faltered. "Sophie was crying . . ."

"Oh God." Bob sat down on the opposite corner of the bed, as far away from her, it seemed, as it was possible to be without leaving the room. He stared hopelessly into the armchair where yesterday's shirts, socks, and pants had collected; his robe hung limply on him as if his whole being had suddenly become inanimate, like a suit valet. Amanda knew that she must say something—she wished to console him, to apologize, to convince him that there had been a terrible misunderstanding—but he had never seemed so remote from her, and Amanda feared that uttering even a gentle word might alienate him further. Instead she picked up the paper again and skimmed the item urgently, hoping that upon a second or third reading it would not seem so terrible, but every time she read it, it only got worse and she flung the paper down, sick to her stomach.

"I don't know what I'm going to do," Bob said, as if to some invisible third party.

"Bob, I'm sorry. I didn't mean—" Amanda edged nearer, hesitating before placing her hand upon his shoulder.

He shrugged it off and stood. "I better get going." Without looking at her, he fetched his clothing from the closet and took it with him to the bathroom to change.

Amanda curled up under the covers. She felt paralyzed; she did not think it possible that she would be able to leave the bed. It was only when she heard noises from Sophie's room that she raised her head. Her eyes strayed across the headline again— STRANGE BEDFELLOWS—and she buried her face tightly in the pillow, moaning, "Oh God, oh God, oh God."

The light padding of feet told her that Sophie had entered the room. "What are you doing?"

"Mommy doesn't feel well."

"Mommy need medithine?"

"No, honey. Maybe just a hug."

The little girl obliged and Amanda clutched her, trying to banish her horrible feelings. After a few minutes Sophie began singing a nursery rhyme to herself and idly twisting Amanda's hair. Amanda knew that she could not lie there indefinitely; Ben would awaken shortly and demand breakfast . . . and the day's chores would begin their relentless assault upon her, regardless of whether she was able to stand or not.

Actually, Amanda realized, the prospect of a thousand tiny tasks in which to lose herself was not altogether unappealing. She winced once again at the sight of the newspaper, then folded it to take to the recycling bin.

"C'mon, Sophie. Let's get you something to eat."

Downstairs the remnants of Bob's breakfast—a crumb-covered plate and a still-warm quarter cup of coffee left on the kitchen table—caused her stomach to lurch again. He had left without a word of good-bye. What he would face at work she couldn't predict. The only thing Amanda could do was to wait—and to wait without distraction was intolerable. Rather than set out a bowl of cereal for Sophie, she gathered her purse and got the stroller bag ready.

"Sophie, wake your brother and start getting dressed. We'll go out for breakfast. Would you like muffins in the park?"

"Yeth!"

Within half an hour, the three of them had emerged into the fire-wall heat of a Washington summer morning.

They stayed out the whole day. After the park, they ventured downtown to look at dinosaurs in the Smithsonian. Amanda wanted to keep going, but by three o'clock, they were all hot and exhausted and Amanda had spent her last bit of change on ice cream. Reluctantly, she brought the children back home. There were six messages on her answering machine. None of them was from Bob. Four were from the mothers in her play group, including a long-distance call from the odious Patricia vacationing in Portugal. How had she heard? One of the other women must have phoned her, which meant—they were all gossiping about it. Patricia's message, however, was less odious than might have been expected. It was almost simpering: "Heard about 'The Ear' and had to call. Imagine Jim Hochmayer at your house! Congratulations, and can't wait to hear all about it when I'm back. By the way, Meredith has just learned to dive. She's such a little fish!" Amanda ignored the veiled reference to Ben's aquatic shortcomings: he still refused to put his head in the water. Kim's and Ellen's messages were much the same, both offering their "congratulations" on the item. Christine's was the oddest. She called about an event she purported to be organizing "on the spur of the moment" to celebrate her new, postsurgical look ("although I'm only telling *you* that"). Then Christine added, almost shyly, "I'm sorry about the late notice and I hope you and Bob will be able to come, although with your newfound celebrity status maybe you'll be spending the weekend at the Hochmayer ranch. Ha ha!"

Amanda was flummoxed that her friends viewed "The Ear" column as anything but an embarrassment and potential calamity. Was it possible it was less bad than she thought? Then she listened to the fifth message. It was Alan. "Hey, read today's 'Ear.' I guess there's not really anything to say, but—I feel for you." Sigh, long pause. "I'm sorry about the other night, too. I meant to call and tell you how much I appreciated it that you came. I guess I was really just disappointed with everything and—"

Amanda hit the DELETE button.

The last message was from a female editorial assistant at the *Wall Street Journal,* wanting to "fact-check something." Amanda took down the number and automatically began punching in the numbers for Bob's office. Then she stopped. She was too afraid to tell him. *Let the reporter find him,* Amanda thought. *I'm not going to do it.*

Instead she spent the next hour assembling something that reasonably approximated a home-cooked meal—ground beef hastily unthawed from the freezer and simmered in canned tomato sauce.

Bob came through the door around six—not a good sign. Amanda hadn't expected him until past eight. She could see immediately that his mood had improved from that morning, although the kiss he administered to her cheek was perfunctory and not altogether forgiving.

"Bob, what happened today?" she asked tentatively.

"I think it's going to be okay." He sat down by the table and loosened his tie. "God, I need a drink."

"I'll get it. Scotch?"

Bob nodded.

"What did Frank say?"

"He was a bit upset, there's no doubt about it." Bob suddenly looked tremendously weary, as if all the excitement that had animated him through these past weeks of hard labor had been switched off. He slumped slightly in his chair, his eyes as dull as unlit lamps. "But overall he dismissed it as gossip. I assured him of course that Hochmayer and I had discussed nothing improper, that it was entirely a social visit. Frank said to just let it pass."

"Does it hurt the case?" She placed a large dose of Scotch in front of him.

"I hope not. Frith might make a bit of a fuss—but then he fusses about everything. I think Frank's right. Let it pass." He drained the glass.

They avoided the topic for the rest of the evening. Several times Amanda attempted to mention the call from the *Wall Street Journal*, but she could not get it past her lips. Bob took refuge, as she had done, in the distraction of the children, and offered to give them their bath while she cleared up.

By the time she came to bed, Bob had already tucked himself in and was going through a copy of Hochmayer's testimony. She settled in next to him with a book, and they both fell asleep early, exhausted by the tension of the day.

The next morning she was again awoken by Bob. And he was again holding a copy of a newspaper. This time he was not angry, but ashen.

"Amanda," he said, rousing her. "Good God, Amanda, listen to this."

He sat down beside her with the *Wall Street Journal* opened to
the editorial page. In the left-hand column, below the two main
editorials, was a smaller one headlined WHO IS BOB CLARKE?
Bob read it out loud:

Antitrust supremo Frank Sussman has promised to pursue
the government's investigation of Megabyte impartially.
And even though we've been vigorous critics of this Justice
department, we respect Mr. Sussman's reputation as a fair
and open-minded lawyer. We have to wonder, though,
what is going on when we hear that Mr. Sussman's right-
hand man, Bob Clarke, is coordinating the government's
case with Megabyte's competitors over barbecue and beers.

"Oh no," said Amanda.
"Hold on, it gets worse." Bob swallowed and continued:

Mr. Clarke, who has taken an increasingly public role in
the case, had Jim Hochmayer of Texas CompSystems over
for an out-of-the-limelight dinner the night before Mr.
Hochmayer's Senate testimony. While the DOJ refuses to
comment on the record, Amanda Clarke—wife of Bob
Clarke—confirmed to the *Washington Post* that her husband
used the dinner to go over "strategy" for the hearings.

Off the record, Justice insiders say that Mr. Clarke has
been vigorously—even fanatically—pushing Mr. Sussman
to prosecute Megabyte. It's not clear whether Mr. Clarke
is one of this Justice department's hate-success crowd—or
whether he's just spent a little too much time in the company of Sherwood J. Pressman, the colorfully wacky attorney who earns his living arguing that Mike Frith is to blame

for every business failure in Silicon Valley. Either way, America's high-tech industry needs to be put back under adult supervision.

Bob tossed down the paper and put his face in his hands.

"Oh Bob—do you think Frank will be upset?"

"Do I think Frank will be upset?" Bob replied incredulously, almost cruelly. "Of course he will be upset! Unless . . ."

Bob read the editorial again to himself, nodding more emphatically as he did so. ". . . unless he was the source for this. Oh, Amanda," he groaned.

"That's impossible!" she said, horrified by the possibility. "Frank himself said it was just gossip—that we should let it pass."

"*Yesterday* it was gossip," Bob said bitterly. "Today it's news."

Chapter Fifteen

CHRISTINE LOOKED stunning, truly stunning—like an air-brushed version of herself. Her face was pulled as smooth as a freshly made bed. Gone were the squiggly forehead lines, the billowy cheeks, the creases in the corners of her eyes. She had done something new with her hair, too: it seemed lighter, more sun-kissed, and styled in such a way as to appear prettily mussed; only when Amanda looked more closely did she notice that every strand had been meticulously sprayed in position.

"Bob," Christine effused, as she drew them toward her back patio where the other guests had assembled, "we're all so intrigued by your recent celebrity."

Amanda cast a worried look at Bob. This was their first public outing together since the story had broken. It had taken considerable effort to persuade Bob to venture out of the house. These days he didn't even like to stop at the Fresh Farms to pick up milk in case the cashier recognized him. If they lived in any other city—any *normal* city, Amanda thought resentfully—no one would recognize him. Unfortunately, they lived in Washington, where even the Guatemalan who did the weeding next door called out one morning, "Hey, I see your husband on C-SPAN!"

Bob smiled like a sick man trying to rise above his illness for appearance' sake. Amanda knew he would blame her for Christine's comment, just as he would blame her for dragging him here, against his better judgment, for the sole reason that they should not appear to be "hiding."

"Hungh," he mumbled.

"I *insist* you tell us all about Jim Hochmayer. Amanda never told me you knew him, but then she's congenitally modest about these things. Is he an old family friend?"

They were on the patio now, and Amanda and Bob both assessed the scene nervously. Would people recognize them? Were they a laughingstock?

Christine apparently did not think so. She tugged on Bob's arm the way she might pull the collar of a prize ox, and led them over to a couple standing near the pool. "Let me introduce you to the Fenshaws. They're both terrific. I used to work with Colin at Burgess, Whitehead.

"Colin, Janet," Christine called out from a few feet away, "I want you to meet Bob Clarke. He's involved in the Megabyte case."

"Oh, of course," said Colin, looking him over like a sideshow curiosity. "We've been reading all about it."

Bob twitched but managed a fake chuckle. "Yes, well, it's certainly been in the news lately."

"And this is Bob's wife, Amanda." Christine prodded Amanda forward. "I'll catch up with you all later. And remember, Bob, I want to hear *everything*. Don't you let him give away too many of his best stories, Amanda," she admonished before gliding off to another set of guests.

Both pairs of eyes fixed on Bob. No one seemed to know who should speak first. The Fenshaws appeared to be waiting hungrily for what Bob, in his role as curiosity, would do next.

"So you've known Christine for some time then?" Amanda offered the most innocuous gambit she could think of. Colin Fenshaw repeated that he had worked with Christine, and Janet warbled something about attending her wedding. On any other occasion, Amanda might have felt intimidated in the company of people like the Fenshaws. For one thing, Amanda saw that she had spectacularly misjudged the dress code for the evening. She had interpreted Christine's description of the party as a "casual poolside barbecue" as a green light for her Indonesian drawstring pants and tank top; Bob appeared only slightly less conspicuous in his T-shirt and khakis. Janet Fenshaw, like the other women at the party, was decked out in full suburban cocktail party regalia—pearls and a dress patterned in the lurid flora of Palm Beach. Her husband wore a jacket and no tie, but he seemed uncomfortable without one—his hand kept nervously checking his open collar as if to make sure his head was still attached at the neck.

But this evening, Amanda had too much else to be self-conscious about to worry about her clothes. When her initial gambit died, she ventured another.

"Such a lovely house, isn't it?"

They all obediently admired the lit hull of the Saunders residence. "It's a perfect night for a party, too. The rain seems to have cooled everything off."

Bob, who had been looking desperately around for a drink, grabbed a glass of white wine from a passing tray and took several large gulps as if it were lemonade. Amanda, sensing she might be called upon to drive later, accepted a glass of mineral water.

At that moment Colin Fenshaw, abandoning all pretense, tugged at his throat again and said, "Caught you last week on *Left/Right*. Thought you did well. You were in a tough spot."

Bob's face lost its hunted expression. He shifted bashfully and said, "Not as tough as this week."

"Yeah—must be quite a thing to be the target of a guy like Mike Frith." Fenshaw shook his head, impressed. "You must be doing something right."

"That's one way to look at it, I guess."

"It's the only way. I mean, where does Frith get off acting like a martyr? The guy's a bully. If you ask me"—here Fenshaw nodded deferentially at Bob—"not that I'm an expert in antitrust or anything—but the whole case raises important issues of whether consent decrees are going to be enforced . . ."

Fenshaw began dissecting the case as if it were a law school exam problem. More guests began to drift over, and soon a small huddle of people had gathered around Bob. Bob, rather than shrinking from the attention, entered into a friendly debate with Fenshaw; Amanda noticed that the other people's interest fell off when Fenshaw began to speak and only revived when Bob replied.

Presently, Christine returned. She directed everyone to help themselves to the buffet and find a seat at one of the small, candlelit tables overlooking the pool.

"Of course, Bob, *you* must sit next to me," she insisted, sparkling with charm, and leading him away.

If Amanda had suspected this party was not the last-minute affair Christine had claimed, her first glimpse of the lavish array of food confirmed it. No caterer could have thrown this together with just a few days' notice. There were two chefs working at opposite ends of the buffet table, one carving a huge side of beef, the other preparing pasta to order. Waiters dipped in and out to replenish serving dishes heaped with salads, shrimp, and chilled lobster.

"That's Bob Clarke—you know, that guy from Justice who's involved in the Megabyte hearings," Amanda heard the man ahead of her in line say to his wife. They both paused to watch Bob and Christine cross the patio. By the time Amanda finished filling her plate, all the chairs at Bob and Christine's table had been taken. Bob was regaling the other guests with a story about Sherwood J. Pressman, his face flushed, his hands making exaggerated gestures in the air, while Christine laughed gaily and egged him on.

Amanda took a seat at a nearby table, where two women were engaged in conversation. Her eyes fastened on Christine and Bob, and then on Christine alone, and she marveled at the subtle, yet astonishing—or maybe astonishing because it was so subtle—transformation of her friend's appearance. Watching Bob's obvious enjoyment of Christine's company—apparent every time Christine shook her hair and showed off the trussed cleavage visible through a sheer black blouse—Amanda did not feel jealousy—not exactly. Her friend was cheering Bob up, and Lord knew the man needed cheering. Amanda just wished that it could be she who was applying the balm. Her first impulse in the hours after the story broke had been to defend herself against Bob's unspoken accusations: yes, she shouldn't have spoken to "The Ear" reporter, and yes, it was her friend Susie who had brought this all upon them. But wasn't Bob culpable, too? He was the lawyer, not Amanda, and he should have known better than anyone the risks of entertaining Hochmayer. And hadn't it been Bob who raised the topic of the hearings at dinner? Bob might reply that the discussion had been ethically in bounds—that his words had been willfully misconstrued—but didn't that excuse apply to Amanda, too? Hadn't her remarks been perfectly innocent until taken out of context?

Yet Bob had steadfastly refused to discuss what had happened, even as the story grew bigger and bigger by the day. Amanda still did not fully understand why the barbecue had become such a huge story; she only knew that it had. Within twenty-four hours of the *Wall Street Journal*'s editorial, it seemed that every cable news show, political reporter, and gossip columnist in the country had called her house. The phone rang again the instant it was set down. Amanda gave up answering it, and learned to ignore it the way she would a constant jackhammering outside their house. Sherwood J. Pressman left several messages, as did Cathy O'Toole, who threatened a weekend "cover story" in the conservative *National Standard* to which "Bob might like to respond." Amanda's e-mail became so overloaded that her computer crashed; at one point, she had to eject a *New York Post* photographer from her front stoop.

Miraculously, the children remained wholly unaware of the turmoil. Ben and Sophie went about their daily routine unconscious of the sharp jolt of dread that awoke Amanda every morning, uninterested in the lengthening silences between mother and father. To the degree Bob said anything to Amanda, it was to insist that he was not angry with her. In the past it had always been Amanda who withdrew in times of trouble, and Bob who pulled her back. Now it was Bob who shrugged off all Amanda's attempts to console him. He answered her questions in precise sentences or with an exasperated "I have no idea what's going to happen." She read that the Justice department had issued a short statement—barely a bleep in the "Federal Watch" column—condemning the news stories as "without substance," but Amanda also knew that Sussman had asked Bob not to attend any more of the Senate hearings so Sussman could do damage control on Capitol Hill. Amanda did not ask how Bob occupied himself all day. He didn't give her the chance. When he came home at night, he retreated almost immediately to the bedroom.

Any hope Amanda harbored that Bob's notoriety might quickly fade was dispelled on the final day of the hearings—yesterday—when Megabyte's Mike Frith himself took the stand and promptly launched into a long, self-pitying complaint about his persecution by the Department of Justice. The cable channels carried his testimony live: with his pointy-collared beige dress shirt, brown knit tie, and goofy perm, Frith looked exactly like a high school graduation photo snapped in 1977. Yet instead of provoking mockery or the merciless grilling that Bob had predicted, this eccentric corporate baron somehow managed to capture the sympathy of the committee and the press. And when Senator Benson pressed Frith for evidence of persecution, Frith waved a copy of the *Wall Street Journal* editorial and identified Bob (!) as the ringleader of "those faceless bureaucrats who have been working day and night to thwart innovation in this country."

With that, Amanda's pity for Bob, her pity for them both, came crashing down upon her. It no longer seemed important who was to blame. Bob's situation was undeniably worse than hers, and that very evening Amanda sought to make amends with him. Maybe she should have gone about it differently— maybe, she thought now, she shouldn't have opened with, "Look, Bob, we both have our sides in this . . ."—but the effect was to shut him down even further. When words failed, she tried touch. She rolled closer to him in bed, but his very skin seemed to radiate hostility toward her. She had never known him to be physically indifferent to her—he had always welcomed her rare initiations of intimacy—and his rejection left Amanda feeling drained of all her power; she hugged her pillow, careful not to let even her ankle stray near his lest it cause him to jerk away.

Two men joined Amanda's table—husbands, apparently, of the women already seated—and the talk shifted to the sudden explosion of stock prices that summer. Megabyte shares might have slumped, but the rest of the market, which experts had called dangerously overvalued in the spring, was now rocketing rewardingly upward—to the benefit of everybody at the table except Amanda.

Amanda studied the female faces around her. They seemed almost enviably indifferent to everything except their children, their houses, and the stock market. They picked delicately at their plates and inserted an observation whenever a pause in the men's conversation permitted it.

"Do you go to St. Cuthbert's as well?" a voice asked from Amanda's right. It belonged to a woman of about fifty, wearing what looked like a floral housecoat, who seemed politely concerned that Amanda should feel included in the conversation.

St. Cuthbert's was Christine's Episcopal church, a membership in which she took as much pride as in her club: two Supreme Court justices and the last vice president worshiped there.

"Oh—uh, no," Amanda stammered, as she tried to pull her thoughts out of their whirling tempest. "I don't." She'd nearly added *go to church* but realized that it might seem offensive to this thoroughly inoffensive woman.

"Yes, I didn't think I'd seen you there, but then it *is* a large congregation. Do you go to another in the area?"

"No, we live in the District," Amanda said, as if that settled it. Seeing that it did not—the woman was still looking at her quizzically—Amanda rummaged around in her mind for the name of a nearby church.

"Christ Church is lovely, if you're in Georgetown," the woman continued. "And I've always adored the Foundry Methodist—the building at least—"

Amanda nodded, all the while thinking to herself, *C'mon, c'mon—there is that one over by the supermarket, and then that large modern place we pass on the way to school*—what is its name?— *where every Christmas on the front lawn there is a live reenactment of the crèche scene . . .*

"We go to . . ."—*what is it?*—"St. Paul's."

"St. Paul's Catholic Church?"

"Oh no, not *Catholic.* The St. Paul's on Massachusetts Avenue."

The woman looked surprised. "You mean the *new* St. Paul's *Baptist* Church?"

"Er, yes." *Jesus!* How did she stumble into that one? Amanda took a large forkful of pasta to tie up her mouth for a few seconds.

"That's very interesting."

"Not really."

"Why, yes it is. I wouldn't have guessed you were a Baptist."

"Really?" Amanda sat up stiffly, as if the woman were implying something derogatory about Baptists, her newfound people. "Why do you say that?"

The woman caught the implication and flushed.

"Oh, no reason in particular. It's just that you seem so . . . so . . ." It was now the woman's turn to grasp for the right answer, and Amanda was not displeased—perhaps it would put an end to the cross-examination.

". . . progressive," the woman said finally. "Progressive people are not usually Baptists. They're usually *ex*-Baptists." And she laughed as if she'd just made an especially witty *bon mot*.

Amanda did not return the laugh.

"How did you come to be a Baptist?" the woman persisted. "Your parents?"

"Look, we belong to a new movement of Baptists," Amanda said desperately. "*Neo*-Baptists. We're quite different."

The woman looked puzzled. "I've never heard of it before. How is it different?"

Amanda fumbled around for what could be a plausible distinction between traditional Baptists and her hypothetical progressive Baptists.

"Well, our minister—she's a lesbian."

"I see. That *is*, er, progressive." The woman made such a considerable effort to sound nonjudgmental that Amanda suddenly felt guilty for leading her on. Why didn't Amanda admit that she didn't attend church in the first place? She wasn't ashamed of the fact—if she just hadn't been so upset . . .

Amanda abruptly excused herself to get more food. She took a circuitous route to the buffet, passing Christine and Bob's table. She paused behind Bob's back.

"Are you doing okay?" she whispered in his ear.

Bob turned his head, startled.

"Yes, yes, I'm fine."

Amanda sat down in her chair again, and pushed around a small second helping of pasta. Both of her tablemates were now engaged in separate discussions, leaving Amanda to her worsening mood and untouched food. When the meal ended and the other guests rose to take dessert and coffee in the living room, she stuck to her seat, hoping Bob would come and collect her.

He didn't, and Amanda ended up trailing everyone else through the grand French doors.

Bob stood by the mantel drinking an amber shot of something, surrounded by a fresh cluster of guests. The alcohol had capsized his usual discretion, and his voice was louder than Amanda had ever heard it in company. What little remained of her instincts warned her that she had better pull Bob out of there. She approached him and gently grasped his elbow.

"Bob—"

He was midsentence and ignored her. "—my opinion was that the DOJ was getting scared—"

"*Bob*," she interrupted, this time more emphatically.

The members of the cluster looked to her, and the loss of their attention momentarily cut Bob off. Amanda pinched her husband's arm in the universal marital code that indicated, *I'm ready to go.*

Bob did not move. Instead he said, "Oh, this is my wife, Amanda."

"Hello, Amanda. We haven't had the chance to say hello yet this evening." Brian Saunders, Christine's husband, leaned over to kiss her lightly on the cheek. He was a pleasant, golf-shirted man with whom Amanda had never exchanged more than three sentences of conversation. He introduced her to the group, including the Fenshaws again, who all turned back to Bob, eager to hear him finish his sentence.

"I'm sorry, Bob, but I'm really quite tired. Do you mind? . . ."

"In a minute," Bob replied stubbornly.

"I really think—"

"Oh, I'm tired, too," announced Janet Fenshaw, with a knowing look at Amanda.

"About time we thought about heading out, too," one of the

men said to his wife, catching on. He began patting his pockets for his keys.

Bob saw his audience dissolve.

"Let's go *now,*" Amanda insisted, and to her surprise Bob turned suddenly docile. He followed her to the front door, where their hostess was waving good-bye to the couples who had preceded them. Amanda thanked her, and Christine hugged them both. "Hang in there, Bob. We're all rooting for you . . . except my husband, of course. He's annoyed about the stock."

"You better let me drive," Amanda said when they reached their car. Bob surrendered the keys without a word.

"I'm sorry to have pulled you out of there." She started the ignition. "You—you were going to say something you'd regret."

"I'm not exactly the one with that problem, am I?"

Amanda absorbed the blow as she had the others. She pulled out into Christine's quiet street and began navigating the familiar route home while trying out different retorts in her head. *I wasn't the one staring down Christine's dress.* No, that was not going to be helpful.

Bob switched on the radio and fumbled with the buttons until he found the news. Amanda never thought she would be so happy to hear a story about homicide. There was not a single word about Megabyte.

"Bob," Amanda ventured slowly, hopefully, when the news was over and jazz music crackled through the speakers, "I'm as sorry as you are about what's happened . . ."

She didn't dare look at him.

"I know you blame me—and I agree, much of it is my fault, I accept that, but being angry with each other doesn't help anything. We've got to get beyond our anger or it's going to start affecting our marriage . . ."

Bob made no reply. They were approaching the entrance to the Beltway, and for the next minute or so Amanda concentrated on merging into the stream of cars.

"Look, I know you're angry and you probably don't want to talk about this right now, but I really think we have to—for the sake of our marriage, for the sake of everything."

Amanda changed lanes and, when the road was clear, glanced sideways at Bob. His face was briefly lit by the oncoming head-lights.

He had fallen asleep.

Chapter Sixteen

THE FOLLOWING MONDAY, Amanda was sitting in the back garden, watching the children splash in the wading pool, when she heard the screen door open.

"Daddy!"

Bob pulled up one of the deck chairs next to Amanda and greeted the children, not seeming to mind wet handprints all over his suit jacket. Amanda checked her watch—it was only two o'clock.

"What are you doing home?"

He waited until Ben and Sophie had returned to the pool before answering, "It's worse than I thought."

Bob unfastened his briefcase and brought out a copy of the current *National Standard*. On the cover was a cartoon of a saintly-looking Mike Frith lashed to a cross, with ghoulish caricatures of Frank Sussman, Jim Hochmayer, Senator Benson, the attorney general, and the president gathered at the base, rubbing their hands in glee. Just in case the symbolism was lost upon the casual browser, an accompanying headline read: THE CRUCIFIXION OF MIKE FRITH: WHY THE ADMINISTRATION IS OUT TO DESTROY MEGABYTE.

"Oh no."

"Look inside."

She turned to the article—by Cathy O'Toole, naturally—and quickly skimmed the paragraphs. ". . . Administration captive of Silicon Valley donors, all of whom have an interest in the Justice department handcuffing Frith . . . abusing the antitrust laws to advance special interests. . . ."

"Middle column, first page."

Amanda read:

More evidence of Justice's cozy relationship with Megabyte competitors emerged just last week. As the *Washington Post* reported, Bob Clarke—the department bureaucrat who is leading the charge against Frith—invited Jim Hochmayer to his house for dinner to plot strategy the night before Hochmayer's testimony at the Senate hearings. According to the *Wall Street Journal*, sources inside Justice insist Clarke is a loose cannon driven by ideological hatred of Megabyte. Clarke is reported to be acting in cahoots with the famously loony Silicon Valley lawyer Sherwood J. Pressman, who has long pressured the DOJ to take antitrust action against his clients' formidable competitor. But this explanation sounds suspiciously like department higher-ups trying to take cover. There is no way the Megabyte case could have advanced so far without support from the top: not just from Sussman and the attorney general, but also from the president himself. Jack Chasen, CEO of TalkNet, and Jim Hochmayer are golfing buddies of the president— and both of them contributed hundreds of thousands of dollars in soft money. . . .

Amanda looked up. "But they're saying it's *not* you."

"Yeah, great. That really helps me. It's only my *boss*, who is a pawn of big donors and the president, and who feels the need to trash me anonymously in the *Wall Street Journal*."

"But Frank knows this is all partisan garbage! That they're blowing the dinner out of proportion—"

Bob took back the magazine and rolled it up. "Yes, of course he does. I'm sure that's why he told me to take the rest of the week off work."

He stood, ignoring Amanda's stunned expression.

"I better go change my clothes."

Bob did not descend again until dinner. He wore a pair of old shorts and a T-shirt. Amanda had set the table in the kitchen. She emptied a pot of spaghetti into a bowl and tossed it with some tomato sauce from a jar. Sophie and Ben began eating eagerly. Amanda helped herself before pushing the bowl over to Bob.

"Did you know, Daddy, that nobody's ever seen a giant squid?" Ben asked.

"Really?" Amanda replied, when Bob did not.

"Yup. They live too deep in the ocean."

"Where did you learn that?"

"From my *Sea Monsters* book."

"That's very good, Ben."

"Daddy, guess what a giant squid likes to eat?"

Bob was picking at the pasta but not really eating it. "I don't know, Ben. What?"

"Thpaghetti?" guessed Sophie.

Ben shot her a contemptuous look. "*No*. Dead sharks."

"Huh." Bob stood up. "I'm going to catch the news."

"Thpagetti ith *my* favorite food."

"Have some more, sweetie."

Amanda's eyes followed Bob as she cut Sophie's second help-ing into manageable strands. It was one thing for Bob to be angry with *her*, but why must he take his anger out upon the children?

"Could you take us to the museum tomorrow, Mommy?" Ben asked. "The one where they have the giant whale?"

"Gosh, Ben, we've got some errands to do."

"I'm bored of errands."

A thought occurred to Amanda. "Perhaps Daddy could take you. He's going to be home this week."

"He is?" Sophie's tomato-splattered face burst into a smile.

"Yes. Daddy is having a little summer vacation."

She watched her words carry over to Bob. He was on his way to the stairs, but he stopped to register them with a look that said, *Thanks a lot.*

"Could you take us swimming, too, Daddy?" Ben asked.

"Maybe."

"Yay!"

Ben and Sophie charged off after their father, who was mut-tering that he'd missed the top of the news. Amanda finished cleaning up the dishes. She heard the children's excited yells drown out the low intonations of the newscast, but she could not make out anything Bob said except for an irritated com-mand to "stop jumping on the bed!" Amanda lingered down-stairs after she had dried the last glass, reading a magazine until it was time to give the children their baths. This was usually Bob's job, but when she didn't hear the taps switch on by eight o'clock she went up to do it herself. Their bedroom door was shut, and Ben was playing with Sophie in his room.

Amanda bathed the children and tucked them into bed. She ran a tub for herself and soaked for an hour in a fruity bubble bath, her toes idly fidgeting with the taps. By the time Amanda padded into the bedroom wrapped in a towel, the television was switched off. Bob was asleep in his shorts. His light was still on; a book rested on his chest. The tension had drained from his face, and he appeared far away, untroubled by anything but the brightness of the lamp, which caused him to twitch unconsciously. Amanda turned off the light and stole around the room like an intruder, removing her pajamas from a drawer and slipping into her side of the bed unnoticed. Delicately she removed the book from Bob's chest and placed it on her table. So long as he lay still, she could bear to share the room with him. But she did not know how much longer she could stand to share the house with him awake.

"Christ, Amanda," Bob complained the next morning. "I don't exactly feel like going to the museum."

He stood by the refrigerator in his robe, holding a cup of coffee. Amanda had risen early and was already dressed.

"You promised the children—"

"*You* promised them."

"Well, they're expecting to go. I've got errands to do. I've got to go to the grocery store. I was going to pick up the vacuum from the repair shop. A dozen stupid things like that. Frankly I'd appreciate the time without Ben and Sophie tagging along. It takes me twice as long."

They were facing each other with about eight feet of space between them. Bob took a long sip from his mug, and said nothing.

"Besides"—Amanda proceeded cautiously—"I thought it might be nice for you to spend time with the kids. It might . . . be distracting. I know they want to spend time with you."

"I'm just not up for their company, that's all." Bob turned his back to her to pour himself another cup of coffee. She glared after him.

"Then whose company are you up for?" Amanda exploded. "You're not up for mine. Now you're telling me you're not up for your children's company? Honestly, Bob, I'm at a loss. What else are you going to do around here all day except stare at the wall and feel sorry for yourself?"

Bob leaned on the counter, with the hand that had been gripping the mug now clenched in a fist. His body was rigid except for his head, which nodded in a knowing way as if to say, *This is exactly what I expected from you all along.*

At that moment the telephone rang. Neither of them made a motion to answer it. Amanda counted the rings until voice mail intercepted the call. But the rings only started up again— someone was determined to reach them. Amanda brushed past Bob to answer it, and a glimpse of his face told her that her decision had lowered his opinion of her one more notch.

"Amanda, thank God you're there. It's Susie."

She had not spoken to Susie since "The Ear" incident. Immediately she regretted picking up the phone.

"Yes?" Amanda said neutrally, as if she were speaking to a phone solicitor.

"Look, can I come over this morning? I have to talk to you."

"Today would not be good. I'll be out."

Amanda looked over at Bob; he was staring out the window above the sink.

"Where are you going? Maybe we could meet for a coffee?" Susie had not detected anything untoward in her tone, but that hardly came as a surprise.

"Possibly," Amanda relented.

"What about the Coffee Hut near you? Ten o'clock?"

"That will be fine. Good-bye."

Amanda gathered her purse and keys from the kitchen table. Her hands were trembling.

"I'm going now," she informed the terry-cloth expanse of Bob's back. "I'll be home later."

Amanda paused for a reaction, but when none came she carried on, out the front door.

Halfway down the walk, Amanda realized she had walked out without the shopping list. Well, she sure wasn't going back in for it.

It was already blazing hot; the street was empty and quiet except for the rattle of cicadas. The heat from the interior of the car hit her face like a blast furnace. She rolled down the windows, expecting to see Bob come chasing after her. The front door remained shut. She drove the few short blocks to the Coffee Hut, feeling lighter and happier the farther she got from her house. *Let Bob see what it's like to be depressed and to have to entertain children. Let him for once have a taste of my life.*

By the time she found parking, Amanda was as giddy as a sailor on shore leave. For once the day held unscripted possibilities. For the next few hours at least, she was unshackled—she'd shed the Velcro monkeys!

Her spirits were dampened only by the sight of Susie slumped over a cappuccino at a tall round table at the back of the café. As Amanda stood in line, waiting to pick up a coffee for herself, she realized that she had only begun to reckon how furious she was with her so-called friend. Amanda had heard from Susie only once during the turmoil of the past week—a perfunctory phone message left the day of "The Ear" column, in which Susie had expressed surprise that the reporter had written a different item from the one Susie expected. But she had not apologized. She had not even expressed any interest in how the item might have affected Amanda and Bob. Amanda suspected, in fact, from the edge of defiance in Susie's voice, that Susie was inwardly quite pleased; the item had, after all, achieved exactly what Susie wanted it to achieve, which was public acknowledgment of her relationship with Hochmayer.

Amanda half hoped that Susie's urgent call today had been prompted by belated remorse. But as Amanda approached Susie's table, she saw immediately that her friend was cocooned inside her own bubble of misery. She barely looked up when Amanda sat down.

"Hi."

"Hi."

"So what's up?"

"I—I needed to see you. Oh Amanda, it's just been so bad." Susie raised her eyes piteously, and had Amanda not been so exasperated she might have warmed with sympathy. But Amanda's first thought was how tired and drawn her friend appeared. Susie's beauty for once provided no protective mask against her inner distress. There were fresh, small lines around her eyes and mouth. Her usually golden complexion had gone flat; she had pulled her hair back into a limp bun rather than bother with styling it.

"Yes, it has been bad. For everyone."

Susie went on, heedlessly. "Jim's not returning my calls. He left town after the hearings. I tried him on his plane, his cell . . ."

"You *didn't* call him at home?"

"No—" Susie hesitated. "Well, I did, but he wasn't there."

"Who answered?"

"Just the housekeeper. She said they had gone away for a couple of weeks."

"Thank God. Is it possible he didn't see 'The Ear'?"

"Somehow I doubt it. I'm sure someone would have brought it to his attention. It's not like Jim not to call or return my messages or—not to tell me he's leaving town. What am I going to do?"

"What *is* there to do?"

For the first time Susie seemed to register Amanda's impatience. But rather than grow defensive, which was her customary reaction to anything less than total agreement, Susie simply looked wounded.

"I don't know. I thought maybe I should write to him, to let him know how I feel—and remind him of some of the things he said to me."

Amanda returned Susie's hurt look with one of amazement. "And what would that accomplish?"

"He might call."

"Or not. And I think the likelihood is not. Susie, don't you see that he doesn't *want* to call you? That by making this public you embarrassed him? He obviously didn't want his adultery exposed—"

"Don't call it that," Susie replied, eyes flashing. "That's such an ugly word. And it wasn't like that. Jim—Jim said he could honestly imagine falling in love with me. That he *was* falling in love with me."

Amanda was too disgusted to enter into a debate over the nuances of Hochmayer's feelings. She only felt foolish for being drawn—once more!—into Susie's emotional shell game.

"Okay, call it what you like. But I'd appreciate it if you could manage to leave other people out of it this time."

"What do you mean by that?"

"I mean like us. Bob and me."

"You? How does this affect you?"

"Susie, where have you been? Have you thought at all about what that 'Ear' column did to Bob? Did you see the *Wall Street Journal* editorial? Did you hear Mike Frith's testimony at the hearings? It's on the fucking cover of the *National Standard*!"

"I don't read that magazine." Susie took a sip of her coffee and glanced about as if she were afraid Amanda was making a scene.

Amanda lowered her voice. "Well maybe you should—this week anyway. Bob might lose his job."

"That's ridiculous," Susie said, disbelieving. "There was nothing in that 'Ear' column that could possibly cause that. *I'm* the one who's been hurt by it."

Amanda traced a pattern of swirls on the table in a bit of spilled foam. "Yes. Yes, you have been hurt by it. But so have we. And so has Jim. And so has his *wife*. Why don't you think about *her*?" She slammed her hand down. "I've got to go."

For the second time that morning, Amanda found herself walking out on someone.

The sun dazzled her eyes, and for a second or two Amanda was uncertain which direction to walk. Her hands were shaking and her heart pounding, and the dense heat seemed to further constrict her already labored breathing. She felt urgently that she had to get away—but to where? There was the grocery shopping to do, but she could not face that right now. She needed to be somewhere cool, anonymous, somewhere she could sit down and think straight. Amanda climbed in her car again and headed toward a mall. The nearest one was up Wisconsin Avenue in Bethesda. Amanda drove slowly, aware of her unsteady nerves; several times cars accelerated up to her rear bumper, only to veer and roar past her in frustration.

She had not waited for Susie's reaction. Was Susie dumbfounded? Furious? Amanda would probably never know. She didn't care to know.

The windowless concrete front of a department store jutted out from the mall at an angle, like the massive prow of some futuristic galleon. Amanda parked in the gray dungeon of a covered lot and emerged from an elevator into the mall's interior courtyard. For a while she just wandered, pausing by brightly lit shop windows advertising clearance sales. Already the merchants were seized with that peculiar midsummer impulse to restock their racks with heavy sweaters and jackets. Amanda bought herself a take-out sandwich and ate it on a bench under the shade of a gigantic potted tree. Gradually she felt her internal meters returning to normal. It was fine sitting here with nothing to do, watching the other mothers haul their wailing infants in and out of strollers.

Amanda finished her sandwich and walked around some more. Eventually she found herself at the entrance to the department store. It occurred to her that she needed a new swimsuit, and that swimsuits would probably be on sale with the rest of the summer merchandise. The purchase of a swimsuit gave new purpose to her outing.

She strode into the store and rode the escalator up two levels. But to Amanda's disappointment, most of the swimsuits were gone—only half a dozen one-pieces were left in her size. Amanda hesitated over a black, designer bikini. It was the sort of swimsuit Christine would wear. Impulsively, she pulled it off the rack and took it into the dressing room with her more practical selections. She'd give it a go. It might even be funny.

Each suit looked worse than the last. Amanda was baffled by the cross-straps on one; another she couldn't tug over her hips. And what was it about artificial lighting that revealed new pockets of fat that her critical eye had not yet detected at home? God, her thighs looked like topographical maps! And why was her stomach so bloated? Soon all the swimsuits except the bikini were piled on the floor. Amanda gamely tried it on—struggling with the tiny bottom and hooking the top without looking in the mirror. Then—voilà. Amanda turned around. It wasn't . . . funny. It wasn't bad, either. All her flaws were there, and perhaps more on display than they had been in the other suits, but somehow they seemed less framed. The bikini top lifted her breasts attractively and the bottom triangles barely covered what they were supposed to—could she possibly wear such a thing in public?

Amanda checked the price tag—70 percent off ninety dollars. She could afford the risk. She changed back into her street clothes and took the bikini to a register.

Amanda expected the saleswoman to police Amanda's purchase—"I'm sorry, ma'am, but I'm confiscating this for your own protection"—but the clerk, whose own figure made Amanda feel gratifyingly skinny, merely commented that the suit was "very pretty." Amanda waited, tapping her credit card on the counter, wondering if she should buy the damn thing after all.

When she stepped back onto the escalator, Amanda began to second-guess her decision. The saleswoman had mentioned that she couldn't return or exchange the swimsuit. And when Bob saw the bag and suspected she had spent the day idly shopping . . . Well, whatever—the bikini made her feel good about herself, and that was what was important, right?

Amanda passed into the glittering landscape of cosmetics. Usually she was immune to the siren calls of the clerks and would bustle by their long mirrored counters, ignoring their offers to "try the latest Seduction." It was all shamanism, she thought, propagated by the high priests of the makeup industry. Today she intended to pass right by them—but a display of pale lipsticks caught her eye. They were similar to the delicate shades Susie wore. Amanda paused—long enough, alas, to catch the attention of one of two saleswomen, both wearing identical gray tunics, chatting a few feet away.

"May I help you?"

"Oh, not really. I'm just looking—"

"We've got some lovely new shades. May I show you?"

"Well—" Amanda caught sight of her own naked face in a mirror and compared it unfavorably to the saleswoman's: she wasn't much younger than Amanda, and not especially attractive. Her features seemed to have been arranged according to the asymmetrical principles of feng shui, especially her nose, which jutted off to one side. But the woman had skillfully used makeup to highlight her eyes and lips while minimizing the effect of her nose.

Amanda examined one of the testers. "All right."

"Please, take a seat."

Amanda sat herself on a tall stool while the clerk busily pulled tubes from their testing slots.

"Have you worn this brand before?"

"No." Amanda would not admit that she bought her makeup in the pharmacy aisle of Fresh Farms where it had the virtue of being untested on animals, and also the virtue of being cheap.

"Let's try this one." The saleswoman brought out a pencil and a little brush.

"First let me line your lips—do you use liner?—and here, this brush helps the color go on smoothly."

Amanda rubbed her lips and agreed the pinky beige shade suited her.

"But now look how pale the rest of your face looks." The clerk frowned, and pushed a stray lock of hair from Amanda's forehead. "When was the last time you had your colors done?"

"I haven't—"

"May I just try something more—if you have time?"

Amanda made a show of checking her watch. "Not really—"

"It will just take a second."

"I really only need lipstick." Amanda had not actually intended to buy the lipstick but could see no other way of extricating herself from the saleswoman's chair.

"That's fine, that's fine. But you'll be amazed how fabulous I can make you look."

The other saleswoman was listening to their conversation, and drifted over.

"Oh yes, you must let Gina do you. Gosh, Gina, look at her eyes! You're so lucky to have such big eyes."

Amanda, who had never thought of herself as having especially large eyes, wilted under the pressure of the two saleswomen.

"Well—if you can do it quickly."

"Of course."

The first saleswoman rummaged under the counter and brought out several trays that resembled artists' palettes. Then she took some sponges and began dabbing at Amanda's face as if at a canvas.

"You have such beautiful skin. What do you use on it?"

"Um, soap. A little moisturizer."

The clerk paused, worried. "My goodness, you need to take better care of it than that! Do you see these little lines?"

Amanda was well aware of them.

"We have a product that takes care of them. I'll show it to you afterward. Now look—see how well this foundation covers?"

Gone were the circles below Amanda's eyes, the red blotches on her nose and chin. The other salesclerk watched approvingly until another customer drew her away.

"I'm not finished," the first saleswoman continued. She produced a case of brushes. For the next few minutes she worked intensely on Amanda's face, instructing her to look up or look down as she painted around Amanda's eyes, or to turn her head this way and that as she added color to Amanda's cheeks.

"Now, look again." The woman moved the standing mirror closer to Amanda, and angled it so Amanda could see her whole face. "Gorgeous, huh?"

"It's—it's very nice," Amanda replied—untruthfully, for she was astounded by how much prettier she appeared. Her skin—it had that elusive, rich glow of Christine's.

The clerk stood back to appraise her. "Now if you plucked your eyebrows a little bit, and tied back your hair perhaps—perfect. But my job is done." She smiled.

"Which cosmetics did you use?"

"Let me assemble them for you."

"Oh, I don't think I want to buy all of them—"

"It's not much. I'll just get you the products that are essential."

The saleswoman rooted around some drawers and pulled out a number of small, gold-banded boxes. She lined them up in front of Amanda.

"This is the rouge, the eye shadows, the lipstick, the lip pencil, the eyeliner, mascara, foundation, powder . . . will you need brushes?"

"Uh, no."

"It's important to use the right brushes."

"I'm okay."

"Do you want me to show you the moisturizing cream you should use?"

"I don't think so."

The woman raised her eyebrows.

"I'm sure." Amanda's mind was quickly trying to calculate how much the cosmetics would cost, and what she could ask the clerk to take back without seeming to be unable to afford them.

"All right then. I'll ring these up," and the saleswoman took them away before Amanda could protest. When she returned from the register, the saleswoman said, "The total is one hundred ninety-seven dollars and fifty cents with tax."

Amanda panicked. That would wipe out her housekeeping budget for the next week. How would she explain it to Bob? How *could* she explain it?

"I don't really need the lip pencil—or the mascara. And I have an eyeliner already."

The clerk made no comment but removed the offending items. She went away to ring it up again.

"The total now is one forty-nine sixty-seven."

Amanda could not send anything else back at this point. She either had to tell the saleswoman she would not take anything but the lipstick, or somehow squeeze the money from the household expenses. The woman was beginning to wrap the boxes in pink tissue paper. Amanda bought time for herself by rummaging through her handbag for her wallet. She could probably find a way, she reasoned, if she cooked a lot of pasta and used up the cans of chickpeas and tomatoes at the back of her cupboard. But then the whole sorry predicament of Bob's job came crashing down upon her—what if he were fired? What if he found out how much she had just thrown away on cosmetics at a time like this?

And yet, and yet—why should she *not* do something nice for herself, *especially* at a time like this? She was not like some wives, always demanding new things. Christine would spend this sum of money without thinking about it. Why couldn't Amanda indulge herself once in a while, too? And Bob was being so awful to her these days. She deserved to do something nice for herself—

Amanda presented her credit card to the saleswoman and allowed her eyes to rest covetously on the beautifully wrapped boxes, all hers.

The clerk returned with the card. "Do you have another? This one was declined."

Mortified, Amanda searched through her wallet and pulled out the card she and Bob reserved for emergencies.

The clerk snapped it up and turned on her heels, pausing to simper at an elegantly dressed woman who was examining bottles of nail polish. "I'll be with you in just a moment."

Amanda signed the slip, and the saleswoman thrust the package at her.

"Have a nice day."

Amanda thought it best to leave her new purchases in the trunk. She assumed Bob and the children would still be at the museum, and was surprised to find the front door unlocked.

"Hello?" she called into the house.

There was no answer.

"Bob? Ben? Hello?"

The back door was open as well, but the yard was empty. Was it possible Bob left the house this way when he went out? No— a floating bucket in the wading pool indicated recent activity. Amanda, worried now, returned to the front hall and stood by the staircase.

"Hello?"

She heard the muffled sound of a man's voice in a room upstairs. Amanda crept up to the top of the stairs to listen. The voice was coming from behind their closed bedroom door. The children's rooms appeared empty.

She edged toward their door. It sounded like Bob speaking to someone, but the conversation was one-sided—there was no other voice. She opened the door.

Bob was sitting on the end of the bed, talking on the telephone. He was still wearing his robe and boxers. He looked at her but did not hang up.

"Uh-huh. I realize that, but listen—"

"Where are the children?" Amanda whispered.

"Huh? Could you hang on a moment?" Bob covered the bottom of the receiver. "What are you asking me?"

"The children—where are they?"

"They're playing outside."

"No they're not."

"They were a minute ago."

"They're not," Amanda insisted. "The doors are wide open and no one's there."

"Just a moment." Bob returned to the phone. "May I call you back in a few minutes? I have to deal with something here."

Bob rose and retied his robe.

"You're not even dressed!"

Bob walked past her without answering and began calling for the children. She followed him to the backyard.

"They were right here."

"You left them *alone*—with a wading pool?"

"There's only a little water in it."

"Bob, children can drown in *one inch* of water! You know that!"

"I just stepped away for a second!"

Amanda was growing hysterical. "Where the fuck are they, Bob?"

Bob searched among the scrawny bushes as if they might be hiding behind them. Amanda ran to the front walk.

"Ben! Sophie!"

Bob joined her. He looked worried now too but was trying not to show it. "They can't have gone far."

"You've lost them! You've lost our children!"

"They're *not* lost. Look, you go that way."

They jogged up and down the short block calling out the children's names. When there was no answer, they returned to the driveway of their house.

"I'm getting in the car," Amanda said frantically. "I'll drive around the streets. Do you think we ought to call the police?"

"Not yet."

They heard the phone ringing inside. Amanda dashed ahead of Bob to answer it. It was Marjorie, who lived three doors down and was the mother of Hannah.

"Amanda—you're there!" she exclaimed. "Ben and Sophie are at my house. I've been trying to reach you, but your phone has been busy for the past hour. I even sent Hannah over to knock on the door, but no one answered. Is everything okay?"

"Yes. Oh, Marjorie, thank you." Amanda was breathless. "I'll be right over."

She hung up and turned to Bob. "They're at Marjorie's."

He raised his hand as if to say he had known that all along; the gesture had the same effect as if Bob had just casually tossed a match into a pile of oil-soaked rags.

"How dare you!" Amanda erupted. "How *dare you* act like that! You didn't leave them for 'just a second'! You were on the phone for a whole hour!"

"It wasn't that long."

"Yes, it was—Marjorie just said so!" Amanda grabbed up her purse and keys. "And who the hell were you talking to anyway? Grace Bertelli? I can't take this, Bob. I just can't take any more of this."

The children were sitting in front of Marjorie's television set sharing a huge bowl of popcorn.

Amanda practically fell upon them and held their bodies tightly to her. Ben squirmed.

"Mom—it's *Space Rangers*."

"I'm sorry for this, Marjorie," Amanda apologized. "Bob, he's . . . home sick today. I went out to do some shopping and, well . . . he must have fallen asleep. Thank God they're okay."

"They rang my doorbell and said they were explorers from another planet," Marjorie said, amused. "I'm just glad I was home."

"So am I." Amanda clapped her hands together. "Okay kids, time to go."

"But *Space Rangers* isn't over yet!"

"Who wants to go to Burger Chalet?"

"Me!"

"Me too!"

Amanda hustled them down the sidewalk and into the car. Through the screen door, she saw the shadow of Bob in his bathrobe, waiting for them. Go to hell, she thought.

Chapter Seventeen

THE NIGHTMARE WAS indifference. It was always indifference. She never dreamed about divorce, or illness, or death. Instead her life would be shown exactly as it was, except that Bob no longer cared about her. This time she came home and found Bob speaking on the phone to Grace Bertelli. He didn't bother to hide the fact from her. He said, "May I call you back in a moment, Grace?" and when Amanda confronted him— "Why?" she yelled soundlessly, "why?"—he merely shrugged. "I just got bored."

Amanda awoke with the terrible sense that there was no division between the nightmare and her real life. Bob was not sleeping beside her. She opened her eyes, instead, to the sight of the living room, and the bed she had made for herself on the pullout sofa. In the past, when they had fought, it had been Bob who slept down here; Amanda had always claimed the territory of their bedroom. Last night, Bob seemed determined to punish her for taking the children out rather than bringing them home directly; in his mind, Amanda's defiant act trumped his negligent one of losing them in the first place.

"I did a stupid thing," he'd argued, "but you were deliberately cruel, taking them away before I could see them. You had no right to do that. Didn't you think I was worried, too?"

"No," she'd replied, "no, I didn't think you were worried, because I didn't think you cared—I don't think you care a damn about any of us."

"You really think that? You really think that, don't you?"

Amanda could not remember Bob being so furious with her; and yet the argument that ensued—as explosive as any the two had ever engaged in—lacked the heat of the others, as if all the sparring and fighting of the previous weeks had brought them to the critical final round, but neither had the strength to deliver the knockout blow.

Instead, Amanda struck out at him wildly—"I do think that—in fact, I'm surprised you haven't left us. I'm surprised that you haven't left us . . . for Grace Bertelli."

The moment she said the woman's name she saw that she had miscalculated: rather than crumpling, every fiber of Bob's body seemed to rebound. He stood up from the table in the kitchen— for that's where the fight took place, after Amanda had put the children to bed, without so much as a good night to their father— and crossed the room to the doorway, moving, it seemed, with great effort to control the anger coursing through his limbs.

He fixed her with a look of such disgust that Amanda wished desperately to recall the words out of the air. She could not, though, so she blundered on, hoping to justify herself. "Well, why wouldn't you? She feels free to call here."

"And why wouldn't she—unless she had something to hide?"

"I don't know. You tell me."

"Okay, I will. She provided expert testimony for our case, and she had a question. I couldn't talk to her when she called me at the office, so I told her to call me later at home, when it would be quiet. Anything else?"

Amanda could not refute the devastating logic of Bob's answer so she tried swinging from another angle. "Okay, maybe not Grace—maybe not anybody. But you've been so angry with me I *am* surprised you haven't walked out. Really—what's stopping you?"

"This, for one, is stopping me, Amanda," he said, holding up his left hand and pointing to his wedding band. "I don't know about you, but I plan to honor the promise I made."

"That's what men always say," she said, more bitterly than she felt, for the truth was, she was weary of fighting, she was weary of everything, she just wanted this whole damn business to end. "And then they change their minds."

"I'm sorry you think I'm like that."

"I'm not saying you're like that. I'm saying that people don't always know—look at Hochmayer—"

"I'm going to take a shower," he said curtly.

Amanda did not follow him upstairs. She didn't know what to do. She knew, simply, that she had begun the evening in the right and had ended it feeling miserably in the wrong. And as she lay there the next morning, the sunlight spilling onto her spare set of floral sheets, the sheets she had bought for their first double bed together, that feeling of wrongness had not gone away.

She would have to begin her day conceding this much to Bob—that her accusations last night had been unfair. But how much would he be willing to concede to her? And as she churned this over, and all the other things she had to make right (*I'll make those calls about finding work in September; I will restart my life!*), Amanda remembered something else, something that had been pressing at the edges of her mind, something that she had kept pushing away during the turmoil of the past few days, something she should not put off any longer . . .

No one else was up yet. Amanda was able to dress, slip out of the house, and return less than half an hour later from her errand. By the time she heard the first stirrings of the others, she was locked securely in the bathroom, grasping a slim litmus wand and following the progress of a spreading stain.

According to the instructions on the box, the liquid would reach first an "indicator" line, then a "test" line. If this latter line turned pink, however faintly, she was "to assume that you are pregnant and contact a medical professional as soon as possible." The result could take as long as three minutes.

Amanda had held these wands many times before. She had even saved the tests that had offered the first scientific proof of the existences of Ben and Sophie, putting them in a keepsake box along with other odd mementos that were not exactly "album" material and yet she could not throw away: their locks of baby hair, their first teeth, the tiny woven caps the midwife had pulled on their heads within moments of their emergence from the womb.

This test she approached in quite a different frame of mind. She held the wand away from her, her whole body tensed.

After a few seconds, there was no doubt. From the very instant the liquid touched the strip, the pink raced forward. The first line was crossed and reddish tinges almost immediately revealed the second line.

Amanda sat upon the closed toilet and cradled her face in her hands.

*   *   *

When she came downstairs, Bob was in the kitchen, reading the newspaper. It was him Amanda had heard rising; the children, apparently, were still asleep.

If Bob remained angry with her, he did not show it. He was absorbed in whatever article he was reading but not so absorbed as to avoid looking up when Amanda entered. He greeted her with a mixed expression—one that could easily swing between friendliness, if she were to encourage it, or hauteur, if she decided she was not speaking to him. She knew Bob well enough to see that he was praying for the former, but a slight stiffening of his jaw told her he was also preparing himself for any fresh blow Amanda might land.

She placed the wand on the table and sat down opposite him, saying nothing. He folded down the edge of his newspaper, glanced at her again and then at the little stick. His eyes returned to hers, inquiringly.

"Look at it," she said hoarsely.

Bob knew what it was, but he seemed unable to fathom it. He picked up the stick and examined it carefully. Then, like an expert witness about to pronounce himself baffled by Exhibit A, he placed it back on the table and began to say, "I'm not sure what—"

"It is what. It's exactly what. I'm—" She found she couldn't say *pregnant*. "—it's . . . positive."

"You're? . . ."

"Yes. Seems so."

"But we haven't . . . in ages!" he managed to say, and Amanda was grateful that he restrained any hint of resentment. "I don't understand—how could it have happened?"

"I don't understand either."

"Sophie took four months of trying," he added, almost wistfully. "And I just assumed you were using your—"

"I must have forgot. Don't ask me how I could forget. I'm not like that—but maybe that time, when you just . . ."

"Yes."

". . . it's possible I forgot then. I've been so distracted with everything." Amanda rubbed her eyes. "Dammit! Why don't I use the pill?"

"You hate the pill."

"I know, but—"

"It makes you sick."

"Yes, but—"

"And moody."

"I feel so stupid! Like a goddamn teenager—" Amanda wiped away a tear and rose to pour herself a cup of coffee. She did not want to fall apart in front of Bob—the fight of last night still hovered between them, and if only out of pride she wanted to hang on to her composure—but the moment she stood up, Amanda burst into tears.

She felt his arms around her immediately, and she sobbed and sobbed, clutching him back, crying out, "It's so awful! It's just so awful!"

"Shh. There we go. Let's sit down."

Bob guided Amanda back into her chair. When her crying had subsided, he got a cup of coffee for her. The shoulder of his robe was soaked.

"So what do you want to do?" Bob asked gently, sitting down with her and refilling his own cup.

"What do *you* want to do?"

"It doesn't really matter what I want to do."

"Why do you say that?" Amanda said, looking up with surprise. "Of course it matters. Three children to support—and God, this Megabyte business."

"That at least is all over."

"What, the scandal? Yes, I suppose there can't be much more of that now that the hearings are over."

"I don't mean the scandal. I mean everything."

"I thought you still had the whole antitrust case to pursue—"

"Not me."

Amanda stared at him. Bob reacted by returning his attention to his collapsed newspaper, which he'd thrust down when she'd fallen apart. He folded it up carefully, smoothed it, and pushed it aside. The stick still lay on the table, radiating its two irrefutable bright pink lines.

"Look, I didn't want to tell you this," he said, "and it sure isn't the moment to tell you—I was waiting to see what Frank was going to do. But basically, before Frank sent me on this little 'vacation,' he told me that it was possible he would have to call in the division's ethics officer."

"What does that mean?"

"That someone would be brought in to investigate my relationship with Hochmayer and, you know, to determine whether I had acted improperly."

"Does this mean you've been fired?" Amanda asked, stunned.

"No—not yet. They don't fire you until you've been found guilty. I'd probably be transferred or suspended while the investigation was taking place. But even if they find me innocent, my career at Justice—well, it's pretty much over."

"Bob, I had no idea. I had no idea it was this bad."

"I know." He got up and wandered over to the counter, mostly, she sensed, because he felt too ashamed to face her directly. "And I know I've been acting like a jerk. I'm sorry. I just don't know what to do."

"And now . . . this," Amanda replied sadly.

"We have a little time, right, to think about that?"

"I guess so. I was planning to go back to work next month. I could have helped us—I could have taken some of the load off you. But if I go ahead—if *we* go ahead—with this . . ."

She let the sentence die.

The morning turned into one of those August days in which it was too hot to go outside but too stuffy to stay in. The gray sky was bloated with moisture, but for all its threatening rumbles, it didn't rain, and the air grew heavier each hour. Their window units choked and gurgled, and their house felt cast in funereal gloom. Bob was too preoccupied to do anything but sit on the sofa with a magazine, halfheartedly supervising the children and replying to their constant questions with a distracted, "Sorry—what did you say?" Amanda absorbed herself in housework and tried to take comfort in the fleeting satisfaction provided by a swept floor and freshly wiped counters; yet everywhere she looked she envisioned a baby—eating in a high chair, plopped down in the hallway, napping in a crib in their bedroom. When Amanda was not imagining a baby, she was visualizing Bob testifying in a government committee room before a tribunal that included Frank Sussman. What would the punishment be if Bob were found guilty? Amanda was afraid to ask. She passed by the living room on her way upstairs with a basket of clean laundry.

"Would you like anything?"

"No, thanks. You?"

"No, thanks."

The anger, at least, was gone.

In Ben's room Amanda knelt to collect a mess of plastic figures and blocks before running the vacuum over the floor. She rearranged them in a little city upon one of his shelves, something for him to come across as a surprise. For all Ben's "issues," Amanda found her son much easier to deal with at five than as a baby. She had not been much good with babies. She could not decipher the language of their cries, nor did she ever master the schedules of their sleep. At ten months old, Ben had still awoken two and three times a night. Amanda consulted an array of child development manuals and did what they told her to do. She took Ben for walks, she dangled new objects—mixing spoons, black-and-white shapes—over his crib, she played classical music while he slept, she charted his month-by-month progress. But she rarely felt confident she was doing the right thing, and it had been a great relief when her maternity leave ended.

When Sophie came along, things went a little easier. Amanda might not know how to amuse her, but Ben did, and Sophie was one of those babies who figure out how to sleep through the night on their own.

It was only recently that Amanda had begun to enjoy her children. The pleasure of their company was gradually exceeding the labor they exacted. When they left the house together, they no longer resembled a Himalayan expedition, bulging with knapsacks, water bottles, and emergency food supplies. But, Amanda told herself, switching on the vacuum, if she were to proceed with—with *this*—she would be yanked back to those burdened, sleepless days. They had all advanced so far up the ladder. Now she was about to be sent plunging down the chute.

Amanda did a quick calculation. The baby would be due sometime next spring, after she turned thirty-six. She would be forty-one by the time the child would be ready to start school full-time, forty-nine when it entered high school. It would not be ready for college until Amanda was . . . fifty-four! She and Bob had hoped to travel. They had hoped to do so many things. Would it really be another decade before they would be able to enjoy even a night out without racing home to a sitter . . .

Amanda stopped cleaning and hunted for one of the old pregnancy books she stored on a high shelf in her bedroom. She sat on the edge of the footstool and thumbed through it. Gosh, how it all came back to her! And the book—it was so relentlessly upbeat, illustrated with drawings of earthy mothers cradling their wrinkly newborns. Amanda turned to the diagram that showed the growth of a fetus during the first trimester. "By the end of the first month," it read, "your baby is a tiny, tadpolelike embryo, smaller than a grain of rice."

This grain of rice had the power to upend her whole life.

Amanda stroked her abdomen and returned to the vacuum.

Later in the afternoon, Bob volunteered to take the children to fetch milk. The moment they left, Amanda phoned her friend Liz.

Liz had her mouth full of nails. "I think it's fantastic news." Actually, this came out more like, "I thimk ith vamtathtic newth."

"Hold on a second." ("Helld un unthecond.")

Amanda heard banging, and Liz returned to the receiver with her mouth empty. "Fixed it. It was a loose step on the back porch. I had to get to it before one of the kids broke their necks."

"I'm just miserable, Liz. I don't know what to do."

"What *can* you do?"

"I—I don't have to go through with it."

Amanda waited for Liz's usual outburst of advice, but it did not come. Instead Liz asked, with uncharacteristic diplomacy, "What does Bob think?"

"I'm not sure. I think he'd support whatever I decided to do."

"Huh." It was a noncommittal *huh* and Amanda grew vexed.

"Well, what would you do?"

This elicited a chortle. "You know what I'd do. That's why I have four of them."

"That's why you have *one* of them," Amanda corrected. "The other three were by choice—or so that's always been my understanding."

"Yeah, I suppose."

"Look, I really need help figuring out what to do. I need *your* help. Talk to me, Liz! God knows you used to be so outspoken about this—"

Boy, had she. A dozen or so years ago, Amanda and Liz had stood outside a clinic near their college, linked arm-in-arm with hundreds of other students before a tiny knot of anti-abortion protesters. She remembered the protesters' inflamed eyes and the way their mouths twisted as they yelled their slogans, "It's a child not a choice!" and "Murder!" and the gruesome pictures of dead fetuses they held aloft, cardboard crucifixions stapled to plywood. Liz had grabbed the bullhorn and shouted back, "Get your laws off my body!"

"I don't know," Liz said. "I guess I've gotten older."

"That hasn't stopped you from having opinions."

"True, but this is different."

"Why does it have to be different?" Amanda prodded. "Can't

you just look at the situation objectively for a minute—or at least from my point of view? Let me spell it out. Liz, I am *pregnant*. I don't know how pregnant, but probably just a week or two. All I know is that it couldn't happen at a worse time. Bob may be out of a job thanks to this Susie business—"

"Shit. Really?"

"Yes." At last Liz seemed to be getting the seriousness of the situation. "That makes the need for me to find some sort of job in the fall more urgent."

"Uh-huh."

"So it really doesn't make sense, does it, for me to go ahead with—this?"

"Uh-huh."

"Is that a yes 'uh-huh'?"

"Oh, Amanda, please, don't ask me to decide this for you."

"Objectively speaking, what is the right thing to do?"

"I can't speak *objectively* about this," Liz said. "It wouldn't matter what else was going on in my life. I'd have the baby."

"You would?" Amanda was astonished.

"I would."

"Even if—you didn't want it?"

"Even if I didn't want it."

"Well, that's a hell of a change. What happened to all that 'every child a wanted child' business we used to chant?"

"I'm not saying, you know, there aren't circumstances when a woman might need an abortion—*should* have one," Liz said, uncomfortably. "I'm not saying what other women should do. But come on, Amanda, let's be honest. You and I—we're not twenty years old anymore. We don't sleep around. We're married. We've been through pregnancy. And frankly, I can't regard it as blithely as I used to."

"*Blithely?* No woman undergoes an abortion *blithely*. We always understood that it wasn't an easy choice."

"No—no we didn't. We *said* we did, but how could we possibly know? Having a baby—it was so abstract. We couldn't even imagine getting ourselves knocked up. We were so bloody knowledgeable. Hell, my own mother got me the pill when I turned sixteen."

"Mine took me to Planned Parenthood at fifteen. You'd think I would have learned something by now."

"So you've been stressed lately. You forgot. It happens. But what happens if you don't go ahead with it?" Liz continued. "Let's say you do have an abortion. Are you certain you will feel afterward that it was the right decision? Years from now, will you look back and feel confident that you did the right thing?"

"Maybe—I don't know."

"All I know is that if I were to have an abortion now, well, I'd be haunted by it. I'd feel like there was this missing piece in my family, this lost child. Zoe, Sarah, Rachel, Zak—I mean, they were all clumps of cells once. Wait, hang on a second."

Amanda clutched her end of the receiver while Liz shouted "No, not another!" and a cry erupted in the background.

"Sorry," her friend said, returning to the conversation, "but one of my clumps wanted a second Popsicle."

"Mine are at the store getting milk." Amanda felt her eyes burning. It all seemed so hopeless. She was hopeless. Her life was hopeless. Amanda swallowed. "It's just so much to get through again. Honestly, I don't know that I can face it."

"I know, hon. I wish I could be there. It must be terribly difficult for you," Liz said soothingly. "But listen, one of these days, you're going to realize that motherhood is not something to be *gotten through*. It is not some fleeting phase of life—it *is* your life, and it will be, for a long, long time, whether or not you choose to have this third baby. The sooner you recognize that, the better it will be."

Bob suggested they go to the Sheik Kabob for dinner.

"I think we all need to get out of this house."

"Can we afford it?"

"This week we can. Maybe not next week."

Amanda had not yet had the courage to tell Bob about her shopping blowout the day before. She had waited for everyone to fall asleep to carry the department-store bag in from the car. By night's end, it all seemed like such a folly, and she had taken soap to her new face and stripped it off.

Now Amanda went quietly to the secret stash of cosmetics she had hidden under the bathroom sink and began applying them the way the salesclerk had showed her. She tied her hair back and dressed in the same black skirt and blouse she had worn to Jack Chasen's cocktail party.

Bob seemed slightly bewildered by her appearance. "You look—nice."

The restaurant was packed even in August, when everyone who could had fled the capital. The waiter showed them to a large round table for six—the only one left—at the back of the restaurant. Amanda sat next to Bob with one child on either side to minimize the potential for mischief. Ben immediately started fishing for the ice in his water while Sophie struggled to turn the pages of the menu.

"Chianti?" Bob asked.

"Yes. Actually, no." She glanced down at her belly.

"I'll just have a beer then."

Amanda gazed around the room, remembering the last time they were here—the night Bob had announced his good news about the Megabyte case. It had felt then as if something magical was about to transform their ordinary world. Tonight there was no fairy-dusting to coat the dusty paper lanterns and startled mounted fish. The Sheik Kabob had all the atmosphere of a lodge dance hall at the end of a long, hot summer. The tables sagged under their layers of stained cloth, and the waiters sweated through their red vests even though the air-conditioning was turned up so high as to leave most diners shivering.

"Ben, please, get your fingers out of your water, okay? You're just going to spill it."

Bob, too, was idly fiddling with his glass. When the waiter appeared Bob seemed momentarily confused, as if he was unsure which of a hundred questions running through his head he was being asked to answer.

It was the same waiter as before. He acknowledged them with a brusque smile before asking his usual question, "Vat is your choice thiz ev'ning?"

After they had given their orders, Sophie reached for a sugar packet and poured its contents down her throat.

"C'mon, Sophie, stop it," Bob snapped, taking the empty packet from her.

"I want one!" Ben complained.

"Both of you," Amanda muttered. She rummaged through her purse and handed them each a pen and a small pad of paper.

"Here, draw Mommy a nice picture."

As they waited for their dinner to arrive, Amanda glanced uneasily at the two extra chairs across the expanse of white tablecloth. She imagined a booster seat strapped to one, containing a toddler banging a spoon on the table. *What is your choice this evening?* What was her choice indeed? The little grain of rice was dividing itself as she sat there. In less than a month, it would resemble a cocktail shrimp; a month after that, a funny combination of squid and hippopotamus, with a bulging, translucent head and the flutter of a nascent heart; a month after that, every aspect of it human, but in miniature, a dollhouse baby. Amanda might not yet be attached to it, but it was attached to her. Within its spirals of genetic coding, as mysterious and beautiful as a nautilus, the story of Bob's and Amanda's ancestors could be traced back generations, just as, when Ben was born, Amanda could trace in his tiny face the soft outline of her grandmother's forehead, her mother's nose, her grandfather's brown eyes. Whatever her child would become was already contained in the grain of rice; it just needed to unfurl itself—if Amanda would let it.

Could she live with the knowledge of the empty chair?

"Bob," Amanda said, suddenly aware of the clatter of cutlery and plates being put down in front of them. "I don't think I could—"

She didn't have to say anything further. Bob looked at her sheepishly, as if they had both wasted time elaborately working out a problem whose answer was obvious from the beginning.

"I know. I wouldn't ask you to. I wouldn't want you to."

"*Really?*"

"Really. I'm—I'm ashamed you thought I would ask you to do something like that."

"But you said we should think about it. That there was time."

"If you didn't want to go through with it, I didn't want to put pressure on you. I suppose the right thing to do was to have acted overjoyed."

"No. I think you did the right thing. I needed to think it through."

Bob raised his beer bottle in a toast.

"Then if there's nothing to do but celebrate, we should celebrate."

A light rain had dampened the heat. They left the restaurant and began walking in the direction of their house. Ben for once seemed content to trot alongside without volleying a thousand questions. Bob pushed Sophie's stroller, and Amanda held his arm.

"When will you know about your job?"

"When I go back on Monday."

They crossed busy Connecticut Avenue and turned down their side street. All of a sudden it was lush, peaceful. At this time of year, Washington was overrun by foliage, like an ancient city crumbling into obscurity. Untended ivy clambered over fences and spilled onto the sidewalk. Hedges too tall to clip sprang unruly new shoots, and shaggy green branches cloaked the rooftops of houses. The sun was sinking a little earlier, and Amanda enjoyed the glimpses into other lives offered by lit windows. What did their cracked brick dwelling, with its tricycle on the front porch and scorched geraniums, show to the world?

Just this, Amanda thought: here lives a family, another family, with small children, a mortgage, a car that needs replacing, and not enough time or money to fix the place up.

Not great—but maybe not so bad, either.

Bob collapsed the stroller. Amanda went inside and checked their phone messages. There was just one, from her mother, threatening a visit.

"It's hot as hell in New York, and I assume it's hotter than hell down there, but at least I could be catching the new show at the National Gallery. I've gotta get out of this stinking city for a few days."

"What should I tell her?" Amanda asked Bob.

"Maybe she could put it off?"

"You can't tell my mother to put things off."

"Then I suppose she'll have to come."

"But it's the worst possible timing."

"Why should that be different from anything else?"

Chapter Eighteen

SHE ARRIVED EARLIER than either of them expected. On the Monday morning that Bob returned to work, Amanda's mother telephoned at seven-thirty from Penn Station. She was boarding the eight A.M. Metroliner from New York City and would arrive in Washington at eleven. Bob bolted for the office as early as he could. He promised to call Amanda as soon as he emerged from his meeting with Sussman. At eleven-thirty precisely, Amanda's mother barged through the front door, carrying a knapsack and a battered paper shopping bag from Macy's.

Ellie Burnside Bright was a stout woman in her mid-fifties who had long ago shorn away every aspect of her appearance that might be misconstrued as feminine. As a young woman she had worn her thick brown hair long and flowing, but now it was lopped off and razored at the sides like a man's. She dressed in functional clothing that could be rolled and unrolled over her shapeless figure without the fuss of pressing: today she wore a wide purple T-shirt, jeans, and orthopedic sneakers. Her once sharply defined cheekbones could still be discerned underneath a padding of flesh, like the lines of a wire hanger beneath a bulky winter coat, but she never bothered with cosmetics and was untroubled by the two unruly whiskers that sprouted out of a mole on her left cheek. Her most striking feature remained her eyes, which glowed in their settings like two fire opals. These had not faded with age; if anything, they burned more intensely than ever. Pinned to her shirt was what she called her "trademark," a political button she changed daily. Today's unfortunate choice was MY GRANDCHILDREN ARE WANTED GRANDCHILDREN.

"So how is the future first female president of the United States—oh, and my little Supreme Court justice?" Ellie Bright kissed the tops of her grandchildren's heads.

"You're looking—weary," was her greeting to Amanda. "Where do you want this?" She indicated the knapsack.

"Just leave it. I'll move it out of the way." Amanda hauled it to the living room like a stevedore, trying to suppress her irritation at her mother's remark. Every time she saw her mother, Amanda presented a cheerful front—and every time the front collapsed in a matter of seconds.

Her mother, meanwhile, withdrew two presents for the children from her shopping bag.

"Look what I brought for you." She handed Ben a package labeled Sand Art. She offered Sophie a kit to make a small plastic bulldozer. Both children failed to conceal their dismay.

"You can make beautiful pictures with colored sand, Ben." Their grandmother's enthusiasm was undiminished by their reaction. "See the directions? On the back? You can make a sunset or an elephant . . . Sophie, honey, that's a *really good toy*, but you have to construct it. It's very simple." And to Amanda, "I checked—they're age appropriate."

"Isn't that nice of Grandma?" she prodded the children, in a happy falsetto. "Can we say 'thank you' to Grandma? Ben? Sophie? Say thank you!"

"Thank you, Grandma," they said, without looking up.

"Why don't you go play with those wonderful toys now. I'm going to give Grandma some tea."

The children headed toward their rooms. Before they had moved eight paces away, they had negotiated a swap.

"I'm going to make a pwetty picture!"

"And then I'll bulldoze it," came Ben's cheerful reply.

Ellie Bright affected not to hear them and followed Amanda into the kitchen.

"So tell me everything that's going on with you."

Amanda set down a pot of black Chinese tea, the only kind her mother would drink.

"Not much," Amanda said. "The usual."

Amanda had learned to answer all maternal questions about her life with the wariness of a suspect under interrogation. She knew her uncommunicativeness disappointed her mother. Each Christmas, Ellie Bright gave Amanda a clutch of new novels about warm, earthy mother–daughter relationships: novels in which mothers and daughters fought each other, laughed together, and in the end confided in one another, "coming to terms"—as one of last year's dust jackets put it—"with the quiet truths of living and loving and simply *being* women." So long as Amanda could remember, she and her mother rarely laughed together, and they confided in each other even less. On the few occasions that Amanda had been lured into unburdening herself, her mother, eyes flaring, demanded to know "how any daughter of mine could possibly think that way."

"Really? You don't look so well."

"I'm tired. Sophie woke up in the middle of the night."

"That's not it. You seem unhappy."

"Mom, you just walked in the door. Why would you instantly assume that I'm unhappy?"

"I can see it for myself. I'm your mother."

"Honestly, I'm tired. That's all." Amanda thought of her secret baby. She had already determined she would not speak to her mother about it.

"Fine. Have it your way. Tell me about Bob."

Bob had lately become their safe topic, which was surprising given her mother's mistrust of husbands in general and her opposition to Amanda's marriage in particular. Ever since Bob had become involved in the Megabyte case, however, he had earned her highest accolade: he was now a "crusader."

"I've been following the whole thing," her mother continued when Amanda hesitated to answer. "Imagine! Bob attacked by the *Wall Street Journal and* Mike Frith—in one week! I've been telling everyone he's my son-in-law. He's giving them real hell. You must be so proud."

"Yes—" Amanda wondered how much she should say. "It's caused a bit of trouble for him—"

"*Pshaw.* You can't take those right-wing bastards seriously. They're always exaggerating."

"Well, the Justice department is listening to them. Did you see the article in the *National Standard*?"

Her mother sipped her tea. "I never touch that rag."

"Neither do I. Not usually. But it ran an article last week saying that Bob might become the fall guy. Hochmayer's a big donor to the party. The *Standard* said that's why the president wants the case against Megabyte pursued. Sussman—you know, Bob's boss—is upset about how it all looks. We're both actually a little worried about what's going to happen."

"More right-wing propaganda," Ellie Bright said dismissively. "Although I'd agree on one point: the whole system is corrupt.

But Bob will be fine. The Justice department should be treating him like a hero."

"We'll see, I guess."

Amanda began to remove the tea things.

"I'll be off then," Ellie Bright announced, standing up. "I've got three galleries to do before supper."

"Did you maybe want to do something with Ben and Sophie? I've got an appointment this afternoon and—"

"Maybe tomorrow. I'll check the papers, see if there's any children's theater going on. Wait, I'm visiting some friends tomorrow . . . Well, we can discuss it this evening. What time do you want me back for supper?"

"I don't know. Six-thirty?"

"Fine."

Her mother marched down the front walk, a fanny pack strapped to her waist and a floppy canvas fishing hat perched on her head. She paused at the street to consult a map of the Washington subway system, and then headed off briskly in the direction of the station.

Amanda closed the screen door and went upstairs to check on the children. They had scattered the colored sand all over Sophie's carpet. Ben was bulldozing it into little piles. Sophie had created a beach for one of her dolls and was in the midst of supplying it with an ocean carried in from the bathroom sink.

"Oh God."

Before Amanda could clean it up, Bob telephoned from his office.

"Everything's okay," he said.

This was unreassuring—it was the way he might have prefaced an account of an accident with the words *No one's dead.*

"I don't want to go into it now," he continued, "but I'm still—employed—"

"Is there going to be an investigation?"

"No. I don't think so."

"You *don't* think so?"

"No. But please, let's discuss this when I'm home. It's awkward right now—I just wanted you not to worry."

"Okay."

"Is your mother there?"

"She's gone out to the galleries."

"That's good, I suppose."

"Yes."

"I'll see you tonight then."

"Bob?"

"Yes?"

"I—I love you."

His voice warmed. "You too, darling."

The midwife worked out of a medical building a short drive from Amanda's house. Ben dived headfirst into the elevator when it opened, nearly knocking down an elderly woman with a walker.

"So sorry—" Amanda pushed the button for the third floor. As they stood in silence watching the numbers change, Amanda's hand fixed tightly on the back of Ben's collar, Amanda remembered all the other times she had been here, in this same paneled elevator, her ankles swollen, her belly fat with Ben, then Sophie . . .

The office was at the end of a corridor of identical pale blue doors. Small silver signs identified the practice of each, but outside the last door there were two: one listing a group of obstetricians, the second stating simply, SARAH BLUMSTEIN, MIDWIFE.

Amanda knew that Sarah Blumstein would have preferred to work out of a less institutional office. The medical building was an odd location, after all, for a woman who believed that modern birth should take place as naturally as on the African veldt. But as Blumstein explained, *some* of her patients preferred to give birth in hospitals, rather than in their bedrooms or homey birthing centers, and the only way she could accommodate them was to affiliate herself with an obstetrical practice. (Amanda belonged to these unfortunate *some*. Despite pressure from both her mother and the midwife, Amanda had succumbed to the lure of the hospital labor room with its movie channel and push-button reclining bed and painkillers—the last of which Amanda had pleaded for when the midwife had left the room.) Blumstein referred to her impersonal surroundings as "high-techy" and in retaliation she had decorated her small office like the embassy of a developing nation, with colorful tribal prints, masks on the walls, and a hand-knotted rug on the floor. Over her examining table she had thrown an orange batik tablecloth that she removed when the table was in use.

"Amanda Bright!" Blumstein exclaimed, wandering into the waiting room and embracing her. "How wonderful to see you again. Are these *my* babies?"

Blumstein crouched down to look at Ben and Sophie, who were absorbed in trying to inflate surgical gloves that a nurse had brought in to amuse them.

"My, aren't you both so big!"

She turned to Amanda. "Can you give me some urine?"

The other patients—most in advanced states of pregnancy—averted their eyes.

"Uh, yes, I'll go back."

"Fine. I'll meet you in my office."

This was another aspect of Sarah Blumstein's philosophy: there was to be no squeamishness about bodily functions. Cramping, bleeding, breast-feeding—all must be talked about proudly and loudly.

Amanda left her children under the watch of the receptionist. She entered Blumstein's office a few minutes later bearing a filled plastic cup.

"Just put it on the side table. I'll have a look at it in a sec."

Blumstein was sitting on a comfy, well-worn sofa. She did not use a desk ("too hierarchical"). She patted the seat next to her and Amanda joined her.

"So, a third! Are you happy?"

"I think so. It wasn't exactly planned."

"Just came on like the rains, huh?"

"That's a good way to put it."

Blumstein asked Amanda a number of questions about her recent health and then examined Amanda's urine, holding it up to the light like a connoisseur of fine wine.

"It's a nice rich straw color."

She gave it a lusty sniff. "Good smell too. Very healthy."

Amanda worried the midwife might taste it as well, but Blumstein replaced it on the table and began performing a test.

The office was tranquil; Amanda appreciated the soothing, oceanic strains of New Age music that washed gently through speakers hidden in the walls. Sarah Blumstein was about the same age as Amanda's mother. She looked like her, too: the same ample body, the same cropped hair, the same casual clothes. The midwife eschewed lab coats and hospital scrubs, except in the delivery room, and today wore a baggy navy blue jogging suit. But where Amanda's mother's edges were hard, Blumstein's were soft. Her opinions may have been as forceful as those of Ellie Bright, but they were expressed in the lilting, earnest cadence of a guidance counselor.

"Hmm, I think you're right, Amanda. Let's have a look inside. Get out of your clothes, put on that terry robe hanging over there, and I'll be right back."

Amanda prepared herself and waited on the examining table. In a few minutes Blumstein returned with a young female obstetrician pushing a computer-laden trolley. This was another source of discontent for Blumstein—the medical center's rule that only real doctors could use the equipment.

"Is this the patient?" the woman asked.

"This is my *client*, Amanda Bright," Blumstein corrected her. "We don't treat pregnancy as an illness in *this* room."

"I'm Dr. Stark. I'll be performing—"

"helping with—"

"—the sonogram."

The two women fiddled around uncomfortably inside Amanda's lower regions. Amanda watched the ultrasound's computer screen. A fuzzy black-and-white image of Amanda's uterus flickered into view. There was an unmistakable oval shape floating in the middle, larger than she expected.

"There it is!" Blumstein said excitedly. "There's your little bean!"

The doctor tapped at the keys and small white arrows surrounded the oval.

"I would estimate five weeks," the doctor murmured. "Would you agree, Sarah?"

"For sure."

The doctor hit another key and printed a copy of the picture.

"Here you are," said Blumstein, snatching the picture from the doctor and presenting it to Amanda herself. "The first photograph of your baby!"

There it was, indeed. Amanda studied the picture while the doctor removed the trolley. It was real now, no doubt about it. Already she could feel the changes taking place: the waves of sleepiness, the slight nausea, a burning below her heart. But Amanda felt too—was it possible?—a twinge of eagerness. Despite everything, she could not be immune to the hard proof of her baby's existence. She glanced at the picture again. It looked like a pebble thrown into a black pond, small circles radiating outward, circles that would continue to radiate outward, eventually touching all of them.

"Amazing, technology, isn't it?" Blumstein allowed, after the doctor had closed the door. "Sixteen years from now you'll be looking at that picture, wondering where the hell it all went."

When Bob returned home, he looked as though he'd been to see a doctor as well—one who'd told him that while his disease was not terminal his life would be gravely restricted from here on. He tossed his jacket over the downstairs banister and riffled through the mail without really looking at it.

Amanda handed him a Scotch before he asked for it.

"Where's your mother?"

"She's taking a shower."

"The kids?"

"They're watching a video."

"Let's go in here." Amanda guided him toward the couch in the living room. He sat down and rose again, and began pacing in front of her, clutching his tumbler of Scotch.

"Here's the upshot," he began. "I'm not going to be investigated . . ."

"Oh, Bob, what a relief."

"... nor am I going to be fired."

"So it's all going to be okay then?"

"Not exactly." He took a large gulp of his drink and winced slightly as the liquor burned a path down his throat. "They're moving me off the case."

"*What?*"

"Frank spoke to the division's ethics officer. I think he also spoke to Hochmayer and maybe even to Chasen. Everyone is convinced that I did nothing that warrants investigation. But Frank also feels that appearances have been compromised, and it would be best if they transferred me somewhere else. You know how politically sensitive this is—"

"So the *National Standard* was right," Amanda said grimly.

"Maybe. Jeez, I don't know."

"Where are they transferring you to?"

"I'm not sure yet. They'll let me know in a few days."

"Who will be taking over the case?"

"Frank's now talking about bringing in some star lawyer from the outside—on a contractual basis, to be the face of the thing."

"He's bringing in someone from the private sector?" Amanda felt truly betrayed.

"Yeah."

Bob shrugged semi-ironically, the way we sometimes greet fate when it deals us an unexpected blow: *Isn't it a queer thing that we should have been standing in that precise spot when the truck careened around the corner? If we had only had the foresight to stand two feet back it might have missed us.* Amanda's mind was cast back to that day, so many years ago now, when Bob had started at Justice. She'd met him for lunch. He waited for her by the main entrance, between two magnificent stone lions. An inscription chiseled above the doors read: THE PLACE OF JUSTICE IS A HALLOWED PLACE. The sleepy majesty of the lions suggested that not only was the place hallowed, but it had long been so and would continue to be so for a long time hence. The department's employees passed in and out: like the lions, they seemed to take it for granted that the nation's justice would be carried out to the punch of a clock. Bob was enchanted by the dingy magnificence of it all: the vaulting rotundas, the Art Deco murals, the silvery leaf that trimmed the moldings, the plaster and yellow marble that covered everything else; this contrasted with the battered government-issue furniture, the drooping flags, and the crookedly hung photographs of the current president and attorney general. When Bob and his colleagues walked into a courtroom to face a slick battalion of private lawyers in two-thousand-dollar suits, he felt—he told Amanda excitedly at lunch—like one of those marshals in an old Western movie confronting the diamond-pinkied elite of a corrupt frontier town. Those folks might have the money, but in his shabby brown briefcase Bob carried the might of the U.S. government—and there was no sweeter moment than the one when those slick bastards discovered that they were outgunned.

And now it was all at an end. After the drama of the past few months, it was a sorry little end. Bob would hang on, he would continue to breathe in the air of the Department of Justice, but it was all over.

Amanda had nothing of comfort to say.

Suddenly a sharp voice shouted from upstairs: "Is that Super Bob?"

Amanda's mother descended, barefoot and dressed in the large muumuu she wore as pajamas, her wet hair spiked around her face like a hedgehog's.

"How's my hero?" She crossed the room and gave Bob an enormous embrace.

"Hello, Ellie."

"I see I'm missing the cocktail hour." She turned to Amanda. "White wine will be fine."

Amanda fetched two glasses and a bottle of wine from the kitchen.

"Aren't you having any?" her mother asked.

"I don't feel like wine right now."

"Hmph. That's not like you."

Ellie Bright settled herself in the sofa, her plump toes not quite grazing the floor.

"So tell me, Bob, what have you done to piss off Mike Frith today?"

Amanda interceded. "They're pulling Bob off the case, Mom."

Her mother looked stricken. "That's impossible! They can't do that! *Why* would they do that?"

"They have their reasons," Bob replied.

Amanda excused herself to check on dinner. She heard her mother's voice rising and cursing. "Don't those assholes realize what they're doing?" Dinner was doing fine. Amanda continued on upstairs to fetch the children, guiltily leaving Bob to handle the wrath of Ellie Bright by himself.

Later, after putting the dishes away, Amanda made a bed for her mother in the living room. It was only nine o'clock, but she was already desperately tired. The sleepiness of early pregnancy overcame her like a narcotic. Ellie Bright was brushing her teeth over the kitchen sink. Bob, in exchange for dealing with her mother before dinner, escaped upstairs with the children afterward.

The meal had gone disastrously, as usual, and only Ellie Bright had not noticed the disastrousness of it—which was also as

usual. Amanda had long ceased to wonder whether this quality
of her mother's was unconscious or deliberate, for its effect was
the same regardless: Ellie Bright would let rip some amazingly
rude observation and then chew her food calmly, apparently
unaware of, or indifferent to, the hurt she had just caused. If
Amanda or anyone else dared to challenge her, she'd respond
with offended innocence. Throughout dinner, Amanda and Bob
had managed to steer her away from the topic of Megabyte, but
this had only resulted in Ellie Bright redirecting her "observa-
tions" to Ben and Sophie. Ben's decision to launch a pea across
the table at his sister incurred a sharp lecture from his grandmother about the decline in table manners among children. "It's
because they watch too much television nowadays," she said
pointedly to Amanda. Amanda and Bob did not bother to argue,
agreeing, with a mutual look, that it was better to let Ellie Bright
feel that she had won the point. Her mother then pounced on
a comment of Sophie's—"Mommy, for Halloween can I be
Thleeping Beauty?"—as an example of the corrupting influence
of fairy tales upon little girls. Amanda, seeing the distress on
Sophie's face, assured her daughter, "You can be anything you
want, honey," to which Ellie Bright added, "Yes, maybe Sophie
could dress up as a soccer star. That's what her mommy did when
she was a little girl."

"Actually, it was Billie Jean King. But I *wanted* to be the
Tooth Fairy."

"You're wrong, Amanda. I remember."

Amanda was tucking in the sheets on the sofa when her
mother padded in from the kitchen. Ellie Bright settled herself in
a chair and followed Amanda's progress over the top of a novel.

"Don't worry about an extra pillow. I can make do with one."

"I've brought two anyway."

Amanda smoothed the blanket and stacked the sofa cushions in a neat pile by the fireplace.

"Okay, Mom, it's ready. I hope it's not too uncomfortable. We keep meaning to replace this old pullout."

"I'm sure it's fine. I've slept on garbage bags in the rain, for heaven's sake.

"The Women's March on Washington, nineteen seventy-five," her mother explained, when Amanda failed to ask.

"Right. Of course. Can I get you anything else?" Amanda waited by the archway leading to the front hall.

"Nope. Got my book. That's all I need."

"Okay then. I think I'll go up and have my bath."

"Amanda?"

Amanda had already started up the stairs. "Yes?"

"You know, I've been thinking about this Bob business."

Amanda glanced longingly at the light shining from her bedroom. "Uh-huh?"

"Well, in some ways it's not all bad. It presents an opportunity for you."

Amanda knew her mother would not let her retreat if she was bent on a discussion. She wandered back into the living room but did not sit down, hoping her mother's point would be brief. This, of course, was a mistake.

"How is it an opportunity for me?"

"I don't know if Bob is going to continue on at Justice—"

"I don't know, either."

"—but maybe this is a chance for you to go back to work and give Bob some time off so he can figure out what he's going to do next."

"Yes, maybe."

"Amanda, you're not listening to me."

"I am listening—I'm just tired of talking about this. It's been a long evening. I can't think about it anymore."

"You ought to think about it. It's only your entire future."

"I will—tomorrow. But right now I just want to go to bed."

"Fine."

This time Amanda made it nearly to the top of the stairs before the pull of her own conscience drew her back down.

"Look, I know you're concerned, but we can talk about this in the morning, okay?"

Ellie Bright ostentatiously absorbed herself in her book.

"Don't do this, Mom. Speak to me."

"You never appreciate when people are trying to help," her mother said without raising her eyes.

"I don't need help. I need sleep."

"That's just what I mean. You don't take anything I say seriously."

"Look, I really don't want to argue."

"Besides, why do you need sleep?" Now her mother looked at her directly. "Why on earth are you so tired? I'm more than twenty years older than you are, I've spent the whole afternoon walking around the city, and I'm not collapsing from fatigue. What have you done today that justifies your being so exhausted?"

"I don't need *justification* for being tired," Amanda retorted, against her better judgment. "I'm just tired. It's not like you've been with two little kids all day."

"Oh, don't give me that. I was a wife and mother long before you were, and not only could I manage that but a hell of a lot of other things as well."

"Yeah, I know," Amanda said, unable to disguise her irritation any longer. "Your generation was tougher than mine. I've heard all this."

"Don't be sarcastic. We *were* tougher. As women we faced barriers you can't even imagine. We ripped them down for you. And now you take all that freedom for granted—or waste it. Look at you! Look at all the choices you have."

"Not so many at the moment."

"That's ridiculous. You just refuse to see them. You just refuse to *take* them. Instead—"

"Instead what?" They were glaring at each other now. "Well, what? Go on, say it."

"Instead you choose to do nothing with your life." Her mother's face was thrust into defiance, as if daring Amanda to contradict her. Amanda felt pushed beyond endurance.

"I *am* doing something with my life," Amanda said at last, her voice barely rising above a whisper. "*This*"—she waved her hand to indicate her home and all it contained—"is not *nothing*. It is *something*.

"And it is more than you ever gave me."

Her mother, trembling, returned her attention to her book.

Chapter Nineteen

"DIAPER DUTY."

This was how Bob characterized his new assignment at the Justice department. His boss phrased it somewhat differently: Bob was being transferred to an important investigation into anticompetitive action by the Cuddly Wuddly Diaper Company.

"It's big, Bob, it's big," Sussman assured Bob. "Look what you've got: false claims about absorbency. Attempts to force supermarket chains in poor neighborhoods to carry only the Cuddly Wuddly brand—you can imagine the financial repercussions for struggling single mothers. And there's even an environmental side. Cuddly Wuddly commercials claim the diapers are manufactured from one hundred percent recycled paper products, unlike those of their competitors. Total crap, if you'll excuse the pun. Obviously, some of this investigation overlaps with the FTC—you'll be working with their people, too.

"Of course, it wasn't an easy assignment for me to get for you, not that I wasn't delighted to push for it. I gave you the highest recommendation. Really, I think this is a tremendous opportunity for you."

It was an early-September evening, and Amanda and Bob were sitting on a bench outside an ice cream parlor on Connecticut Avenue.

"Are you sure it's that bad?" Amanda asked. "From Frank's description, it does sound important. We use Cuddlies, although I won't anymore."

"Maybe it's important, but it's not the same. It's a comedown, there's no getting around it. And all my expertise is in the high-tech industry. It seems a shame to waste it."

"But what else can you do?"

"There are people who would be willing to pay for my expertise. Hochmayer, maybe Chasen. There are plenty of others, too."

"You'd leave government then." Amanda said this with less shock than she once would have.

"I'd certainly consider it." Bob bit into the side of his cone. "Hell, there's nothing really to keep me at Justice—"

"Except principle."

"Yeah, right." He took another bite. "We saw where that got me."

"You don't think Frank was motivated by principle? There was—there *is*—merit to the Megabyte case."

"Sure there is. We wouldn't have acted on nothing. And I'm sure the DOJ will come up with something. But loath as I am to admit it, I think there's some truth to Frith's complaint that the investigation was politically motivated. I mean, I've been pushing this case for two years. Why did they suddenly pick it up? You start thinking it through—Hochmayer's and Chasen's donations to the party, their friendship with the president, Senator Benson's campaign debt . . . A lot of Frith's competitors live in Benson's state. And Frith has managed to make himself unpopular with practically everyone in Washington.

"I don't know. Maybe, like the cynics say, it *is* just about pay-off. And if it's just about payoff, why aren't I at least being paid off in the private sector where I could make some real money?"

"Because you *are* principled."

"Yeah—but maybe I need some new principles."

Autumn came upon Washington as it always does, in the guise of summer. September was indistinguishable from August; the heat, if anything, was worse. The arrival of fall was evident only in the suddenly purposeful stride of the government workers whose bosses had streamed back into town for the return of Congress.

For Amanda, though, the change of season was dramatic. In the space of three months, her entire personal landscape had been bulldozed and replanted. Gone were the familiar hedges and old trees and mossy stepping-stones. In their place was a field of fresh, overturned soil in which thin, tethered saplings and sparse shoots of grass struggled against opportunistic weeds of doubt. Her whole life seemed as yet an unrealized vision, as mysterious and unknowable as the baby growing within her.

Amanda was keenly aware that Bob, too, was trying hard to adjust. There are certain types of notoriety in Washington that command not even a single-line obituary in the collective polit-ical memory: Bob had been obscure—then notorious—and now almost as quickly forgotten. Perhaps Mike Frith's denunci-ation of Bob in his Senate testimony might qualify him for a footnote in some future scholarly text, but among the people to whom the case mattered in the here and now, "Bob Clarke" was already a figure of little more significance than the fly that one afternoon briefly disrupted the composure of the Judiciary committee chairman by landing on his nose. In the antitrust division of the Justice building, manila files were passed along, nameplates on offices were switched, and a new Bob took over the old Bob's desk and chair. For Amanda, however, the scandal left lingering, if perverse, benefits. On the children's first day back at school, Amanda ran into Dr. Koenig in the hall. Amanda, who had failed to take Ben to a therapist over the summer, was ready with an excuse but to her amazement, Dr. Koenig did not even raise the issue. Instead she greeted Amanda with an ingratiating smile. "What an exciting summer you had!" and then—"I've heard Jim Hochmayer is an extraordinary man—quite the philanthropist!"

Bob, meanwhile, discharged his duties with all the passion of a postal clerk. Rather than race out the door in the mornings, he leisurely read the newspaper and took a second and sometimes third cup of coffee; it was Amanda, not he, who shouted at the children to hurry up with their shoes. When Bob returned home again, he would brush aside Amanda's questions about what he had done that day and instead insist upon hearing about her ordeal with the plumber, the confusion at carpool, the funny thing Ben or Sophie had said. It was as if he were seeking comfort in those aspects of their lives that had survived unchanged, and this interest was in some ways more worrisome to Amanda than his arrogant indifference at the height of the Megabyte case. When she occasionally asked whether there were any "new leads" on the job front, Bob would evade this question as well. Only once did he let slip that Hochmayer and Chasen no longer returned his calls; the upside was that Sherwood J. Pressman no longer did, either.

Gradually the trees tinted gold, and the wind carried the first whiffs of autumn—smokiness, chill, dying things. Amanda's waistline thickened around the nutshell of her growing baby. She had not heard from her friend Susie since their last meeting at the coffee shop. From a small item at the bottom of a television column, Amanda learned that Susie's show had been canceled. A few days later "The Ear" reported that "Luscious pundette **Susie Morris** is moving to Los Angeles to pursue other options." The item lewdly implied that those options were not entirely related to her career. Some weeks afterward Amanda glimpsed Susie at a bank machine. Amanda was in her car, waiting for a light to change. Susie stepped aside to tuck her wallet into her purse. The autumn sun glinted off her hair and for a moment she reminded Amanda of a maiden in an Old Master's canvas, if an Old Master had ever painted *Woman Making a Withdrawal on a Street Corner*. Amanda felt a rush of forgiveness. She wanted to roll down her car window and shout to Susie. But why? Maybe it was not forgiveness but that universal impulse to rescue beauty—to save it from its curses and in doing so, to feel superior to it. Susie would not appreciate her pity, nor would she see Amanda's forgiveness as anything but her due. The window remained closed. A second later, Susie vanished into a cab.

Amanda saw little more of her mothers' group friends. She attended only one of their gatherings that fall, at Patricia's house in Chevy Chase.

Patricia's sour, mistrustful housekeeper led Amanda downstairs to the playroom. The formal rooms with their dusted tables and arranged cushions were evidently reserved for grander company; Amanda wondered why Patricia did not take the added precaution of erecting velvet ropes.

The playroom, however, was pleasant enough. Sliding-glass doors led to a garden and a pool covered, at this time of year, by a green tarpaulin. The children romped outside in the leaves, and Ben and Sophie dashed to join them.

Patricia offered Amanda her cheek to brush with her lips, but her eyes nervously followed Ben's progress into the yard. "Just watch that Ben doesn't climb on the *Winged Victory.*"

Patricia's stone statue, which she described as "an authentic Beaux-Arts study" of the famous piece in the Louvre, had been shipped from a Paris flea market the previous spring. Patricia felt its deteriorated condition lent "a tragic, ruined" quality to her otherwise flat lawn, and her pride in it had inspired her to collect other pieces, including a scaled-down cast of Rodin's *Thinker* and a doleful concrete bunny ("Meredith picked that one—she has quite a good eye").

The other mothers greeted Amanda somewhat more warmly. Christine lounged upon a sofa with her legs extended to show off new suede boots.

"How's Bob doing?"

"Fine, thanks." Amanda refused a glass of wine.

"We want to hear all about it," Kim said excitedly. "I can't believe I was away when you made 'The Ear.'"

"There's really not much to tell. It's over now."

"But you had *Jim Hochmayer* to dinner!"

"He was seeing a friend of mine. That's over, too. Patricia, would you mind if I got myself some water?"

"Go ahead. There are glasses above the sink."

"You have to tell us *everything,* Amanda."

"I had Bob and Amanda over during the Senate hearings," Christine boasted, stroking one of her boots.

Amanda spent longer than she might have letting the tap water run cold. It was the first time she had ever possessed a story that piqued the mothers' interest, but she could not bring herself to share it. She knew this was a violation of mothers' group rules—the foremost being that you must share all personal information, no matter how private or trivial, and that of your husband and neighbors as well. It was not only that Amanda was reluctant to revisit the story, although she was, or to reveal Bob's changed position at the DOJ—a fact that had mercifully gone unreported. It was, rather, that she had developed an aversion to exposing any aspect of her life to these women. Why this should have overcome her now Amanda couldn't say; she only knew that for the first two months of the school year, she had avoided their company. She had not at first consciously intended to do so. But when she heard on her answering machine an invitation from Kim to attend their first postsummer gathering, Amanda created an excuse. Something else got in the way of the second meeting—and the third.

Amanda reseated herself with her glass of water.

"How was Portugal?" she asked Patricia.

"I can barely remember, so much has been going on. Too hot, I think."

"*Amanda*," Ellen coaxed. "Don't be modest. We won't accuse you of name-dropping. Tell us about Jim Hochmayer."

"He's—an interesting man."

"Don't push her," Christine said. "A good hostess doesn't gossip about the people who come to her house." She gave Amanda a chummy smile as if to suggest that in return for this protection Amanda would tell her everything later. "Let's move on. What I'*d* like to know, Amanda, is what's the inside dope on the Megabyte case. There hasn't been much in the news lately. And since I own stock . . ."

"So do I," said Patricia, in a way that hinted she would blame Amanda for any further devaluation.

"That's because there hasn't been much going on, I guess. I think they're still trying to get more companies to come forward against Megabyte. But as you know—" Amanda was not sure whether to reveal what she was going to say next, but the anticipation of the other mothers was too keen. "Bob's no longer on the case."

"I didn't know that."

"I didn't either."

"Oh, I thought I'd told you all this," Amanda said lightly. "Frank Sussman promoted him to an antitrust case in another division. I think he was so pleased by Bob's work on Megabyte . . ."

Ellen and Kim nodded credulously, but she could see that Christine and Patricia were buying none of it. Amanda sensed, in that instant, that she had lost the protection of her friend.

"I suppose that's the problem with working for the government," Patricia said, examining her nails. "The pay is low, and they're always shuffling you around."

None of the women inquired further about Bob's "promotion." Amanda sought to compensate Christine's disappointment by sharing her other news.

"There is something, however, I haven't told anyone yet—outside of Bob, I mean." Here she looked directly to Christine, who had resumed her admiration of her boots. "I'm pregnant."

This news had a stunning effect, although not an overwhelmingly positive one.

"Oh, how wonderful. That's lovely," Kim murmured. "How far along are you?"

"Nearly three months."

Patricia reached for one of the pieces of celery she had put out on a serving plate. "I don't think I could *endure* pregnancy again.

Not that Meredith wasn't worth it. But it took me a year to get my figure back."

Christine simply asked, "Why?"

The question flummoxed Amanda. "I—I don't know what you mean."

"I mean that you have the perfect setup, a boy and a girl. I could see it if you had two boys or two girls . . ."

"To be honest, we didn't exactly plan it."

"At our age you don't get pregnant by accident," Christine scoffed.

"It just happened." Amanda had not expected to be defensive about it—not in this crowd—but Christine's reaction was the most unsettling. How often had she spoken about her satisfaction in giving up work for motherhood?

"Think about it!" Christine continued. "Just the *thought* of going back to diapers and feedings. And three! It's just so many . . ."

They were interrupted by a scream from outside. The women all started in their seats but before any of them could rise, Ben ran in, the left side of his head awash in blood.

"Good God!" Amanda raced to him and began using her shirt to mop the blood from his hair. "Patricia—please, do you have a damp cloth?"

"I'm getting one. Watch the carpet."

The other mothers clustered around.

"Is he okay?"

"It looks like a bad scrape."

"They bleed like anything from the head."

"It's not deep. I don't think he needs stitches. The blood's stopping."

"Ben, sweetie, what happened?"

"I f-f-fell." In one hand he clutched a large chunk of stone.

Amanda pried apart his fingers. "What's this, honey?"

There, plainly, was the carved feathered tip of a wing.

Amanda knew, as Patricia's door closed behind her, that this would be her last visit with the mothers.

Through the rest of the fall, Amanda would see one or another of them in the hallways of the school, at assemblies, in the three o'clock carpool. Every time they would pause to say hello and effuse how happy they were to see her and gosh, wasn't she looking well—"Your tummy, Amanda! Can you feel the baby moving yet?"—and every time they expressed regret that "things had been so busy" that they hadn't been able to get together.

Amanda was not wounded by these exchanges. In retrospect it seemed odd that they should have remained friendly for as long as they had. So many of the friendships Amanda had formed in the early years of motherhood had long since fallen away. She never saw the women she used to know in Sophie's infant play group, and yet those friendships had felt so intense at the time—like the friendships soldiers form in battle, a cama-raderie based on the besieged circumstances of the moment. When the shelling ceases, the smoke lifts from the field, and the troops return home to resume the normal lives they thought they would never experience again, there is little left to say to former comrades-in-arms except "Hell of a time, wasn't it?" For now, Amanda felt only relief at not having to keep up with the other mothers as her girth expanded and she became ever more preoccupied with the upheaval of the coming spring.

As for Ben and Sophie, after an initial burst of curiosity and an argument over whether the baby would be a boy or a girl, they seemed to have forgotten about Amanda's pregnancy—except to wonder occasionally where the baby would sleep or whether it would covet one of their toys. Each month Amanda checked in with the midwife; each month the midwife listened for the baby's heartbeat—a swishing sound like windshield wipers going full speed; each month, the midwife announced that the baby was doing well. Amanda felt the baby's movements increase in strength: first tiny flutters, then gentle motions like the finning of a fish resting among reeds.

Amanda barely thought about returning to work anymore. She decided to pass her spare hours volunteering at the public library, sorting books and reading stories to groups of schoolchildren. The satisfaction of helping in the library was as ephemeral as that of housework; the smiles and gaping stares of the little faces gathered before her on the carpet lasted no longer than a clean countertop. But the clean countertop did not run up and embrace her or trill excitedly to the other countertops that "Amanda is here today!" For now, the hours she logged among the library's tiny carrels and overburdened carts would have to fill the space inside her that once held greater ambitions. There would be time later, she assured herself, for dreams that reached farther—and yet those dreams did begin to take shape in her mind. The children's reaction made Amanda think she could be a teacher, a vocation she had never considered before. It was impossible to consider it now, of course, and Amanda kept the vision to herself; but she found herself looking to it, like a beacon on some distant horizon flashing through fog.

Sometimes that fog was dense. Often she would awake in the middle of the night, tormented by doubts. The darkness, rather than cloaking her worries, relentlessly exposed all the cracks and fault lines of her daytime logic. It marched out the exhibits of her life thus far: thirty-five—nearly thirty-six—and what did she have to show for it? What sort of return would there be at the end of all these years of investment in her children? Maybe she would be too old to try something new. Who would hire her? Her own mind framed the accusations her mother would hurl at her, if they were speaking. Mercifully, they were not. The morning after their last encounter, Ellie Bright had risen early, said an unrepentant good-bye, and returned home to New York. When Amanda telephoned some weeks later with news of the pregnancy, Ellie said "Huh." That was it—"Huh."

When daylight came, however, Amanda's thoughts would reorder themselves and settle in their places as solidly as her dresser and bed. If any demons persisted, she'd call her friend Liz, her unofficial exorcist. When Amanda repeated Christine's remark—"you have the perfect setup, a boy and a girl"—Liz sneered that this attitude reflected "pure consumerism—children as items of consumption to adorn a successful lifestyle." To Amanda's distress over her fattening figure, Liz declared, "Carry yourself proudly—like a galleon under full sail!" One day Amanda wondered wearily, "Is every mother wondering all the time about whether she's doing the right thing?" Liz responded with a teacher's enthusiasm when a slow learner finally masters a lesson. "My point exactly! You're allowing yourself to be victimized by our anti-mother culture. You know in your heart what you're doing is right. So stop thinking about it."

"I try, Liz. I just wish sometimes that I felt more comfortable in my own life."

Then, in the weeks leading up to Christmas, Amanda began suffering stabbing headaches. "Your blood pressure is fine," said

Sarah Blumstein, removing the Velcro band from Amanda's arm. "Slightly elevated but within normal range. And my, you've put on a lot of weight this month—that's good so long as it's from healthy foods. I'd suggest you just lie down when the headaches come. Put on some soft music. Take a bubble bath, or have your husband give you a massage."

The massage remedy lasted about thirty seconds. Bob squeezed and poked at her shoulder blades, but he was no shiatsu artist. His clumsiness reminded Amanda of her first labor. Bob's ministrations to her then—the cool cloth on the forehead, the tennis ball in the lower back, his reminders to breathe, everything the books and Sarah Blumstein taught him to do—had only annoyed her and aggravated her pain. Amanda had longed to crawl away to a dark corner and be left alone like a cat, and she hadn't been sorry when Bob became faint during the birth's final stages and had to be led from the delivery room.

More usefully, Bob arranged for them to spend Christmas at his parents' house in Syracuse, sparing Amanda the ordeal of decorating a tree and cooking Christmas dinner. They drove through Pennsylvania in a blinding snowstorm, and stayed the night with Liz and her family in Binghamton. It was hardly a visit: Amanda's headaches were growing more persistent and almost immediately after arriving and getting the children to bed, she had to lie down herself, excusing herself from the elaborate meal Liz's husband, Steve, had cooked.

"Are you cold?" Liz asked, entering the darkened porch that served as a makeshift guest room. "I brought you some of Steve's soup."

"I'm okay. I'm piled with blankets."

"Do you think you ought to call the midwife?"

"She's away for the holidays. There will be no one there but some on-call doctor. Did you get headaches when you were pregnant?"

"Sometimes. Not as bad as yours. Drink some soup."

Liz stroked Amanda's head like a baby's. Her maternal hand was effective, and within a few minutes Amanda was asleep.

The next day, Amanda felt much better.

"I'm sorry I wasn't a better guest." Amanda embraced her friend as Bob and the children waited for her in the car.

"Don't worry. Next time. Get in the car—it's freezing."

The headaches subsided somewhat, and Amanda was able to pull herself through the next few days. Bob's mother, a retired nurse, commented once or twice that she didn't like the look of "Amanda's puffy eyes." Amanda balked at the fuss and reiterated Sarah Blumstein's objections to treating pregnancy like an illness.

"I'm not saying it's an illness, dear," replied her mother-in-law as she stirred gravy for the turkey. "I'm saying you *look* ill. You should be flushed and energetic at this stage. If I were you— not that I'm trying to interfere—I'd call a doctor as soon as I got home."

Amanda suspected her poor health might have been aggravated by the three-day stay with her in-laws. Their little house looked cozy from the outside—a modest suburban box with a big snow-laden spruce on the front lawn. But inside, the thin drywall and warped hollow doors offered little defense against the noise of two bored children and the voice of her mother-in-law as she strained to make herself heard by her increasingly deaf husband. Bob sheltered Amanda as best he could, but the headaches returned, and Amanda was grateful when everyone was finally loaded back into the car, and they were waving good-bye to Bob's parents through frosted windows and puffs of exhaust.

*   *   *

By mid-January, Amanda was back on Blumstein's examining table, her ankles swollen.

"Twenty-nine weeks now, is it? Par for the course, I'd say. Try elevating them when you sit down." Blumstein detected faint traces of protein in Amanda's urine—"nothing to worry about. We'll just keep an eye on that."

"I don't remember feeling this bad last time."

"What's that?"

Blumstein had been distracted by a phone call from one of her other patients, who was in labor. Ten minutes of Amanda's appointment had been spent "talking the client through" some contractions.

"Well, you're older than you were—even a few years makes a difference," the midwife said when Amanda repeated her complaint. "But why don't we see you again next week if you're worried—let's not wait a month. Get plenty of rest until then."

Blumstein bustled off with her "catching kit," as she called it (she didn't "deliver" babies but "caught" them), and left Amanda alone to change back into her clothes and see herself out.

Two nights later Amanda awoke with more pain, this time in her right side. It felt suspiciously like indigestion—she and Bob had gone out that evening for Indian food.

"Are you okay?" Bob whispered sleepily.

"I think it's the curry."

"Can I get you something?"

"No—I'll just lie here for a little bit. I'll be okay."

He fell back asleep, his hand resting on her belly.

*   *   *

The midwife was away for Amanda's next appointment—another "catching." The office was unusually busy: babies, like customers in shops, seem to arrive all at once. One of the junior doctors reviewed her symptoms.

"I've taken down the information, and I'll give it to Sarah," the young man said. "She should be back later."

Amanda read his markings on her chart.

"I've gained five pounds in one week?"

"Seems so."

"Isn't that unusual?"

"Depends. Sometimes it can be water. You look a little bloated."

"I thought so myself."

"Well, we'll have the tests back to see if anything else is up. Baby moving around okay?"

"Not a lot. It seems to have been sleeping a good deal lately."

"Uh-huh." He made a notation on the chart. "Well, I'll pass this all along to Sarah."

The midwife phoned Amanda that evening.

"Your blood pressure's up a little, hon. Still some protein in the urine."

"What does that mean?"

"It means you keep resting. We'll watch this—I'd like you to come again next week."

"Is it serious?"

"No, it's probably nothing. You're otherwise feeling okay?"

"I had some indigestion the other night. Indian food."

"Stay away from the vindaloo," Blumstein said, amused, "and I'll see you in my office."

*   *   *

Amanda finished her lunch and rose to clear her plate from the kitchen table. A sharp stab near her stomach winded her and she sat down again. As she bent over as far as she could, taking a few deep breaths, she caught sight of her ankles: they were hugely swollen and blue-veined, like those of the old ladies she used to see as a girl riding the Madison Avenue bus. All she lacked were the rubber galoshes. Amanda pulled herself up, and her whole body sloshed and jiggled like a pudding. A galleon! More like a garbage trawler.

The telephone rang, and by the time she made it across the room to answer it she was out of breath.

It was Bob. "Are you okay?"

"Just fat and slow."

"You sound terrible."

"Thanks."

"Can you talk?"

"Sure. I have to fetch the kids shortly but I've got a minute."

He lowered his voice furtively. "I've finally got some good news. I didn't want to say anything to you—I didn't want to get your hopes up or anything, but . . ."

Amanda heard someone knock on his door.

"Wait a sec." He placed his hand over the receiver and a muffled exchange took place.

"I'm sorry, but now I have to call you back. Will you be there?"

"Bob!"

"I can't help it—what time can I call you back? I have a meeting in fifteen minutes, so it will have to be after that."

"I'll probably be picking up the children by then—and I was

going to take them to Rockville. There's a sale on baby equipment. I should be home by four-thirty."

"I'll be in another meeting. It'll have to wait until I get home."

"Now you'll have me dying of curiosity all afternoon!"

"I'll try to get home early. Gotta go."

Amanda crossed the icy parking lot carrying Sophie on one hip with Ben tugging on her other arm. To Amanda, THE KID OUTLET, as the ten-foot letters screamed, was a hateful convenience—a noisy, ill-serviced warehouse packed with inventory and jammed into a strip mall—but to her children, its automatic doors opened onto the riches of Aladdin's cave.

"I'm going to the Space Rangers aisle *first*."

"Stop pulling, Ben. We're going to slip. And watch for cars."

Once inside, Amanda took a cart and tried to orient herself. She felt another headache building, and she wanted to get her shopping over as quickly as possible.

"This is our plan, kids," she said, lifting Sophie into the child's seat and restraining Ben from a display of marked-down Christmas ornaments. "Mommy has some things to get for the baby. If you both behave—"

"I want—"

"Shh! Let Mommy finish. If you both behave, I'll buy you *one* treat each—a *small* one—but only when I've got what I need. Understood?"

"Dollies!"

"No—Space Rangers!"

Amanda heaved the cart in what she guessed was the direction of the baby equipment, trying to sort out what it was she needed. The pain in her left temple was increasing. She turned down one aisle, which dead-ended at a wall of party favors.

"This isn't it."

"Can I get these, Mom?" Ben reached for a package of ghoul-ish rubber skeletons.

"No, Ben! Not till I'm finished!"

She craned her head over the racks to look for a sign. Distantly— it seemed a quarter mile away, through a maze of bicycles and toy aisles—Amanda saw what appeared to be a painted icon of a baby above some cribs.

"Let's try over there."

She wheeled the cart back around and pushed it through an area in which every package, shelf, and bit of plastic was fuchsia. Her right temple now chimed in with pain, like the wind instru-ments joining in the overture of strings. Sophie strained in her seat, her hands grasping at every glittering box.

"Printheth! I want the printheth! Oh, Mommy, there's a *car* for dolly—I want the car!"

Ben, for the moment, had gone blind. "Let's hurry," he said impatiently.

They came to the baby section. Amanda hesitated, unsure where to start. The bassoons were now kicking in, along with the timpani and bass. A car seat was what she needed—she remembered that much despite the booms going off in her head—and she paced back and forth, trying to decide which of the many car seats, chaotically arranged, seemed best for its price (ALL 40% OFF AS MARKED!). This one was $49.99, but looked complicated to install; here was one for $59.99, but its pattern resembled vomit. Come to think of it, that might hide a lot— wait, here was a plain blue one, for $63.99, but she couldn't fig-ure out where the seat belt attached . . .

"Mom, *c'mon.*"

"Don't rush me, Ben. Please. Remember our deal."

Sophie was squirming in the cart. "Let me out! Let me out!"

Perhaps Amanda should get a clerk to help her—but there was no clerk in sight. She lifted Sophie down, and the little girl shot off toward a cradle.

"Stay with me, kids—don't run away—"

A sudden stab in Amanda's side joined in concert with her head. It was the same pain from the night of the curry, the same pain from lunch, but worse, much worse. Her vision grew watery. She stumbled toward a rocking chair—SOLID PINE BUY RIGHT AWAY IN STOCK!—and slumped in it.

"Mom!"

"Just a *second*, Ben."

And a new diaper bin. She needed a new diaper bin. Along with the car seat. And another stroller, just a cheap one . . . Amanda tried to rock herself in the chair but with every motion, the pain grew worse. Nursery music crackled over a loudspeaker. It worked its way into the rhythms of her headache like an organ-grinder accompanying the grand instruments of the parade. The lights suddenly seemed too bright. Why were the lights so bright? Now it felt as if someone were jabbing a burning poker into her skull, stoking her brain. The edges of her vision started to curl and blacken. Orange sparks flew in front of her eyes.

"*Mom!*"

She knew that it was Ben's voice, but she couldn't answer. It was too far away.

"Mommy!" Sophie was crying, but she too was far away. *I'm sorry, darling, Mommy can't help you right now.* A hot fissure ripped up Amanda's side, thrusting her forward onto the floor. She gasped; her tongue lolled out; it tasted the filth of the linoleum. The floor felt cool but not cool enough. The flames were leaping higher, she could not breathe . . .

Distantly Amanda heard the loudspeaker, cutting off the nursery music. It said, "Emergency. Aisle ten. Emergency. Aisle ten."

Inexplicably, Bob is here. But where is here?

The orchestra of pain still plays in her head, but it is muted, everything is muted, it is as if she is lying deep inside a cave and voices reach her as echoes. Through the darkness of the cave she can see a round opening leading to the outside, and filling this opening is Bob's face.

His brown eyes look worried. He is saying something to her.

"You were unconscious."

"You collapsed in a store."

"We're at the hospital now."

"They've given you some painkillers."

His words float to her, bounce off the walls of the cave. She does not comprehend them. She must play them again. The rewind takes effort. All she wants to do is to block out the light and drift off to sleep in the nice peaceful darkness. But there is Bob's face. If she blocks out the light, she will block him out. Blinking, she draws nearer to the entrance of the cave, and as she does so, the lights grow more intense and she hears other noises and other voices. Hospital noises. Doctors' voices.

"Blood pressure is one eighty over one twenty. It's not stabilizing."

"Clear signs of toxemia—"

"I've administered magnesium sulfate."

"The patient is severely anemic."

"Have we got the blood work back?"

"It shows bleeding in the liver."

"Let me see."

"We need another ultrasound."

Something is very wrong, but Amanda does not have the strength to ask what. The only thing she understands is Bob's face, and Bob's face is so troubled. He is trying not to look troubled. He is trying to smile at her, but his eyes don't change, only the shape of his mouth.

Please, please tell me. Somehow she transmits the question to him.

"We're waiting for some tests to come back. It looks like you have a pretty bad case of toxemia, but they're treating it. You're in good hands. Everything will be fine."

He anticipates, too, her next question. "Ben and Sophie are fine. They're down the block, at Marjorie's. It's all taken care of."

This is good news. She takes a few steps back from the edge of the cave, but pauses. There is something else, something else that is wrong, but she can't remember what it is. Then it comes to her.

"The baby?" she manages to say ever so faintly.

Bob's lips straighten. His words don't flow so easily.

"The doctors are discussing right now what to do. They may have to operate. We'll know in a little bit. Just rest, sweetheart, don't worry. I'm here."

Yes, Bob is here, she tells herself, and she drifts off under his watch as if in the shade of a mighty tree. He rests his head near hers on the pillow, and she is soothed by the gentle rustle of his breath. She does not know how long she sleeps. She is wakened by another sharp pain in her right side, and a loud familiar voice entering the room.

"Where is my client?"

Amanda opens her eyes. She finds if she shifts the aperture of the cave slightly, she can see a battery of machines—a frightening mass of wires and computer screens, each displaying a moving pattern—and beyond them, the blurry figure of Sarah Blumstein surrounded by doctors.

"Are you her obstetrician?"

"I'm her *midwife*. I got here as soon as I could—you sure as hell took your time calling me."

Bob rises, and Amanda instantly feels the loss of his presence beside her. The cave is open and exposed. She wants him back. She hears his voice—it's too far away!—talking to Sarah.

Sarah's face now fills the mouth of the cave.

"Amanda, hon, I'm sorry about all this . . . It seems to have happened so quickly. Toxemia can do that . . . Never seen a case as bad as this before . . . They don't want me in the room—male doctors!—but I'll be right here, okay? . . . I'll be just outside in the waiting area, so Bob and you can consult with me when you need to. Everything will be fine, okay, Amanda? . . ."

Her face vanishes, and is replaced by Bob's. He looks serious and tries to speak slowly, and as he does he grips her hand, the one without tubes stuck in it.

"They want to deliver the baby right away, Amanda."

This does not make sense. The baby is not ready to come out.

"It's—it's our best hope. They think the baby is strong enough—and they're going to give you some more blood to make you strong enough and then—they're going to put you under general anesthesia. You won't feel anything—"

Bob's voice falters. "But I'm here, Amanda, I'm always here. You'll be asleep—for a long time, maybe even for a day or two, they can't say—but I'm not leaving your side, except when they operate—I'm not leaving your side."

She nods. She has heard everything that matters.

The doctors start fussing around her. They inject fluids into the tubes. Someone fastens what feels like a clamp on her nose, and air begins pumping into her nostils. Her body gradually lightens, as if she is levitating slightly above the bed.

Throughout this, Bob holds her hand; he tethers her to him. So long as she is tethered to that hand, she knows she will be okay. She clings to his hand as she clings to the present moment; that's all there is now, the present moment, but it, too, contains everything. It is here, it is this person, it is this life they have created, it is this life struggling within her, it is this love . . .

She yearns to convey this to him, but she can't speak. She tries to tell him with her eyes, this surge of everything, but they are moving her away. His fingers loosen but remain locked in hers, and he keeps up alongside, with all the equipment swinging around her, the doctors shouting; past the nursing station, past the masked faces in the corridor; past closed doorways and empty gurneys to the operating theater where other masked figures are waiting and the bed veers suddenly and stops.

"I'm sorry—you can't go beyond here," she hears a voice say, and Bob lets go of her fingers. The doors swing shut and her last glimpse of him is through a porthole, watching.

He will be watching, she tells herself, he will always be there, and this thought sustains her as a man wrapped in green sheets introduces himself as the anesthesiologist and prepares to make a fresh hole in her arm. The doctors chatter, but she understands not a word, it is talk about levels and numbers. She can still feel the touch of Bob's hand in hers.

"You can start the anesthesia."

There is an icy sensation in her arm, and then her body is awash with a feeling of pure joy such as she has never known. The joy touches every point in her; it races through her veins to her fingertips and toes; it floods her heart; it breaks into the darkness of the cave and for a moment illuminates her entire being.

The words come back to her, the words she could not tell Bob. *There is this moment, there is this person, there is this love, there is this life. That's all there is, and it is . . . enough.*

Chapter Twenty

LIGHT FALLS on boxes. A whole city of them, arranged as if by some mad municipal planner. Towers of cardboard reach to the ceiling of nearly every room. The living and dining rooms are impassable, and only a small allowance has been made for a path up the stairs to the bedrooms, where mattresses and blankets rest directly upon the scuffed floors.

In the middle of what used to be Bob's and Amanda's bedroom, a tiny life struggles to make sense of the patterns of sunlight. She lies in the center of the double mattress, her fingers waving abstractedly in the golden beams like a sea anemone, oblivious to the tumult of the ocean's surface. Down here it is quiet; down here the cool spring breeze through an open window ruffles her silky hair as gently as a passing current.

Close by, as invisible and yet as necessary to the life as air, lies the infant's mother. Amanda is curled into a semicircle, her legs drawn up protectively around the baby. Half of her mind is attentive to the baby's cries; the other half drifts in and out of consciousness. The packing has exhausted her, but it is nearly done. She has managed a few boxes a day over the course of two weeks, and if she'd ever fretted that her life was not organized, it was now: virtually every object they possess is categorized, wrapped, and labeled with black marker.

Most of the boxes will follow them to Bothell, Washington. There is a large subgroup of boxes, however, marked for charity—as well as their sofa, kitchen table, and an assortment of old chairs. The new owner of their house, a single professional woman who pronounced everything "totally perfect," nonetheless plans to gut the place and "open it all up." Amanda overheard the woman discussing her plans with the real estate agent when they thought she was out of earshot: Ben's and Sophie's bedrooms were destined to become part of the "new master suite," while the kitchen and bathroom would be done over in granite and marble, respectively.

"You'd think they'd have at least freshened up the paint a bit," the buyer said. "Might've fetched a higher price."

"It's amazing what people learn to live with," the agent replied.

Amanda would happily have taken a blowtorch to all of it herself. She had a new house of her own to dream about, a brand-new house with no history whatsoever. It was being built right now as she lay here on the mattress: a four-bedroom modern rambler set in an acre of woods, in a development named Sammamish Landing. No, no, no—it was not *that* sort of development. The house they had chosen had won a West Coast architectural award for its creative design and ecosensitivity. Glass-paneled walls generated solar heating; low-voltage lights reflected off steel-beamed, vaulted ceilings. The development was stepped into hills around a common trail; not far away was the town of Bothell, with its main street and riverside park and band shell. Bob's new office was in the city of Bellevue, a ten-minute drive away—"that's without traffic," the agent warned, but Amanda did not care. Bob's office could be on the moon, she was so happy. As she said to Bob, as they stood by the flagged posts that marked the site of their future house, "We never expected to be like this, did we?"

She was referring to their good fortune, but he replied, "There are a lot of things we never expected to be like."

Amanda replayed the comment several times through her head to reassure herself that he had said it without bitterness. His eyes were surveying the field of churned-up mud. Did Bob see what she saw: the promise of a new life being raised before them? Or did he see, as he had joked, "the aftermath of the Somme," a place that would always be tainted with defeat?

Amanda decided to let his remark go, and remained quietly at his side, holding his hand. The mist that had greeted them upon their arrival melted into a cold drizzle. Amanda called Ben and Sophie, who were poking sticks in mud puddles, and they retreated to their rental car, where the baby was strapped into her seat, asleep. Amanda had already pressed Bob on his feelings about his new job, and he had been adamant that it was the right choice—"If it's good for all of us, then it will be good for me"—but she knew that Bob was anxious not to diminish her own enthusiasm, especially since he had spent so much effort convincing Amanda that the move to Bothell did not constitute a sellout.

"Mike Frith?" Amanda had uttered in amazement, a few days after she had given birth to Samantha. "You're going to work for *Mike Frith?*"

"Keep your voice down, and let me explain."

They were in Amanda's hospital room, which she shared with a heavily medicated new mother and, for as long as visiting hours would permit, the woman's husband and extended family of aunts, uncles, cousins, and grandparents. The other half of the room resembled a florist shop; on Amanda's side sat the lone bouquet of pink roses Bob had brought after she'd regained consciousness. The hospital did not allow flowers in intensive care, where Amanda had spent the first twenty-four hours of her stay—not even flowers brought by so formidable a person as Sarah Blumstein. Despite a prolonged argument over "the sterility of the environment contributing to the poor health of the patients," Blumstein's "life-sustaining" arrangement remained at the nurses' station, where it withered after a day. Amanda was similarly protected from a bouquet sent by her mother. ("Although why she nearly had to die in childbirth, I can't imagine," Ellie Bright complained to Bob. "This is the problem with daughters—they never seek advice from their mothers, even when their mothers are experts. I could have told her she had toxemia, for God's sake.") Amanda herself did not remember being in intensive care. Nor did she remember a single detail of Samantha's traumatic birth. She had lapsed into a coma immediately following her cesarean—a coma that the doctors, in their auto-mechanic way, described to Bob as being "fairly typical" and "nonpermanent." As Amanda lay unconscious, their baby daughter had been whisked from the operating room to the neonatal intensive care unit, where her bright red body—so unfathomably tiny!—was punctured with tubes and sealed inside a Plexiglas tank.

Later Bob wondered aloud to Amanda if he had not had it the worst of any of them: in one room lay tiny Samantha, fighting for life; in another, his wife, unresponsive to words or touch. He did not leave the hospital to go home. He could not face home or the worried eyes of Ben and Sophie. Better the children should remain undisturbed with their neighbor, Marjorie, as if on a little holiday. Bob slept on a vinyl couch in the waiting room, and spent his days wandering up and down the hospital corridors like a shadow trapped in purgatory.

"I must be hallucinating again." Amanda rearranged the pillow behind her head, and, with difficulty, rolled her body slightly to have a better view of Bob, who had pulled an armchair closer to her bed. *"Mike Frith?"*

The laughter and baby-passing on the other side of the room went quiet. Apparently, her roommate's relatives were also curious to hear Bob's news. Bob yanked closed the curtain that divided the beds.

"I'm serious," he whispered. "About a month ago I got this call from his people, feeling me out—you know, a would-you-consider-it sort of thing. It seems they're interested in having someone like me come aboard as a corporate counsel, to help them comply with the consent decree—"

"You told them you wouldn't consider it—didn't you?"

Bob was fidgeting with the control pad of Amanda's hospital bed. "No, I didn't," he said slowly. "I thought it might be worthwhile to hear what they had to offer."

"But why?"

"Because it's potentially a big offer, Amanda."

She took the control pad from him so he would look at her and pushed the button that raised her head.

"I always thought that if you were to leave government, you'd go to work for someone like Chasen—or one of the smaller companies out in Silicon Valley. You know, one of the good guys."

"I'm not sure any of them would fall within your definition of good guy. In any case, Chasen hasn't returned my calls in weeks—you know that. Neither has Pressman, and he's connected to pretty much everyone in California."

"But Bob—really! Mike Frith? He's like Dr. Evil. He's the Dark Side. He's—"

"—like every other entrepreneur with problems with the government. And this could be a real opportunity for me to do some good. Seriously—" he said as she wrinkled her nose—"don't you think it would be something to try to help a company like Megabyte reform itself, if that's its intention?"

"If that's its intention," Amanda replied skeptically.

"I'll find out next week. That is, if you're well enough by then for me to fly out overnight to meet Mike Frith himself."

Amanda was well enough. She was discharged from the hospital ten days after she had entered it, leaving behind, with great anguish, her baby daughter, who needed another few weeks of care. Bob and Amanda took turns doing shifts in the hospital nursery, holding Samantha with sterile gloves, helping her delicate mouth latch on to the ungainly rubber nipple of a bottle, until, miraculously, one day she was able to come home, too. By then, Bob had flown out to Megabyte's headquarters in Bellevue, and the matter had been decided.

"He's an interesting guy, what can I say?" he told Amanda upon his return. His plane had landed late and when he arrived home he'd found himself confronted with the familiar plate of Thai noodles from Fresh Farms. "Very compelling, very persuasive, as all these big guys are."

"They say Satan is charming, too." Amanda was bustling about the kitchen in her bathrobe, putting things away.

"Come on. He's hardly Satan. Look, I had my doubts going in. But he's not what you expect, not entirely," Bob said, chewing thoughtfully. "He's eccentric, sure. I showed up in a suit, and he was dressed basically like a lumberjack, sitting behind this huge, ridiculous antique desk that looked like it came from the First Stagecoach Bank of Kalamazoo, or something. Anyway, he was frank. Said he could understand why I might not want to work for him, and then he made the case why I should. He's planning on retiring from Megabyte in a couple of years, and he's very keen to get the company on the right footing with the government. He said I had integrity—that no one would doubt my commitment to making sure Megabyte complied with the DOJ's orders—"

"He meant you're a good beard."

"Maybe," Bob said, a little irritably, "but you know me, Amanda, and I'm not going to serve as anyone's 'beard.' I told him outright—if I were to come aboard, I would have to have the power to make the necessary changes."

"And?"

"He agreed."

"So what did you say?"

"I said I'd think about it—talk it over with you, et cetera." Bob added, as if an afterthought, "The money he offered wasn't bad, either."

Amanda stopped what she was doing. "How much?"

"Think of the biggest sum of money you can imagine anyone wanting to pay me—"

"Two hundred thousand dollars?"

"—and then double it."

Amanda covered her mouth with her hand.

"Yup. Oh—and did I mention this? We get a car upon signing. Frith recommended the new Volvo station wagon—he drives it himself—but I said I'd have to consult you about that."

"He drives a *Volvo station wagon*?"

"He's got four kids, and he thinks it's the safest vehicle on the road. He's also philosophically opposed to SUVs, which he believes are bad for the environment."

"Don't tell me he's an environmentalist," Amanda said weakly.

"Okay, I won't."

He stared at the remainder of his noodles. "I wonder if there's a Fresh Farms in Bellevue?"

Now Bob was gone. He'd left a week ago to start his new job. Amanda and the children would follow him at the beginning of next month. They'd rented a furnished apartment in Bellevue, which they'd occupy until their new house was finished. Most of their boxes would be sent into storage, a prospect Amanda looked forward to: it would feel as if she were putting most of their old life away, and when it came time to unpack, she would save only those pieces that still seemed desirable.

Amanda shifted herself gently on the mattress so that her face was closer to Samantha's. She closed her eyes and inhaled the sweet soapy scent of her baby's skin. Samantha paddled her little limbs. Amanda began to drift off again, thoughts of moving and packing and new lives washing in and out of her mind, until the baby's cooing gradually increased to fussing, and she was drawn sharply back into wakefulness.

"Here, darling." Amanda reached for a bottle and arranged her arm so Samantha could feed while lying next to her. She watched, spellbound, as the baby's mouth seized fiercely on the nipple. Samantha's gray-blue eyes were as bright as stars and seemed every bit as far away, as if the baby dwelt in some heavenly realm of her own and had not yet joined them in their earthly life. Amanda could gaze at her for hours like this. She had been heartbroken that she was not able to nurse her baby—the Plexiglas tank put an end to that—but she was also amused at herself for being heartbroken. It had always felt like a chore to nurse Ben and Sophie: every two hours, no matter what she was doing, the babies' cries would reel her in. Their demands at night felt vampirelike and left her drained and exhausted.

This time Amanda treasured her baby's every new gesture, every new sound. She mourned the passing of each phase of infancy, as if with this child, Amanda could finally appreciate the brevity of childhood. The cords that connected mother to child were not, as Amanda had once thought, as thick and constraining as ropes, but as thin and light as gossamer. Every day a strand broke and fell away.

Already Ben had lost the dimples on his hands. His skin was taking on the tarnish of an active boy. When he came into the house he always brought a bit of the outside world with him. And Sophie—since the baby had come, she had begun asserting her own superior maturity, demonstrating all the things she could do that Samantha could not, and assuming the role of mommy whenever Amanda left the room. One day—a day not too far from now, Amanda realized—the baby she would cradle in her arms would not be hers but would belong to Ben or Sophie or even Samantha, and she would be its grandmother. Amanda would tell herself that this was not possible because time could not move that quickly. But it does, it does, as her own grandmother once warned her, and what's worse, it only speeds up.

Samantha's eyelids, translucent as onion skin, were closed, and her lips were still moving up and down but lazily now, barely taking in milk. Amanda gently disengaged Samantha's mouth from the nipple, and lifted the baby onto her chest, ostensibly to burp her but more to relish these last weeks when her daughter was small enough to sleep upon her heart.

As Amanda rubbed Samantha's back, it occurred to her that each one of her children had taught her something new. Her first child had taught her how to be a mother. Her second child had taught her how to be a family. And her third—what would this third baby teach her? Maybe, she hoped, how to be a mother and still be herself.

She did not know how she was going to do it. She did not know any woman her age who *had* done it. Amanda admired Liz and took comfort in her friendship, but she could not join her friend's crusade. "This is not my cause," Amanda had found herself saying to Liz one day, after the birth of Samantha, "it's just my life." And what she wanted, dearly, was for that life to feel normal. Had other generations of women doubted themselves like this? Maybe. Maybe every generation has felt that it had to reinvent the wheel. After all, the road keeps changing. Her grandmother's World War II generation had embraced motherhood and rejected careers; her mother's post-war generation rejected motherhood and embraced careers. And Amanda's?

Well, that she did not know. But she did know this: she, Amanda Bright, was a frontierswoman, who, like so many clever, ambitious women of her generation, had one day found herself in the wilderness with a baby on her hip, only to discover that nothing she had learned growing up had prepared her for her new world.

Samantha nestled more deeply into her mother's chest while Amanda continued to rub her daughter's back in small circles.

Her mind was racing now. She was seeking an answer that felt almost within grasp and found it, suddenly, in the motion of her hand. Sometimes your life feels as if it is going around and around in the same place. But in fact the circles are always widening. Each year the rings reach a little farther, like those of a sapling maturing into a tree. The core remains the same. Marriage, motherhood—these are simply new rings. They broaden rather than narrow you. They strengthen rather than weaken.

Yes, maybe that was an answer—or enough of an answer for now. Perhaps all Amanda could really hope for was that someday, years from this moment, there would be many, many rings, and when she looked back, she would be astounded at how sturdy she had grown.

Acknowledgments

Virginia Woolf was optimistic in supposing that a woman needs only a room of her own to produce a novel. Like all books, this one required the encouragement and support of many people before it was able to achieve life.

I am deeply indebted to Melanie Kirkpatrick of the *Wall Street Journal*, who had the audacity and perseverance necessary to launch a serialized novel for the first time ever in that great newspaper; to the spirited James Taranto, editor of *Opinion-Journal*, who agreed to the unorthodox experiment and posted chapters weekly on the *Journal*'s Web site throughout the summer of 2001; to editors Erich Eichman and Joanne Lipman, who gave Amanda a spectacular front-page kickoff in the Weekend section; and to illustrator Ned Crabb, the Lynton Lamb of our day, for his hilarious weekly sketches. Copy editor Brendan Miniter's cheerfulness with midnight changes was also most appreciated. And I am exceedingly grateful to Ken Whyte and Hugo Gurdon of Canada's *National Post*, who brought Amanda to their readers.

Amanda in book form owes chief thanks to my brilliant agent, Jennifer Rudolf Walsh, and to my truly terrific editor,

Caryn Karmatz Rudy. Caryn's wise suggestions and dedicated efforts resulted in Amanda getting the makeover she so badly needed.

A circle of dear friends cheered Amanda on from the start, and I relied very much upon their advice, criticisms, and enthusiasm: Betsy Hart, Amy Kroll, Kate O'Beirne, Mona Charen Parker, Melinda Sidak—and Meghan Gurdon, who must be singled out as the only woman I know capable of offering edits within twenty-four hours of giving birth. My obstetrician, Dr. Damien Alagia, a superb doctor, took Amanda's medical condition seriously and helped me greatly with the technical details of toxemia.

My parents, Yvonne and Peter Worthington, generously kept my family housed, fed, and entertained during the final weeks of the serial. As always, I am left gasping at the thought of what I would do without their unstinting love and support. My children displayed much unrewarded patience throughout the writing of this book (darlings, why can't you do that in movie lineups?): I thank Miranda for being an early, avid reader of the series and for all her excellent editorial advice; Nathaniel for his dear solicitude and eagerness for me to finish, which made me write faster; and Beatrice, who suffuses our lives with such joy.

I simply cannot imagine how this book could have been started, let alone finished, without my husband, David Frum. Not only has he ensured that I have always had a room to write in, but a room furnished with his love and boundless confidence. I dedicate this novel to him, as indeed I dedicate everything else.

ABOUT THE AUTHOR

DANIELLE CRITTENDEN is the author of *What Our Mothers Didn't Tell Us*, a book that resulted in *Vanity Fair* declaring her one of the most important writers and thinkers about women. Her articles have appeared in the *Wall Street Journal*, the *New York Times*, and the *Washington Post*, and she is a frequent commentator on national TV and radio. She lives with her husband, author David Frum, and their three children in Washington, D.C.